PRAISE FOR *THE TWO LILA BENNETTS*

"Intriguing . . . Chapters headed 'Captured' and 'Free' alternate, each describing a parallel reality . . . Along with two perfect endings, this satisfying thriller offers food for thought. Flawless pacing will keep readers on the edge of their seats."

—*Publishers Weekly*

"*The Two Lila Bennetts* is a thought-provoking thriller that will have you thinking about the choices you've made and how your life could change in an instant."

—PopSugar

"Liz Fenton and Lisa Steinke create an imaginative and unpredictable story of modern life, the choices we make, and their consequences. *The Two Lila Bennetts* is an excellent summer read."

—Authorlink

"Buckle your seat belt. All by itself, the title of this book, *The Two Lila Bennetts*, suggests we're in for a ride twice as wild as the average thriller. Coauthors Liz Fenton and Lisa Steinke deliver mightily on that expectation. Page by page, chapter by chapter, these consummate storytellers capture our psyche and our breath as they invite us to solve this 'who's-doing-it' masterpiece."

—*BookTrib*

"*The Two Lila Bennetts* is heart-pounding action from start to finish. It's *Sliding Doors* with a killer twist. I couldn't put it down!"

—Aimee Molloy, *New York Times* bestselling author

"It's trouble in paradise for three best friends struggling to make amends in the latest thriller from the dynamic writing duo of Liz Fenton and Lisa Steinke. *Girls' Night Out* is a chilling page-turner full of secrets and hostility that will leave readers shocked again and again . . . and again. I loved it."

—Mary Kubica, *New York Times* bestselling author of
The Good Girl and *Every Last Lie*

"A wild ride into a high-powered girls' trip to Mexico. Suspense at its best. Liz and Lisa have taken their writing partnership to a new level!"
—Kaira Rouda, *USA Today* bestselling author of *Best Day Ever*

"This suspenseful novel is full of twists and turns and makes clever use of chronology. It will make you think twice about going on a girls' night out!"

—Jane Corry, bestselling author of *My Husband's Wife* and
Blood Sisters

"In *Girls' Night Out*, Liz Fenton and Lisa Steinke guide readers on a suspenseful international tour of friendship at its best and worst. As enviable fun takes a turn through suspicion toward pure fear, you'll find out just how wrong a trip to paradise can go."

—Jessica Strawser, author of *Almost Missed You* and
Not That I Could Tell

"Set against the idyllic backdrop of tropical Mexico, *Girls' Night Out* twists its way through the dark recesses of friendship, proving that nothing is ever uncomplicated or quite as shiny as it seems. An exciting new thriller from a proven team."

—Roz Nay, author of *Our Little Secret*

"*Girls' Night Out* is an utterly enthralling read that is impossible to put down. The dual timelines are captivating, just days apart, as they unfold both the frantic search for a missing friend and the circumstances that led to her disappearance. This is a book that makes you question how well you truly know even your closest friends and also what you yourself might be capable of doing."

—Kathleen Barber, author of *Truth Be Told*

"Liz and Lisa's *Girls' Night Out* is a strong follow-up to the bestselling *The Good Widow*. Three friends go on a girls' trip to Mexico to try to repair their friendship. But when one of them goes missing after a night out drinking—and fighting—they're left trying to puzzle out what happened the night before. Sparkling characters, real friendships, and a fast-paced mystery: What more could you ask for in your next read?"

—Catherine McKenzie, international bestselling author of *Hidden*

"Lisa Steinke and Liz Fenton have conjured up the tropical vacation of your nightmares. After reading the unsettling *Girls' Night Out*, you'll never look at a tequila shot the same way again."

—Janelle Brown, *New York Times* bestselling author of *Watch Me Disappear*

PRAISE FOR *THE GOOD WIDOW*

A *PUBLISHERS WEEKLY* BEST SUMMER BOOKS 2017 SELECTION, MYSTERY/THRILLER

"Fenton and Steinke deliver a complicated tale of love, loss, intrigue, and disaster . . . This drama keeps the pages turning with shocking twists until the bitter end. A great read; recommended for admirers of Jennifer Weiner and Rainbow Rowell."

—*Library Journal*

"Fans of Joy Fielding will appreciate the story's fast pacing and sympathetic main character . . . A solid psychological thriller."

—*Publishers Weekly*

"Fenton and Steinke's talent for domestic drama comes through . . . For readers who enjoy suspense writers like Nicci French."

—*Booklist*

"A fantastic thriller that will keep you on your toes."

—PopSugar

"Accomplished authors Liz Fenton and Lisa Steinke make their suspense debut with great skill and assurance in this enthralling novel of marital secrets and lies, grief and revelation. *The Good Widow* led me along a winding, treacherous road and made a sharp, startling turn that I didn't see coming. Unputdownable!"

—A. J. Banner, #1 Amazon bestselling author of *The Good Neighbor* and *The Twilight Wife*

"Liz Fenton and Lisa Steinke's *The Good Widow* begins by asking what you would do if your spouse died in a place he wasn't supposed to be in with a woman he wasn't supposed to be with. What follows is a gut-wrenching thriller, sometimes heartbreaking, sometimes darkly funny, but always a page-turner. And as you read it late into the night, you'll look over at the person in bed next to you and wonder how well you really know him. A wild, skillfully written ride!"

—David Bell, author of *Since She Went Away*

"An irresistible and twisty page-turner, *The Good Widow* should come with a delicious warning: this is not the story you think it is."

—Deb Caletti, author of *He's Gone*

"*The Good Widow* is both heartrending and suspenseful, deftly navigating Jacks's mourning and the loss of her less-than-perfect marriage. The writing is sharp and evocative, the Hawaiian setting is spectacular, and the ending was a wonderful, twisty surprise. A quintessential summer beach read!"

—Kate Moretti, *New York Times* bestselling author of
The Vanishing Year

"*The Good Widow* is a fresh take on your worst nightmare—your husband dies, and he isn't where, or with whom, he said he was. I ripped through these pages to see where Fenton and Steinke would take me, which ended up being somewhere unexpected in the best kind of way. You will not be sorry you read this!"

—Catherine McKenzie, bestselling author of *Fractured* and *Hidden*

HOW TO SAVE A LIFE

ALSO BY
LIZ FENTON & LISA STEINKE:

HOW TO
SAVE A
LIFE

A NOVEL

LIZ FENTON +
LISA STEINKE

LAKE UNION
PUBLISHING

Text copyright © 2020 by Liz Fenton and Lisa Steinke
All rights reserved.

No part of this book may be reproduced, or stored in a retrieval system, or transmitted in any form or by any means, electronic, mechanical, photocopying, recording, or otherwise, without express written permission of the publisher.

Published by Lake Union Publishing, Seattle

www.apub.com

Amazon, the Amazon logo, and Lake Union Publishing are trademarks of Amazon.com, Inc., or its affiliates.

ISBN-13: 9781542005098
ISBN-10: 1542005094

Cover design by Faceout Studio, Lindy Martin

Printed in the United States of America

To Dad:
I miss you every day.
Love, Lisa

CHAPTER ONE

MAY 2010

This bulge in my pants is making me sweat.

But this is no ordinary bulge. This protrusion is the result of a one-carat round-cut diamond ring sitting inside a small square box. I adjust my position slightly, and the sharp edge of the box stabs me in the thigh. I shift again, causing Mia to ask me if I'm okay. I swallow hard and nod.

But the truth is, *okay* is not the right word. I'm excited. Exhilarated. But I'm also terrified. It feels like that time my best friend, Lance, made me cliff dive in Kauai. I wanted to, I swear. As I stood on the edge of the rocky cliff, I could almost feel the tepid water and my feet slicing through it. But when it was time to vault off, all I could imagine was what could go wrong. Hitting a sharp rock. Nailing the side of the cliff. A hungry great white shark circling below. That's probably why Lance pushed me—he'd seen the way I'd frozen up. But as I flew through the air, all the fear vanished in a whoosh that left me breathless. In that moment, between leaving the safety of the ground and landing in the water, I saw a glimpse of who I could be. A man with no inhibitions.

And now, sitting at the oceanfront table I requested at the Pacific Coast Grill in Solana Beach, I feel like I'm perched on another peak, ready to take a different sort of leap with the beautiful redhead who sits across from me. I watch as she spoons the delicate coconut cheesecake into her mouth, closing her eyes in pleasure. She holds the next bite out to me. "You've got to try this, Dom!"

I open my mouth obediently and make a big deal out of how delicious it is. But I don't taste a thing. I pat the box in my pocket and tell myself what I'm about to do is like cliff jumping. It's scary but also amazing and wonderful, if I can muster the balls to do it. I think of the way I felt when my body hit the surface of the water. Like I could do anything. Be anything. Anyone.

And right now as I sit in this restaurant, the tables around me all filled with people eating their fish and going about their lives, all I know is I love this woman with me. Sure—she's gorgeous. I'll never forget the first time I saw her dancing in the quad at San Diego State. But she is also wicked smart. Incredibly kind. Delicate but also fearless in this wonderful way that makes you want to be fearless too. A life with her would absolutely include cliff diving. And this time I wouldn't have to be pushed.

I refuse to hesitate any longer. I hand the server a credit card as she passes by. "We're ready to go," I say as Mia takes her last bite. I nod toward the beach beyond the window. "It's so nice out. Want to take a walk?" She nods her approval, like I knew she would. The beach is her happy place. And it has also become a living, breathing part of our relationship. I told her I loved her for the first time while the waves lapped our toes down the coast in Ocean Beach, and we kissed with such force that I didn't notice as the tide moved in and soaked us. Or maybe I noticed and didn't care. That's what Mia does—she makes everything else fade away. It is easy to get swept away in her. She's my sea.

Like now, as I take her hand and lead her to the water. We take off our shoes and let our feet sink down into the wet sand, our footprints washed away with each wave that rolls in. The sun is slowly making its way to where the skyline meets the sea. A family of four huddles on a blanket a few yards back, patiently waiting for the sun to set. Men and women in wet suits sit on their surfboards and let the water rock them back and forth. Mia leans down to uncover a seashell, brushing her fingers through the sand until it's free. Time stands still as I pull the velvet box from my pocket and palm it in my hand. Mia uses the seawater to wash off the shell and holds it out, her face shining. "It's perfect!" she declares.

"So are you," I say as I drop down on one knee. Mia's eyes widen. My voice sounds far away, as if I'm listening to someone else. I have a whole speech planned, but my mind is blank. So I say what's in my heart: "Mia, you are the only girl I've ever loved. Will you marry me?"

"Yes!" Mia gasps and jumps into my arms. I hold the ring tight in my right hand and balance her lithe body with my left as we embrace. The perfect seashell drops and is washed away, but Mia doesn't seem to notice. I gently set her down a few moments later and place the band on her left ring finger. Everyone on the beach is cheering so loudly that Mia insists we take a bow. We bend down and wave our arms wide. Mia is grinning. She's in her element for sure. But it makes me feel slightly uneasy, as if we're putting on a show. The thought falls away quickly as the applause fades, and she grabs my waist and pulls me back against her. "We're going to have a great life," she whispers, and I kiss her in response, believing every single word.

CHAPTER TWO

Tuesday, June 9, 2020
Ten years later

At first, I'm not sure it's her.

She reappears in the damnedest of all places—a hipster coffee shop wedged between a refurbished-furniture store and a hemp-purse boutique on Coast Highway in Oceanside, California. Somewhere I would never ordinarily be. But I am. And so is she. I nearly choke on my flat white when I realize the woman with the thick strawberry-tinted hair debating between a hot or iced vanilla–almond milk latte is the one who got away. My biggest regret for the past ten years.

It's a fluke that I'm at Revolution Roasters today. The man behind the counter with the dark-blue beanie and the handlebar mustache is not my barista. Mine is Diane, a short woman with a shock of white hair and a smile that always makes my morning.

Yet here I am.

And there she is.

Mia.

It took me nearly forty-five minutes to drive to Oceanside from downtown San Diego to meet a source for a possible story. When he'd suggested it, I had balked at the location, but he'd convinced me—something about his college-age daughter working here and the lattes being well worth their eight-dollar price tag. He's the source, and I'm in desperate need of a story, so of course I said okay. As I nurse my coffee, which is, in fact, quite good, I check the time. My source is late. By almost thirty minutes. I begin to wonder if I should leave. I study the moose taxidermy on the wall, the long wooden oars hanging next to it. I watch the man at the table next to me, who is wearing a baby and studying something on his phone; a plate of half-eaten avocado toast sits in front of him. I can see the side of the child's cherub cheek, his eyelids, which are closed. Next to the man is a longer table packed with people with their noses deep in their laptops. I start to wonder, as the journalist in me often does, What is everyone's story? Is the man the baby's father or manny? Is the woman nearest to me—clad in shorts, a tank top, and Birkenstocks and studying the stock market on her computer—a student? Or the owner of a million-dollar tech company? And what would any of them think of me? A Latin guy with a head of unkempt curls wearing khakis and a button-down, with sleeves I rolled up after feeling firmly out of place? I hope the stories in their heads are better than the actual one—single, thirty-four, a local-news producer who hasn't found a hard-hitting story since his Daytime Emmy five years ago. Should I add that I have a roommate? Own a leather couch? Probably not.

My phone buzzes, and I quickly swipe up. But it's not my source.

I'm about to stand up to leave when I hear her voice. Melodic. The tone of it instantly taking me back to years ago, when I last heard it. When she said the words, "I can't. I'm sorry. You should go." My stomach flips as I start to swivel my head toward the sound. She's asking about her latte—Is it better hot or cold? I'm almost afraid to look over. Because it can't be her. It's never been her. The hundreds of false alarms over the years have taught me that. When I thought she was in line in front of me at the grocery store. The time I was sure she was driving the car next to mine. Or when I placed my hand on what I thought was her shoulder, and the woman turned and stared at me wide eyed, startled by my touch. It's my mind playing tricks on me. But still, I look.

I notice her hair first. It's a bit shorter now but still falls in soft waves past her shoulders. I hear her double-check that she said almond milk because she can't have dairy. I pick up my keys and phone and start to leave. It's not her. Mia used to drink whole milk straight out of the carton. Then she turns. I see the profile of her nose first. Slightly upturned. Then the freckles that dot it. More pronounced now. The curve of her cheekbone. Her long neck.

It's her. It's Mia.

She looks over as if sensing someone watching her. Her blue eyes meet mine. It seems to take her a second to register it's me. She smiles, timidly at first, and then her entire face lights up. I feel dizzy. The sight of her takes my breath away.

She rushes over and stands only inches from me, all five feet, seven inches of her. Her body still long and lean. "Oh my God. Dom?"

I am reaching toward her for a hug before I realize what I'm doing. But thankfully, she accepts my embrace. I want to hold her forever, inhaling her floral scent. But she pulls away quickly. "Were you leaving?" She looks at the keys in my hand.

"I was, but now, no. No way."

She smiles, then points at the empty bench across from me. "Could we sit for a second?" I nod, thinking that we can sit here forever.

The man with the baby on his chest glances over, and Mia coos at the child. The baby stretches its hand toward her, awake now.

I lean across the table and whisper, "Do you think he's the dad or the manny?"

"Still playing your game, I see."

I smile. She remembers. What else has stuck with her?

"What are you doing here?" I ask. "Last I saw on Facebook, you were still living in Glencoe."

"I moved back last week. I'm at Hailey's here in Oceanside."

A million questions come to mind. Why is she back? Is she staying for good, or is it temporary? Why is she living with her sister? Does she have a boyfriend? I glance at her ring finger. It's bare. She catches me, and I wait for her to call me on it, but she doesn't. The barista calls her name, and she gets up to grab her latte, and I watch her walk over. I see her pick up the mug—turns out she went with hot. I want to ask her why she drinks almond milk now. What her favorite TV show is. If she still loves to go to the movies and order the large buttered popcorn with extra butter. What does she think of our president? Did she ever take that trip to the Great Wall of China? How quickly did she move on from—

"Dom?" I look up to find Mia is back in her seat.

"Sorry. I was thinking that I can't believe you're here."

"I know. I can't either," she says, something flickering in her eyes. But she quickly looks down at the perfectly drawn leaf in her latte and takes a careful sip so as to not spill.

"What brought you back?" I ask.

She laughs. "So many questions about me! How are you?" she deflects.

"I'm good," I lie. But wait—I *am* good. I thought I was, anyway. Until I came to a coffee shop thirty miles away from my home and ran into her. Now what the hell do I do?

"You're good? That's all? What else? I want to know everything!"

So do I. About you. But why do I feel like I can't ask?

"Like what?"

"Are you happy?"

"Wow. I wasn't expecting that one," I sputter.

Mia smiles, the one where only the right side of her mouth curves upward.

"And I'm not sure how to answer that. It's a big question."

"Well, that's honest," she says and plays with the small silver earring in her right ear.

"Are you?"

"What? Happy?"

I nod.

Mia waits several beats. "You're right. That's a hard one to answer. How do you think they make this leaf design?" she asks, peering into her mug.

"I'll take subject changes for five hundred, Alex."

"Sorry." Mia blushes.

I stare at her for several seconds, and she holds my gaze. I want to touch her again—make sure she's real. That I'm not dreaming. But obviously that would be odd. Although I still consider it.

"Is it really you?"

"What?" Mia asks.

Oh shit, I said that out loud.

"It's really me." She pinches the pale skin of her arm, and I notice there are more freckles there now.

She reaches across the table and touches the longer curls around my face. My entire body tingles.

"And it's really you."

"So we've established that we're both really here and we don't know how to answer if we are happy," I say.

"Good summary." Mia laughs. "So what are you doing up here from downtown? The coffee that good or something?"

"I was waiting for a source who didn't show," I say. "It's lucky we ran into each other!"

Mia furrows the skin between her eyes. "Do you think it's luck or something else?" She sits back and smooths the front of her sundress.

"What do you mean?" I ask.

"What do you think puts the two of us in this coffee shop on a random Tuesday at ten in the morning after all this time?"

"You needed coffee, and I was meeting a source?"

Mia gives me a perplexed look. "You know what I'm asking."

"Like if it was fate?"

Mia nods.

I shrug. "You know I'm not a big believer in that stuff."

"It seems too random to be random."

I laugh. "Okay, I'll give you that." I sip my coffee and realize it's now cold. I drink it anyway. "I'm glad we're both here."

"Me too," Mia says. "How is Channel Seven?"

"Good, Lance and I are getting it done."

"That's good to hear—you guys always wanted to work in broadcast journalism. And look at you now. Getting it done, as you say. I'm happy for you."

I stare at her, wondering if this is true—if she's actually happy for me or if she's making small talk. Her face gives nothing away.

"Thanks. Are you still teaching?"

"I was—up until I left Chicago. The school year just ended."

She doesn't elaborate. I don't ask for more. The air between us is heavy with so many unsaid words.

"So," I finally say.

"So," she repeats, then grins; this time both sides of her mouth curve upward, revealing that megawatt smile.

"It's been so long."

"Too long." She looks at me. Her eyes saying so many things. Or maybe it's simply me wanting her to be sending me silent messages like, *I miss you. I never stopped loving you. No one has ever been as good in bed as you.* I laugh a little.

"What?" She cocks her head, revealing three ear piercings in her left ear. She's added two since I last saw her. "Why are you looking at me like you've seen a ghost?"

Because that's what it feels like.

"It's just so surreal that you're sitting across from me. I honestly wasn't sure if I'd ever see you again." I think back to the last time—nine years ago. In Illinois, at her parents' house. Trying to find the right words so she would understand my regret. So she'd understand that I would never let her down again. But I knew it was over. Because Mia isn't someone you can regrasp once you've let her go. That harsh reality has shaped the past ten years of my life.

"I know. I wasn't nice. I'm sorry."

"You do not need to apologize!" I say, and I picture us standing in her parents' front yard in the house she was living in because I'd driven her back into their arms. She told me as much. That she had to go home. Begin again. It was October, but it had been unseasonably cold for that month. I hadn't dressed right. I was in jeans and a T-shirt, hugging myself to stay warm. I'd jumped on a plane without so much as looking at the weather. Not that it would have made a difference—fall in Illinois is a crapshoot.

Six months before that, I'd taken the equity we'd built in our three-year relationship and smashed it into the ground.

"I still can't believe it." She'd looked down and grinned at the engagement ring I'd given her the night before, moving her hand back and forth as the diamond caught the light. When she'd gazed back up at me, her face had changed. She'd held eye contact until I'd had to look away.

"Mia . . . ," I'd said to the tile floor.

"Dom?" She'd said my name like she'd known what I was about to say but hoped with everything inside of her that she was wrong.

"I'm sorry, Mi." I couldn't look at her. I was such a fucking coward.

"Sorry about what?" Her voice had been ice cold. She was going to make me say it. And she'd been right to do that.

"Mia, I thought I was ready, but—"

"But?" She'd put her hands on her hips. Tears had been pooling in her eyes. She'd been trying so desperately to hold it together by biting her bottom lip.

"But I'm not . . ."

As I look at her now, I think, as I've thought a million times since, I broke it off for what? Because my stomach quivered, making me think I was scared? That I wasn't ready? Looking back, it was easy to see that the moment would have passed as quickly as it had come. But when I was living it, the terror felt insurmountable. It was as if I was unable to grasp what we had as the terror of committing my life to her set in—I couldn't recall what it felt like to run my hands through her copper hair early in the morning as the sun beat through the flimsy paper window shades in the tiny room she rented a mile from campus. I hated staying over there—Mia's double bed was old and creaky, and her clothes often were strewed about the room. But I always stayed anyway. I couldn't resist waking up with my body pushed up against hers.

"I want to apologize, though. I'm still sorry for being so cold to you. I couldn't . . . ," she says to me now, looks at me for several beats, then lets her eyes follow a woman walking her toddler toward the bathroom.

"I understand," I say, because I do. I did the same to her. I couldn't. And then I could. But it was too late by then. I had already broken what we had.

She left that day without saying goodbye. I walked to the cupboard and pulled out Jack Daniel's, swigging straight from the bottle, telling myself to give her time to cool off, and then I'd call. Make her understand this wasn't about her. It was about me. That someday down the road we could try it again. I had no idea as I took another long pull from the bottle that that day would never come.

Until now. Maybe now.

"Have you changed, Dom?" Mia asks, and I snap my attention back to her.

Her question surprises me. "What do you mean?"

"Well, it's been, what, over nine years since that day? Would you say you're the same guy?"

My heart is suddenly working in overdrive. If I answer correctly, will she run out the door? If I lie, will she see right through me?

"Changed how?" I ask, stalling.

"Are you still a creature of habit? Routine? Safe? Still you?"

"What do you think?" I decide to put it back in her court.

Mia sets her mug of coffee down and scrutinizes my face. "Well, it has been a while, obviously. But I'd guess you go to the same Starbucks every morning and order the same drink. Probably know your barista by name. You find comfort in that. In your routine. This"—she points to my flat white, the remnants of the leaf now dissolved into the milky liquid—"is so not your jam."

She's right, but something about her depiction of me leaves me feeling unsettled. Have I really not changed at all in the last decade?

"Am I right or am I right?" Mia sits back, tucking a strand of hair behind her ears.

"Nailed it," I say.

But I've changed in other ways. At least I'd like to believe I have.

Mia looks toward the door. "I should probably get going," she says, and I deflate.

"No, stay," I say without thinking, and my cheeks flush. Only moments ago I felt hopeless. But then Mia breezed in, and it was like nothing else existed.

"But don't you have to get back to work? Figure out what happened to your source?" she says, a hopeful look in her eyes.

I do need to get back to work, but all I want is to stay here with Mia in this hipster joint with my overpriced coffee that is *so not me*. She's right about that. "They'll survive a few more minutes without me."

"I wish I could stay, but I can't." She looks at her phone, then back at me. She nods toward the door. "Walk me out?"

My heart speeds up again. "Sure."

We head outside and nearly trip on a homeless man, and I accidentally kick his bag as I try to keep from falling on him. His belongings roll across the sidewalk. I reach over to pull Mia away, but before I can, she's crouching on the ground, picking up a dirty flannel hat and a partially torn bag of crushed recyclable cans.

"Can we help you pick up your things?" Mia asks the man, who looks to be in his early fifties. His beard is long and dirty, but his eyes are clear.

"Yeah. I'll take it from here," he says gruffly, glancing up at me.

"Sorry about that," I say as his eyes bore into me. But the truth is, I don't really feel bad. He was practically blocking the door.

Mia grabs a few of the empty soda cans that rolled out of his bag and hands them to him before reaching into her purse and pulling out a twenty-dollar bill. "Here."

The man looks at the money and back at me before taking it gently from her hand. "Thank you."

I pick up a few more cans because I'm not sure what else to do.

"What's your name?" Mia asks.

"Bill," the man says.

Mia touches his shoulder. "Good luck, Bill," she says and turns back toward me. "I'm parked over there." She points a block down Coast Highway, and we fall into stride silently.

"He didn't seem very happy for your help," I assess.

"That's because he was embarrassed, Dom. He knows people like you are judging him." Mia says the words lightly, but I can feel the weight behind them.

"I wasn't judging him," I protest. "I don't think giving him a twenty is going to solve his problems." And if I wasn't pissed at Bill the homeless guy before, I certainly am now. I haven't seen Mia in all this time, and now we're discussing social issues in the precious few minutes I have left with her?

Mia stops and turns toward me. "I choose to believe that it will help. And if it doesn't, then at least I tried, rather than acting like he doesn't exist."

"Hey," I say, grabbing her shoulders. "I'm sorry. You're right."

"You were always such a jerk about me giving money to homeless people," she reminds me, but there's a small smile on her face. It was something I'd often tease her about—her endless empathy for people. For animals. For anything, really. And now falling back into that conversation after nine years feels oddly comforting.

"I was, wasn't I?" I laugh. "And yet you never let that deter you from giving money to every single one. I loved that about you. And I love that you haven't changed."

My words sit in the morning air.

"Hey, Mi," I start, then stop, thinking how easily I've slipped back into an ease with her, using my nickname for her. She doesn't seem to mind. There's a palpable electricity in the air between us. Does she feel it?

I can't let her go again.

"Yeah?" she says.

I debate asking her. The words sitting on the tip of my tongue. All I have to do is say them. Because I can't let her walk away again.

"I don't want this to be it. Can I see you again?" I ask before I can lose the courage. "I promise to bring extra cash for any and all homeless people we might trip over."

She surveys me as if deciding if I'm worth it.

My heart thuds. My palms are sticky. Right as I'm about to let her off the hook, she smiles. "I thought you'd never get around to asking me."

And just like that, my life has flipped upside down.

CHAPTER THREE

Thursday, June 11, 2020
7:00 a.m.

My alarm turns on, and without opening my eyes, I reach over, trying to find the button to shut it off. I pound the top of the clock, but the song keeps playing. I start to register the familiar notes. It's "How to Save a Life" by the Fray. It was our song. Mine and Mia's. It played at so many junctures in our relationship: At the party where we first kissed. In the car after I told her I loved her for the first time. It was funny—the song itself didn't have much to do with love. It was about a person trying to save someone else from their fate. But since it seemed to pop up whenever we were having a moment, we decided to adopt it anyway.

I rub my pounding temples. Why the hell did I drink so much last night? I typically don't. I struggle to focus. Lance was ordering tequila shot after tequila shot, and I kept drinking them. Shots! What were we thinking? That we were back in 2008 again? Twenty-two-year-old seniors at San Diego State blowing off steam after finals? I could handle that amount of alcohol consumption in those days. Now? Clearly not. I put the pillow over my head, wishing I could go back to sleep. I hear the shower running. Of course Lance is already up. Probably worked out too. The booze never hits him like it does me. His body bounces back after tying too many on like he's still in his twenties. And his face is still freakishly youthful, the lines around his brown eyes never quite forming. His blond hairline is still right where he needs it to be. I reach up and touch mine, already knowing it's creeping backward like my dad's. But at least I have my moppy curls, as my mom calls them.

It's like Lance was born to be on television. He is the guy who would grace the pages of the sorority charity calendars. Who would incite girl crushes and bromances alike. I've been told I'm more of a boy-next-door type, and I only ever wanted to be behind the camera, producing. So the fact that we ended up at the same news station working together has made work fun and something I could see myself doing until I retire. Although Lance has higher aspirations—to first move into the LA market and then on to *The Today Show* or *GMA* or anything on national TV. And until recently, I believed I was on track to take over as assignment editor when my boss, Alexis, leaves. It seemed a natural progression because I've been climbing this local ladder since I started working here as an intern my last year of college. And staying here involves little risk. Exactly how I like it. But lately I'm not sure I'll be a candidate for her job when it opens. I haven't found that *it* story. The one that will prove I'm not a one-hit wonder. I sit up slightly, wincing from the blood pumping to my head, and look at my Daytime Emmy up on the shelf. Which I often do to remind myself I won. Back when I got it, I was arrogant enough to believe it would be the first of many. That was five years ago. Don't think Alexis doesn't remind me all the time.

"You all right?" Lance says when I shuffle into the kitchen for coffee. "You look like shit."

I take in his crisp blue button-down. His wet hair. His nonhungover face. "Fuck you."

"A peace offering," he says, handing me a mug of steaming coffee.

The smell of caramel wafts up from the cup, and I take a sip. "Last night isn't on you. It's my fault."

"You're nervous about seeing Mia tonight," Lance says. "Right?"

I nod, thinking *nervous* doesn't begin to cover it. Every time I think of seeing her, my stomach flips and my heart speeds up. And my negative internal dialogue takes over my brain.

She took pity on you when she said yes. She has moved on, and you are no longer on her radar. Don't get your hopes up, buddy; she's way out of your league now. Maybe she always was.

"Have you heard from that source who didn't show up to the coffee shop?" He changes the subject, knowing we won't discuss Mia in detail anymore. We haven't since the time I found out one of our good buddies from college was getting married and wanted me to be in the wedding. One minute I was staring at the invitation, and the next I was talking about Mia and crying. It was a very long night involving a bottle of Jack Daniel's and some major man tears. Now, we avoid.

"Nope," I say. "Totally ghosting me. Which sucks. I need a story. A big one."

"Don't be so hard on yourself. You're the best, Dom. Nobody better."

"Except all the producers with golden statues from the last four years."

"But who's counting, right?" Lance laughs.

"Alexis has been on my ass." I run my hand over my chin. I need to shave.

"And mine. I think she's been getting heat from the top. We've slipped in the ratings."

"I'm aware." I sigh and open the junk drawer, searching for Advil.

"She's in love with Devon," Lance says as he places his mug in the sink. "That guy was a weekend anchor like five minutes ago, and he gets hired here and thinks he's the next Anderson Cooper." He frowns but quickly recovers with a smile. He would never say so, but I know he's worried about Devon, who is younger and admittedly more eager. He doesn't roll out of bed and into the station minutes before he's due in makeup like Lance does. He shows up to the morning editorial meeting and chimes in about the stories he thinks should be in the wheel. And because of his assertiveness, he's worked his way into our managing editor Alexis's inner circle quickly, which is not an easy thing to do.

The truth is, Lance will have to step up his game if he doesn't want to lose opportunities to Devon. But I can't tell him that. He's the kind of guy with a very fragile ego. It's best to drop bread crumbs for him. Slowly. And eventually he'll follow them and arrive at the correct conclusion. Right now, he doesn't see *why* Devon is moving into Alexis's good graces. And maybe it's because he doesn't want to see it. All I know is that I'm not going to be the one to tell him. Unless he asks. And then I will tread lightly.

"I don't know if I'll ever hear from that guy again, but when I do find that next big story—and I will—I won't let the assignment desk get their hands on it. And I will make sure Alexis backs me on giving it to you," I say, draining the last of my coffee and pouring more, the caffeine starting to settle my anxious mind.

"Thanks," he says, heading to the fridge and pulling out a carton of eggs. "And listen, man, it won't be hard for you to find that story. I mean, anything's better than the ninety-year-old man swimming to Catalina."

"It sounded good at the time. But you're right—it didn't play well at all," I mutter, remembering the elderly man's pale, wrinkling skin, his bright-yellow Speedo and matching swim cap, and Alexis's frown as the tape ran. Yet he had made the trek rather easily, barely out of breath when he'd reached the island.

"You know what the real headline should have been?" Lance asked. "That the dude had a forty-year-old girlfriend. He's my hero! You buried the lede!"

"Whatever," I say and flip Lance off.

He cracks eggs in a bowl, and I'm about to suggest that he should forgo making himself breakfast and get into the office—send an intern out for a breakfast sandwich instead. That Devon's probably been there for two hours already. But he's a grown man. He'll figure it out.

I step into the shower and picture Mia's face at the coffee shop again. Seeing her after all these years has brought so many lingering doubts to the surface. What would have happened if we'd gotten married? Would her free spirit have liberated my conservative one? Or would my spirit have squashed hers? Or would we have grown together, our differences eventually making us stronger?

It's a thought that has trailed me, like smoke from a fire that has long been extinguished. It's probably hindered me from settling down with one of the many nice girls I've dated. I may have been accused of being terrified to commit beyond a few months. And maybe that's true. I've always told myself I had to be sure this time. But there is a small part of me that wonders if I've been stuck in a mental cul-de-sac, a part of me waiting for Mia.

And now she's here.

I shower quickly, bypass Lance as he sits at the dining room table, feasting on bacon and eggs, and head to the elevator. I hit the button for the lobby instead of the parking garage, deciding to walk for a while, then Uber the rest of the way to work. I need to clear my head. As I head out the front door of our building and onto Seventh Avenue, I notice the homeless man who camps out in front of the Simon Levi Company building next door, and I remember Mia and her genuine concern for Bill outside the coffee shop.

Over his shoulder I spot his belongings—a rusty bicycle, from which two canvas bags hang, and a blanket stuffed into the basket attached to the handlebars—leaning against the red brick. This is a good location for him; the entrance to Petco Park is only a few hundred feet east. When he asked me for money once, I asked him why he needed mine when surely he took in at least a couple hundred bucks on game days. He shook his head at me and told me to forget it. He didn't need my money. And his name was Chuck, by the way, if I cared. I wonder for the first time what his story is. I have never understood why home-less people can't get out from under it. How hard can it be to stay in a shelter, save the money you've been given, move into a halfway house, and then get a job? But having watched Mia give so easily to that man two days ago makes me dig into my wallet now. "Chuck, right?" I say, handing him a five-dollar bill. "Grab something to eat."

He looks like he's about to say something but thinks better of it and clears his throat instead. He folds the bill in half and puts it in the inside pocket of his flannel jacket.

I give him a quick wave and walk down to K Street, trying to live in the moment. To appreciate the early seventy-degree sun, though it's a constant in San Diego. To take in the sights of my East Village neigh-borhood that I've walked by a hundred times before—the shiny high-rises a stark contrast to the gritty dive bars and ultrahip farm-to-table restaurants with handwritten signs out front listing the specials of the day. But the negative thoughts about seeing Mia start working their way into my consciousness. *She's only meeting you tonight because she was too nice to say no. She'd been back a week and hadn't called you. If you hadn't run into her, you may not have ever known she was back.*

I force the thoughts away and replace them with positive ones.

She will give me another chance. Tonight is the beginning of a beautiful life together. Okay, maybe that last one was a little too optimistic. *Slow down, Dom. Breathe.*

I make it to the corner of Seventh and K Street and wait for the light to turn green. To my right is a man wearing a SeaWorld T-shirt holding a map out as he and a woman study it. Two small children in San Diego Zoo hats dance in circles on the sidewalk next to them. To my left is a woman clearly still wearing last night's clothes—a black bandage dress and three-inch heels, out of place at eight o'clock in the morning. Her hair is thrown into a messy ponytail, and I would bet anything there's a serious amount of smudged mascara beneath her oversize sunglasses. I should look away, but there's something about her that keeps me watching her. She has an air of confidence despite the fact that she's clearly in the midst of a walk of shame.

The woman looks in my direction, and I give her a nod of understanding. I've done the same walk many times, but never with my head held as high as hers. Did the person she spent the night with let her walk out this morning, not bothering to escort her home? Or did she sneak out? I'm going to guess the latter.

The light changes, and the woman begins to step off the sidewalk. At the same moment a white Toyota Camry rounds the corner, but I sense that it isn't going to stop at the red light. In a split second I make a decision and grab her arm, pulling her back onto the sidewalk. She stumbles and grabs my shoulder, nearly knocking both of us over. "What the hell—" she begins, but she's cut off as the Camry doesn't slow down, continuing on through the intersection and slamming into a city bus. The sound of metal crunching is deafening. I hear screams coming from the family, which thankfully was too distracted to cross when the light turned. Someone yells that he's calling 911.

I realize I'm still gripping the woman's arm. I let go.

"How did you——" she starts, but I'm already jogging over to the Camry to check on the driver. He's alone in the car. He's dazed, the airbag deployed into his face. But other than that he seems okay. I ask him if he can move, and he says yes, so I help him out of the car. The front of the Camry is crushed like a soda can—it's a miracle this man is okay. I look inside the bus, but it's mercifully empty of any passengers.

In my line of work, I've been to hundreds of accident scenes in my career, but this one feels different. Maybe because it involves me. I'm shaking as I sit down on the curb and bow my head, the crash in front of me a haunting reminder of what could have been had I not been here.

A hand on my shoulder makes me jump slightly. It's the woman I stopped from crossing. "If you hadn't stopped me, I don't know what would have happened. I might have been killed." She removes her sunglasses, and it turns out there is a good amount of mascara under her eyes. Her shockingly bright-green eyes. "Thank you," she says, her voice sounding far away. I think I hear her tell me her name is Amanda.

I wonder for a moment if I'm in shock. There is a buzzing in my head, and everything feels foggy. I start to get up, but the scene around me starts to spin, so I sit back down.

"Are you all right?"

"Yeah. It's strange. The Camry wasn't driving erratically, but something told me to pull you back."

"Thank God," she says and sits down beside me. "You have good instincts."

I see Mia's face. *Not when it comes to love.*

"I'm Dom," I say and outstretch my hand.

She waves it away. "The guy who saved my life gets a hug!" She embraces me, and her ponytail rubs across my face. It smells like strawberries. When we pull apart, she thanks me again as sirens whir in the distance.

"I'm happy you're okay," I say, looking over at the bus driver and the Camry driver exchanging insurance information. "That no one is hurt." I push myself up, finally feeling strong enough to stand, the shock starting to fade. A small crowd has gathered as I say goodbye and start to cross the street, looking both ways and waiting several extra beats before I begin to walk.

"Can I get your number?" she calls after me.

Without thinking, I turn and say the first thing that comes to mind. "What about your friend whose place you just left?"

"A, what makes you think I'm hitting on you, and B, why do you think I've just left someone's place?"

"I'll start with B," I say, then simply give her a dramatic once-over from her heels up to her face.

"Touché," she says, a playful smile forming on her lips.

"And as for A, I don't think that at all; I was joking," I say, because I was. I'm seeing Mia tonight. I'm not flirting with random women on the street.

"Well, for what it's worth, he's a douche. I sneaked out, not that he could have heard me over his animalistic snores!" She laughs. "Anyway, I wanted to be able to contact you so I could send you a proper thank-you."

"You've already thanked me," I say but pull one of my cards out of my wallet and give it to her anyway.

She hugs me again. "Thank you so much. I'm going to rethink a lot of things. Including random hookups on Tinder," she says and turns back in the direction from which she came, sliding my card into her purse as she does.

"Be careful crossing the street," I call after her, then look both ways again and run to the other side, not wanting to take any chances myself. I walk for a few blocks, allowing my heartbeat to slow down to a normal pace, then stop and call an Uber. While I wait for my car, I replay the accident. It all happened so fast. How did I know the Camry wasn't going to stop? That it would blow through that light? I shudder at the thought of how it could have ended. Amanda lying in the street, seriously injured, or worse. The driver of the Camry arrested, a very different future ahead of him. Three minutes later, Joel in a black Subaru Outback picks me up, and I lean into the smooth leather seats and shut my eyes, still unable to believe what happened at that intersection but thankful I had the foresight I did. Although I have no clue where it came from.

I can't help but smile as I think of Amanda's vow to quit random hookups. There will be a lot of sad men in San Diego as a result.

~

When I arrive at the studio ten minutes later, the accident is still playing on a loop in my mind. I try to shake it off as I head to the assignment desk to see what's happening in the news before the nine a.m. editorial meeting. I'm a line producer, and I oversee the five p.m. and six p.m. hours during the week. I decide how each wheel—or each hour—will look. Which stories we will lead with at the top of the hour and which will go after. Alexis is the managing editor who oversees the morning and evening line producers. I scan the list—a boat accident in the harbor, an overturned semi on the 805, a shark attack in Pacific Beach. I picture the crumpled car from this morning. As scary as what I witnessed was, everyone is okay—the only damage superficial. Amanda, the drivers, me—we will all go on with our lives because a split-second decision on my part changed the course of events. I'm struck by how much I take life for granted. How easily I—or anyone I care about—could be a part of any of these stories that make the papers.

Mia. Knowing I'm seeing her tonight is what will get me through today. Help me focus on work so I can move on to what really matters—reconnecting. I keep reading through the stories of the people who didn't have a bystander there to save them, and they all make me feel a mix of emotions I don't usually experience when I read the news. I'm normally able to separate my own thoughts from what I'm reading—not get too invested. That's how we all get through what we do. Because most of the news is sad and dark. I'm drawn to a feel-good piece about a bulldog. Maybe a happy story is what our viewers need. When I say this to Janet behind the desk, she rolls her eyes, thinking I'm joking. This type of segment isn't my usual fare or, to be honest, what I need to be focusing on right now if I want to find that wow piece. The story is about a bulldog named Duchess who has developed quite a following because she skateboards through Mission Bay every weekend with her owner, Duke, a fit, long-haired twentysomething. She's been drawing quite a crowd recently—as many as one hundred people gathered during her latest "ride." And she has over ten thousand followers on Instagram. We will want to jump on this before Channel

Nine does. They are always scooping us on the good dog stories. All the stories, really.

I stare at the picture of Duchess. Her white coat and brown spots. Her teal jeweled collar. Crouched next to her is her owner—a man with bleached-blond hair tied into a man bun. I notice Lance's office is dark, his door closed, so I text the story to him, circling the picture of the trainer and adding, That's one way to meet girls—and of course he has a man bun! I know how much Lance respects how far other men will go to score dates with women. He pings me back immediately with a GIF of the Rock sporting a man bun, and I laugh so hard that a table of interns scanning the wires looks up at me. I text him back that I saved a woman from getting hit by a car on my way to work, and he responds, That's a hell of a way to meet a girl. Why didn't I think of that? I don't reply and shove my phone in my pocket, grab my coffee mug off my desk, and head to the break room. Brian, one of our photogs who handles field shoots, intercepts me before I can get to the Mr. Coffee pot. "Hey, man, how are you?"

"Good," I say, forcing a smile, trying not to look over his shoulder longingly at the half-empty carafe. I squeeze my coffee mug tighter.

"Got a sec? I need to ask you something." Brian and I have always had a good relationship. We started at the station at the same time and will grab a beer from time to time after work.

I nod in response. "Mind if I get some coffee while we talk?"

"One of those nights?"

"And mornings," I say, and Brian gives me a look like he understands. But he has no idea.

As I'm pouring the brew, Brian starts in. "So, I caught Julie in a lie last night. There was a flirty text from her trainer on her phone, and she denied it."

We chat for a while, and I tell him to do whatever he can to figure it out with her. Julie is his longtime girlfriend—one he's told me he wants to marry. I add that he doesn't want to let her go and regret it for the rest of his life. I can feel Mia's presence in my response and wonder if it's heightened because she's back and I'm seeing her tonight. Would I have given the same advice to Brian last week? I don't know.

I keep my head down until the editorial meeting, where I take my usual seat next to Alexis.

"What have you got, Dom?" she asks, staring at me from behind the tortoiseshell reading glasses she always has perched on the end of her nose.

I clear my throat. "I think we should take a left turn today. Do something different. I scanned the breaking news, and it was all so dreary."

"Yeah, it's the news," Devon, the anchor, interjects.

I shoot him a dirty look. "Anyway, instead of starting with a story about a jackknifed big rig or another shark attack—"

"Another attack?" Alexis interrupts. "Where?"

"Pacific Beach, but the person survived, punched it in the nose or something," I say and start to continue with my pitch, but she jumps in again.

"That's, what, three already in Southern California this year?" Alexis says to no one in particular.

A production assistant calls from the back of the room, "Yes, that's right."

"James," Alexis says to one of our field producers, "get a quick package together on the other two. And get some man-on-the-streets commentary at Pacific Beach today."

James says okay and leaves the room.

"So what's your story, Dom?" Alexis looks at me.

"There's this bulldog named Duchess, and she skateboards—"

"A skateboarding dog? You can't be serious."

I start to tell her that I am serious. That we need some levity in our programming to balance out all of the depressing stories. But the look on her face tells me it won't go over well, and I'm already failing her by not giving her that big story she wants from me.

"Of course I'm not," is all I say, catching Devon smirking at me from across the table.

Alexis corners me after the meeting, her dark-brown eyes blazing. "What's gotten into you? What's with your positivity speech? We are the number one—" Alexis catches herself. "We *were* the number one news station in San Diego until we let Channel Nine beat us." She pauses, and I am reminded that our rival station has been scorching us in the ratings. "We certainly aren't going to take back the lead with Duchess the celebrity skateboarding dog!" She reaches back and smooths her jet-black hair. "I thought we talked about this—I need *you* to break the news. *You* need to find the story that hasn't been told."

"I know," I say, seeing the smoke rising from the front of the Camry this morning. The weight of what could have been still resting firmly on my shoulders. I decide to be honest with her. "I saw the story, and it made me smile. And I thought maybe going in a different direction for once would be original. Refreshing. That our viewers might need a break from all the doom and gloom."

"Dom, if you want to tell those types of stories, I'm sure there's a home for you at *The Dodo*." She crosses her arms over her chest.

"Ouch," I say and try to read her frown. She's been increasingly critical of me the past few months, and I'm annoyed at myself for allowing this morning's accident to make me soft. I don't have a ton of wiggle room right now at work.

"If the Facebook page fits."

"Sorry. I had a near miss with a Toyota Camry this morning. I stopped a woman from getting hit, and I'm shaken up."

"Is that what's going on with you? Thank God!" Alexis throws her head back and presses her hands together in prayer.

My jaw falls open. She really is ruthless.

"You had me worried there. I thought you meant all that positivity shit, but it's only because you had a near-death experience!" She laughs. "Find me the story that nobody is telling," she says and turns on her heel, disappearing down the hallway before I can say a word.

~

I stare at my computer screen for the next hour, unable to focus. Thoughts of Mia dance through my mind every time I try to concentrate on a news article I'm reading. I can't stop thinking about seeing her tonight. I texted her yesterday to make a plan for our date, and she suggested the San Diego County Fair. I stared at the text for several minutes, not knowing how to respond. There's nothing about the fair that interests me. I hate fast rides, high rides, pretty much any and all rides. The idea of strapping myself into something that was assembled by God only knows who—and trusting that something won't go wrong—seems insane to me. What if the guy forgot a bolt or a wire? Then what? But Mia loves carnivals. Loves rides. I remember she wanted to go back when we were together, and I flat-out refused. Maybe this time she's testing me to see if I've changed. Before I could type, she texted me again.

Well?

I'm in! was all I wrote. And I hoped I could be. All in. Present. Able to put my feelings aside to support hers.

Wow! I did NOT expect that response!

I toyed with several replies and finally settled on: I'm a changed man!

I hoped it was true.

Finally I give up on trying to get work done and text my mom to see if she wants to meet for lunch. Between the accident this morning and my conversation with Alexis, I'm off balance. My mom has always been my beacon when things feel chaotic. Being around her makes me feel better when I'm anxious. But I'm not sure if I'll tell her about this near miss this morning, because it would only worry her. She responds that she'd love to see me at our spot and that my dad is going to come as well. I sigh. I wanted to see my mom alone. My dad changes the dynamic—always takes my mom's side, never seems to have an opinion of his own. Or if he does, he's apprehensive to share it—my mom has a bad habit of bulldozing opinions that don't match her own. And I know going in that the topic of Mia will be a tense one, so it would be easier to discuss it one-on-one versus one-on-two.

When I walk into the restaurant, I see my mom and dad at a table with a bright Mexican blanket that serves as the tablecloth under the glass top. Her practical brown leather purse is on the chair beside her, and my dad sits quietly beside her in a pressed white button-down and tan trousers. Five years ago she retired from the law firm where she'd been a paralegal for most of her adult life, and my dad sold his dental practice.

Not long after that, she promptly did a Yelp search to find a res-taurant where she and I could have lunch as often as my work would allow. I have almost always welcomed these times to see her because we're close, but she'd see me every day if she could, so I don't always say yes. And this year she's started bringing my dad to get him out of the house more. She located Chiquita's and approved of its 4.4 star rating and its two dollar signs. She scouted it by herself first so she could sign off on the food as well (she needed to make sure the carnitas were up to her standards), and then it became our place.

"*Mijo*," she says as I kiss her on the cheek and shake hands with my dad. She gives me her usual once-over. "What's wrong?"

"Nothing," I say, deciding I would at least like to have a tortilla chip before I complain about Alexis.

She wrinkles her nose and glances over at my dad. "You're lying, and I think I know what's going on, but let's order before I grill you." She smiles. "What are you getting?" my mom asks, scanning the menu, though I already know she'll order her regular, the carnitas. And my dad will get the shredded taco combination plate.

"The shredded taco combo plate for me," my dad announces, as if this is news.

"And my usual as well," I say, referencing the Black Angus carne asada burrito topped with the red sauce and extra cheese that I always order. "But it won't be as good as yours," I add for good measure.

"No, it won't." She smiles. My mom takes a lot of pride in her cooking—I grew up with soft, warm homemade tortillas, perfectly slow-cooked carnitas (why she's so snobby about them), and salsa with exactly the right amount of bite.

Our waiter comes. We know him by name.

"The usual all around?" Salvador asks.

"You know what?" I say, looking at the menu again. "I'm going to change things up—walk on the wild side today."

"Chile relleno?" Salvador suggests.

"Nope. I'll get a salad."

"A salad? Dom!" My mom puts her hand over her heart as if I've told her terrible news.

"What's gotten into you?" My dad frowns. "Since when do you eat salads?" He scrunches his nose as he says the word *salads*.

"I'll add shredded beef," I offer.

Salvador laughs. "Should I come back?"

"No! He'll have the same burrito he always gets, and I'll have the—"

"Carnitas." Salvador supplies the answer, and my mom grins. He nods at my dad. "And the number three combo for that guy coming right up."

My dad nods and pats his stomach. "Can't wait."

I shake my head slightly as my salad plans vanish along with Salvador. My mom's determination is both her best and worst quality.

"Like I said, I think I know what's going on, but you tell me," my mom says.

"Can't a guy make a departure from his normal order?" I joke.

"But a salad?" My mom laughs, but her smile quickly fades.

I start to tell both of them about my run-in with Alexis, but my mom speaks first. "Is it Mia?" she asks, and I feel an anger start to rise inside of me. Of course she would think it's about Mia. I called my mom Tuesday to tell her Mia was back, and her response was lukewarm.

"What? No!" I say more sharply than I intend, feeling defensive. My mom looks hurt. "Sorry," I say. "It's not Mia. It's only a salad, Mom." I've lost the desire to talk about work, so I turn toward my father. "So, Dad, what's going on with you? Read any good books lately?"

My dad starts to answer, but my mom cuts him off. "Don't change the subject!" she warns. "The woman you never got over walks back into your life, and you order a salad." My mom folds her arms across her chest, covering the gold cross she always wears around her neck. My dad gave it to her for their tenth wedding anniversary. They've now been married thirty-nine years. "Nothing is normal about either of those scenarios."

I shrug and shoot a pleading look to my dad.

"If the boy says it's not about Mia, we should trust him," my dad says, and I could kiss him.

My mom pauses for a moment, and I think she's going to back off. "I don't think reconnecting with her is going to be good for you," she says, her lips set in a straight line, her lipstick worn off at the corners.

I take the bait. "Why not?"

"You know why not."

"Remind me," I say, my tone now intentionally hard.

"Son," my father says, his voice low. "Don't talk to your mother like that. She's worried about you. Last time you were involved with Mia . . ." He lets his sentence trail off, because we all know what happened last time.

This isn't a battle I'm going to win. Not ten years ago, not now.

"I gave you my ring, mijo. What more could I have done?" She sighs dramatically and looks at my dad.

"She's right," my dad says.

And as I'm about to tell them I'm grateful she offered the ring, she speaks again. "You're the one who didn't want to marry her. There must have been a part of you that knew it wasn't a good match."

I do my best to push my anger down. "I was twenty-four. I was too young." And I took bad advice from Lance. But I don't mention that to my parents. They can't know that he told me backing out was the right thing. That I hadn't been to Europe yet. Europe! As if being married and traveling to Europe were mutually exclusive.

I believed every single word. After all, Lance was echoing that fearful voice inside of me. It was too easy to believe them.

"It had nothing to do with your age and everything to do with your gut. Since you were a kid, you've always known what you've wanted. You go after it. You get it."

"This isn't about becoming fifth-grade class president, Mom."

"If you had wanted to marry her, you would have." She folds her arms across her chest.

"She's right," my dad interjects. "With your mother, I knew. I never had a single doubt. And I was twenty."

"It's only after Mia wouldn't return your calls and you chased her out to Chicago and she wouldn't give you another chance that you convinced yourself she was the one and *you'd* screwed up," my mom piles on. "Haven't you ever thought if she had truly wanted you, if you were truly meant to be, that after having a few months to think about it, she would have jumped into your arms in Chicago?"

"Don't hold back, Mom. Tell us how you really feel!"

"She's worried about you," my dad interjects softly.

"She has a funny way of showing it," I say like she's not there. "What about you? What's *your* opinion?" I ask my dad.

He clears his throat, then looks at my mom.

"*Your* opinion," I repeat.

"Your mom told me she was back." He takes a drink of his water. "And honestly, my initial response was worry."

Of course it was.

My mom gives me a smug smile. "I know you think I'm being harsh, but I'm trying to help you see." She puts her hand over mine. "Let me ask you something."

"Fine," I say.

"Have you ever had a *real* relationship?" She pauses as Salvador sets down a basket of tortilla chips and salsa and hurries away, pretending he didn't hear her question.

"Since Mia?" I ask, feeling defensive and leaning away from her.

"Ever." She takes a bite of a chip.

This hits hard. "Mia was real." I pause. "*Is* real. Why don't you want me to be happy?"

"I do; it's why I'm saying *not* to reconnect. You have been caught up in her for years. It's not healthy, Dominic. It never was. So hot and cold. So intense."

"I know *you* thought that. That we were a fire that could explode. But we were young."

"Yes. But why has the fire continued to burn so strong for you? When you had the chance to enjoy it, you extinguished it. Then you spent all these years wanting it back."

"What's wrong with that? I made a mistake. I realized that after," I say, my stomach hardening.

"Or you simply became obsessed because that's easier than finding a person you could make a life with?"

"Why did you give me your diamond when I proposed? Why didn't you try to talk me out of it if you thought we were wrong for each other?" My words come out choppy. My blood pressure is rising now.

My dad leans in and gives me a long stare. "Because we love you, and sometimes you need to let your kids make mistakes."

"Then why don't you let me make one now?"

"Because this is not healthy," my mom interjects.

"So now I'm not healthy? You know what, guys? Enjoy your food. I'm not going to sit here and take this from you anymore," I say, the color rising in my cheeks. To not have my parents in my corner hurts. Why can't a decade make someone *more* ready, not less? I stare at them for a beat, realizing they're not going to budge.

"But isn't it why we're here? You wanted us to tell you not to go tonight."

I stop for a second and stare at her. Had I wanted that? Was it why I'd asked her to lunch, not the other way around? Over the years she's always tried to steer me away from Mia. Has always wanted me to find another relationship. My lack of desire to settle down after I broke off the engagement has been a point of contention between us. In my twenties, my family found it endearing. My dad would slap me on the back. Tell me he loved my mom but wished he'd had more time to sow his oats too. As the calendar clicked into my thirties, his back pats became more scarce. My mom's bachelor jokes became more and more passive aggressive. Now, as I knock on thirty-five's door, my mother has become laser focused on my single status. Sending me links to women she found on Match.com. How she did that, I have no idea. My mom wants those grandchildren, and she wants them now. Without any siblings, I'm her only hope.

Why did I expect her to say anything other than *Don't go out with Mia tonight*? Because to her, Mia is a distraction, not a solution. But instead of softening toward my mom like I usually do, I turn and huff out of the restaurant before the food arrives, suddenly feeling more like thirteen than thirty-four. Part of me wanting to cry and part of me wanting to scream. And not one part of me wanting to admit defeat. I step onto the concrete, refusing to look back.

I keep myself busy the rest of the afternoon. A small plane crashes into a neighborhood in Oceanside after taking off from Palomar

Airport, and it sends the newsroom into a frenzy to break the story before the other local stations. Miraculously, everyone survives. The six o'clock newscast ends. As I'm walking outside to meet my Uber and rush to meet Mia at the fair, I get an email. I open it. It's Amanda from this morning. She thanks me again for saving her life, then quips that she's joined a walk-of-shame support group. They have awesome coffee and donuts if I'd ever like to join her. I laugh to myself and flag it for later, my nerves tingling with the thought of seeing Mia soon.

CHAPTER FOUR

Thursday, June 11, 7:45 p.m.

I walk nimbly toward the entrance of the San Diego County Fair as the sounds of screaming patrons riding rides and the whir of roller coasters whizzing along their tracks fill the air. Northbound traffic was heavier than I expected, and it took my driver forever to maneuver through the parking lot to drop me off, so I'm perfectly on time, which is late in my book. I scan the line to the entrance and the crowd of people in the area for Mia. My eyes dart back and forth, but she's not there. I pull out my phone—no texts. I look around again, searching the area. What if she didn't come? Changed her mind? There's an empty feeling in the pit of my stomach as I consider this. If she doesn't show up, if I don't get another chance with her, I don't know what I'll do. From the second I saw her in that coffee shop, I vowed to win her back. To right my wrong. And while I didn't plan to lead with that when she showed up tonight, I feel panicked thinking I may never have the opportunity.

I look again, and a woman pushes her stroller away, and then there she is, the people around her all falling out of view. My breath catches in my throat as if I'm seeing her for the first time. She's wearing cutoff jean shorts and a white blouse, her hair tucked behind her ears, gold earrings dangling from her lobes. She doesn't see me, and I watch her for a few moments. She smiles at a little girl with blonde pigtails, tells her mom how cute she is. And then she looks over, her eyes locking with mine. Suddenly every negative thought I've had about today disappears from my psyche. Because she is here. I am here. We are together.

"Dom, you have to stop looking at me like that. You're going to give me a complex!" Mia laughs when I reach her.

"Sorry!" I say, feeling my cheeks warm. I look away to compose myself. "So, shall we?" I ask.

"Yes! I'm dying for some good old-fashioned carnival food," she says, and my stomach rumbles. I never ate after I stormed out of the restaurant.

I buy our tickets, and we navigate the crowd, through the exhausted-looking parents with sticky-faced toddlers on their hips and the gaggle of midriff-baring teenagers pushing through impatiently, anxious to get to the rides, glowing bands adorning their wrists.

"There! I see food!" Mia says, walking faster toward a giant yellow stand with pictures of polish sausage dogs, all-beef hot dogs, and corn dogs.

"I think you've hit the jackpot." I smile as I watch her surveying the menu, her eyes like saucers.

She orders two corn dogs, a basket of fries, and two giant lemonades. She pulls her wallet out.

"No way, my treat." I hand the man my card.

"I went pretty big."

"I'm glad you like to eat," I say, thinking of the women I dated over the years who overthought everything they put in their mouths, frowning at the menus when nothing suited them. And for the dozenth time since Mia walked up tonight, I feel reaffirmed that she's still the one.

"I sure do," she says and takes a bite. A glob of ketchup remains on the side of her mouth. My instinct is to wipe it away, but I hand her a napkin instead.

"So I have a question for you," Mia says as we take turns dipping our fried dogs in the same tiny paper cup full of ketchup.

"Okay," I say, my knee starting to bounce. I put my hand on it.

"Have you been here one time in the last ten years?" She sets her half-eaten corn dog in its paper tray and grabs a french fry.

"To this hot dog stand? Nope," I say, biting the last of my corn dog off its stick.

She elbows me in the ribs. "You know what I mean."

"I haven't been to the fair either."

"Why not?" she asks, her head tilted to the side.

I shrug, wondering if this is a test. Was I supposed to be strapping myself into roller coasters while we were apart?

"You still don't like the rides. You weren't all in on coming, were you?"

I freeze, and my adrenaline spikes. Does she need me to be all in on the fair? And if I'm not, will she want to leave—worried I'm still the same old boring Dom from before? I try to access what's in her head before I answer, but her face is impassive.

"Well?" Mia raises an eyebrow.

"You caught me!" I confess, trying to keep it light. "But I've changed in other ways."

"Mm-hmm. You're still wearing your hair the same." She smiles. "You still work at the same place." She sips her lemonade. "And I'm going to go out on a limb here, but I'm guessing you're still a mama's boy."

"Harsh!" I say with a smile, but inside I'm crumbling. Worried she's saying these things because she was hoping I would have changed. That I've got no shot with her because I haven't.

"You either saw her or talked to her already today. Am I right?" she says, the straw still in her mouth.

"We had lunch," I say, then quickly add, "But my dad was there too!" Leaving out the part about how things went sideways when her name came up.

"Listen, I'm not knocking you. You're you."

"What does that mean?" I ask, my jaw clenching. I force myself to loosen it.

"It means I'm not surprised that you're still a creature of habit."

I don't like how that sounds. *Creature of habit.* It makes me sound boring. Dull. Safe. I stand up from the bird-poop-stained bench we've been sitting on. "Let's go on the fastest, scariest, most obnoxious ride right now," I say, grabbing her hand and pulling her up.

"You don't have to prove anything to me, Dom."

"I know that. But it's time I lived on the edge. Did something different."

"I was thinking we might let our food digest before we hit the big-boy rides, but I don't want this window to pass!" she says, dramatically power walking toward the rides.

My heart does flips as I watch her striding ahead, her hair bouncing against her back with each step. She glances over her shoulder as we enter the Fun Zone, the sights and sounds of the carnival rides backlighting her heart-shaped face. Evidence of the decade we've been apart is apparent only in the faint lines around her eyes that crinkle when she smiles. How did she earn each one? Who made her laugh so hard that it caused a permanent fissure? Did they also make her cry? Where are those scars hidden? Because this is not only a date. This could be the beginning of the rest of our lives. That thought bolsters me, makes me walk faster so I can be closer to her.

"Coming," I call out and quicken my pace until we're locked in stride.

On our way, I spot one of those carnival games—it's basketball. A total waste of money because there is zero chance of winning. I read once that the nets are smaller than standard, but the balls are regulation size. But of course they don't tell you that. The safe and boring Dom would never play this game. He'd make a comment that he might as well burn cash, as it would be the same difference. But right now, being around Mia makes me feel invincible. I pull a twenty-dollar bill out of my wallet. "Wait a second—I'm going to win you a prize!"

Mia stops and turns. "Basketball?"

"Sure, why not?" I say, and the carny running the game smiles, revealing a missing front tooth. He thinks he's got a schmuck on his hands. And maybe he does.

"You get three tries," the carny says, handing me a ball.

I shoot the first one, and it sails toward the basket, and when I'm sure it's going in clean, it hits the rim and ricochets off.

"You've got this, Dom!" Mia says from next to me. I feel a drip of sweat form on my brow.

I shoot again. This ball hits the backboard and bounces right back at me. I catch it, and the carny laughs.

"Last chance," he says to me, and I glare at him.

I take a deep breath and release the ball from my fingertips. It sails through the air and slips straight through the basket.

Mia cheers. "All net!"

"Third time's the charm," I say to the carny.

"What does she want?" He points to the large stuffed animals hanging from the top. "She can have any of those."

"I'll take him!" Mia squeals.

The carny pulls down a three-foot-tall soft brown bear with a pale-pink bow tied around its neck.

"He's almost as big as you," I laugh and try to determine if she's proud of me for winning the bear. Hoping that she is. Hoping she thinks I've changed. That I know better than I did at twenty-four.

"I'm going to name him Beary."

"How original," I deadpan.

"Whatever," she says, giving Beary a kiss on his nose. "There she blows." Mia points to the Zipper ride to our right. "The scariest ride here without a doubt. Not for the faint of heart."

By the look of its rusty oblong frame, aging paint job, and antique-looking cable, I'd say it's already had one ride too many. My stomach twists as I watch the red, yellow, and blue lights flashing while each car flips end over end on its axis. The high-pitched screams coming from the passengers almost drown out the Avenged Sevenfold song blaring from the speakers. As the cars fly by, I stiffen, rethinking my earlier proclamation. I prefer both feet planted firmly on the ground, thank you very much. I look at Mia, and she's having the polar opposite reaction to this ride. She's grinning and bouncing on her toes as she watches it. And I know, despite the alarms that are ringing inside of me, that I'll go on this ride. Because I'm desperate to please her. Then I hear a joyful *woot woot* sound coming from one of the cars and feel my shoulders relax. How bad can it be? Mia is already getting in line. She's always been such a force of strength and confidence. Convincing me to do things I never would have on my own—both big and small, but all impacting me for the better. Like climbing the thirty-foot tree in the backyard of her childhood home in Glencoe, Illinois, when she took me there for the holidays six months after we'd met. She encouraged me to apply for an assistant producer job at the station, even though I was only an intern at the time, hadn't graduated yet, and would be competing against people with far more television experience. I ended up getting the position, Alexis saying she admired my gusto. And now—Mia was pushing me to ride the Zipper.

"We're really doing this?" I walk up to her and smile nervously as I look into her eyes. That brilliant cobalt that reminds me of the ocean after it rains. Still sparkling like they did all those years ago when she was standing in her parents' front yard telling me to go to O'Hare. Fly back to California. "Because there's still time to go get our teeth whitened," I joke, referring to the booth we passed a few minutes earlier.

"See! You're so damn practical!" Mia says, falling into line behind a gaggle of long-haired teenage girls dressed in crop tops and short shorts.

"Is getting your teeth whitened practical? Feels more like a luxury spend to me." I smile widely, hoping I don't have a piece of corn dog stuck in my teeth. I don't remember the last time I've felt this nervous. It feels like I'm riding one of the roller coasters here—my emotions spiking with joy and then plummeting with anxiety in a matter of minutes. It's both exhilarating and horrifying.

Mia swats me lightly, and my whole body tingles at her touch. "Come on, Dom. You suggested this. So stop stalling."

"I'm not stalling, but is now a good time to tell you I already averted death once today? So maybe I won't be so lucky this time?" I say, looking up at the cars flying above us. My earlier internal bravado waning.

"What?" Mia's mouth falls open.

I tell her about the Camry that didn't stop at the light and how I pulled Amanda back onto the sidewalk. How the front of the car looked like a soda can someone had stepped on.

"Holy shit. Are you okay?"

"I'm fine. It was ludicrous, and the woman was super thankful, vowing to change her life," I say, leaving out the part about her email to me.

"A near-death experience will do that to you, I'm sure."

I nod. I've been feeling that way all day. That life is short. That I need to revel in the moments. Like this one. "True."

"I'm going to ask that guy to hold Beary for me." Mia points to the carny in a skin-tight Metallica T-shirt taking tickets. The man mumbles something about not being responsible if something happens to the bear.

I wince as I take in his belly poking out from under the taut fabric of his shirt. "You may have to give Beary a bath after," I say under my breath, so only Mia can hear.

"Stop it." She covers Beary's ears. "Beary will be fine. Stop worrying so much. You overthink everything."

42

I look down at my Vans and let her words dangle in the air, understanding she's not talking about the bear or the ride. I need to snap out of it. Put my unease on a shelf. This is the chance I've been waiting for. She's here, now, and I don't want to waste it.

The line moves quickly. Too quickly. My heart beats faster with each step we take. I think about what Mia said about my tendency to worry. When she and I were together, I let fear win out most of the time, my mom's voice in my head. She raised me to be careful. *Look both ways before you cross the street, mijo; then look again. Don't ever trust your first check. Always check twice. Things can go wrong. Think about what bad things could happen before you try something and act accordingly.* She'd been pregnant before me, and she'd lost that baby in the middle of her second trimester. She blamed herself—said that she could have taken it easier than she had. She'd been working double shifts at the law office—the caseload intense, but the extra overtime paycheck propelling her. It was my dad who, on a rare occasion of sharing personal details with me, told me she changed after that. Became hypercautious.

I remember a time when Mia wanted to skinny-dip in the ocean after a walk on the beach. It was long after the sun had set, the sky like blackout shades, the area was deserted, and Mia would be naked in my arms, but still, I said no. That we'd get a ticket if caught by the police. But she rolled her eyes and pulled my shirt off me anyway. Then she removed her own. I found myself following her into the waves, my fears quieting with each stride. We dived in, the cold water shocking to my system but also making me feel wide awake and more alive than I had felt before. Why didn't I let myself follow her more often? All these years later, I'm still worried about things that don't matter, rather than what's right in front of me. I glance up at the ride soaring above us and then at Mia.

The line continues forward, and I take a deep breath as the ride operator calls out that he'll take the next group, including us.

Mia takes my hand as we step through the gate, our car with a cage door awaiting. Her fingers are soft and narrow, exactly as I remember them, and I'm instantly comforted.

Mia places Beary on a chair next to the carny, the bear's face pointed toward the night sky. "So he can watch," she offers when she catches me eyeing her.

"We certainly don't want him to feel left out." Then I stage-whisper, "He'll be upset if he hears we ate corn dogs and fries without him. We should take him for a deep-fried ice cream after this."

"Oh, he can't partake. He told me he's dairy- and gluten-free," she deadpans.

I roll my eyes. "Of course he is."

"Southern California bear—what do you expect?" she shoots back.

The carny lifts the cage door to our awaiting car, revealing giant sweat rings under his arms. His name tag reads THEO.

"Hey, Theo?" I say.

"Yeah?"

"How long is the ride?"

"One minute and thirty-five seconds," he says, then gives me a once-over. "I need you to shit or get off the pot, sir." He motions toward the car, and I hear giggling. The teenage girls in front of us in line are watching.

"I'm coming. Was hoping the ride would be *longer* than that," I say, puffing out my chest and glancing at Mia, who doesn't seem to be listening.

Theo mutters something and rolls his eyes.

Mia jumps in and settles herself quickly, patting the worn black pleather bench seat. "Here, I'll sit next to the door, and you can have the inside," she offers after I don't move toward her.

I step over her and sit down, though something doesn't feel right. But my emotions have hit so many highs and lows since I saw Mia at the coffee shop that I'm not sure I can trust the twist in my gut. Her presence has heightened my senses. I feel each pause in her speech, every catch in her breath, all of her glances in my direction. I am a mess.

Get it together, Dom.

Theo slams the cage door shut and slides a pin through the lock. I jump slightly.

"It's not going to feel as fast on the inside," she says when she catches me staring at her. I know she's lying, but I don't call her on it. "You ready?" she asks, resting her hand on my knee.

"Yes," I answer, putting my hand over hers. "I am this time. I promise."

Her eyes widen. "Dom," she says, but the rest of her sentence gets caught in her throat as the Zipper roars to life and sends us swinging into the warm summer air. She threads her arm through mine tightly and begins to scream as we flip over again and again. Her touch makes me feel brave, and I relax and begin to enjoy the ride.

Our car crisscrosses through the air as we gain height and speed, the long arm of the Zipper thrusting us and the other passengers up and down. I grip the lap bar tightly and glance over at Mia. She smiles widely. We are moving so fast that it takes me a moment to realize with horror that our cage door has come open and is flapping wildly on its hinge, ramming against the side of our car with an intense force over and over. Mia screams, the sound of her cry absorbed by the door pushing against our cab. I grab onto her just as the lap bar flies upward, our bodies thrusting forward. We land on the floor of the car, I slam into Mia, and we fall toward the opening. "Hold on!" I scream, but I'm not sure she hears me. I grab onto her arm and try to pull us both backward using my legs as leverage, but the g-force is too strong. My muscles clench in fear as we rock back and forth. I gasp for air. Mia's eyes are wide and glassy. Her smooth fingers grasping mine like a vise. My heart is pounding wildly, bursting against my chest, and I can barely breathe as the force slams us both down again—our bodies coming together and splitting apart as we fall closer to the doorless opening. The car twists again, thrusting both of us against the back side of the cage. My head slams against the side, but I feel nothing. I'm able to grip Mia's arm again. I use all of my strength to hold on to her and keep us from falling out, but I feel like I'm trying to swim upstream in white-water rapids. I lose my hold on her, and she starts to fall. I scream in fear, but then the cab turns, and I'm able to grab her again. My arms and shoulders are fatiguing, and I start to panic. She pulls herself closer to me, and we twist again, but this time, Mia's body is thrust into the doorway. She grabs onto the side of the cage, and I watch in horror as she loses her grip and starts to slide out the door.

"Mia!" I grab onto her shirt with my other hand and pull, but it rips, and she is thrust outward farther. I'm holding on to her with one hand, but it's wet with sweat, and our fingers are being separated millimeter by millimeter, until finally I lose my grasp on her and she is ripped from me. "Mia!" I cry again as the g-force launches our bodies into the sky, nothing below us but the hard ground fifty or sixty feet down. I try to breathe, but my chest is frozen. We are both falling to our deaths.

Mia flies farther away from me, her mouth open in surprise, as if she can't believe I've lost her. I flail my arms in vain, trying to reach her. My body is shooting through the air, spiraling fiercely toward the ground. Fear pierces every organ of my body. I'm falling at a breakneck speed, but everything in my mind slows to a snail's pace, and I process that I likely have only seconds to live. There's no way I will survive this. I've found Mia only to lose her again. I desperately search the air for her. "Mia!" I wail but am only met with silence. No Mia. My breaths are shallow, and I'm shaking uncontrollably as the fair below me blurs out of focus. I hear myself howl, a terrifying sound I'm sure I've never made before. The ground becomes closer and closer every second. I cover my head with my arms and brace for impact. Everything is loud—and then silent all at once.

~

I wake to people screaming. My head is pounding. I can't feel my arms or legs. I see Mia sprawled out several feet away from me, blood streaming from her head, her eyes open but not registering me. "Mia." I push my voice to be loud, but it comes out as a whisper. "Mia, don't leave me. Stay with me. Please. Is she okay?"

"He's conscious!" someone calls out. I hear scattered applause.

"Don't move," a paramedic says as he leans over me. "Can you tell me your name?"

"Dominic Suarez," I sputter. "I'm okay. Help Mia." I nod in her direction. "Please." I try to move toward Mia, but my right leg won't cooperate. I manage to drag myself a few inches, but the pain in my ribs and chest is searing hot. I reach as far as I can until my fingertips are touching hers. "She's warm!" I say. "She's still alive. She'd be cold if she was dead. She'd be cold." I'm crying now. I can barely get the words out.

"We have to work on you too. You're injured." I watch as another paramedic puts a finger to her neck and then her wrist. He waits a few beats, and I watch the color drain from his face as he begins chest compressions. I start to shake. I feel numb from shock. A scream sits at the base of my throat, wanting out, as I helplessly watch him work to save Mia. The carnival sounds feel out of place, indiscernible, but loud, and I squeeze my eyes shut, wanting silence. The paramedic who asked me my name jars me and begins to tend to my injuries. He's asking me more questions, but all I can do is watch the other man squeeze the bag valve mask for ventilation. He repeats this process several times. Chest compressions. Squeezing the bag, blowing oxygen into her airway. My lungs burn and my chest is heavy. I can only manage short, shallow breaths. I'm sobbing so hard I can't see. I watch him working on Mia, and I pray she'll live. *I will do anything,* I promise. *Anything. Save her, please. Please.*

Finally, after another round, the paramedic quickly inserts an IV before pulling her lifeless body onto a stretcher and into the waiting ambulance. They continue to perform CPR, but it's obvious to me that their efforts are in vain. I can feel Mia leave this world as they pull away, lights flashing.

My heart shatters inside of me as I lie on the concrete.

"No!" I scream. I attempt to sit up, but the pain is too strong. Why did I avert death twice today? Why am I alive and Mia dead?

"We need to get you to the hospital," the paramedic says.

"But—" I don't finish my thought. I try to move, but shards of pain shoot through my chest. It's more than my physical injuries that I'm feeling—there is an incredible ache at the realization before me, so strong that I can barely breathe. "Mia!" I yell, even though she's no longer here. I scream her name louder, again and again, until the paramedic gently tells me I need to lie still so they can get me on the gurney. That they need to save my life. It's unspoken that they couldn't save Mia's. The thought empties me.

I lie back and close my eyes, wondering how I'll survive losing her a final time.

CHAPTER FIVE

Thursday, June 11, 9:45 p.m.

The sirens from the ambulance drone as we speed down the 5 freeway toward UCSD Medical Center. My body is fatiguing against my will, the injection of a sedative they gave me after breaking the news Mia had passed away beckoning my consciousness.

I think about Mia. Where is she right now? I hate that she's all alone. On some gurney somewhere. I gave them her sister's name and the ancient phone number I had for her. But what if she's changed it? What if they can't find her?

Hailey will be devastated. Her parents will be beside themselves. So many people will be at a loss. How will this world move forward without Mia? Without her playful spirit, her kind and open heart? She loved her sister and her parents with every ounce of her being. That's how she loved—100 percent. There was no middle ground. She was either all in or all out. People, animals, it didn't matter. She could never pass a dog without asking if she could pet it. She would always murmur in the animal's ear as she stroked its fur. Once I asked her what she had said to a yellow Lab with a pink jeweled collar. "I told her that she is beautiful." She smiled at me. "That she is good."

Why didn't I use my time with her at the fair to tell her these things? I wish I had wiped that ketchup off the corner of her mouth.

Touched her when I had the chance. I wish I'd told her I was sorry. I wish I'd asked for her forgiveness. I wish I'd had the balls to use the chance I finally had with her to tell her how much I'd missed her. Missed us. But I played it safe yet again, having no idea that our time together would soon run out.

My chest constricts, and I gasp for air. A machine makes a beeping sound. The paramedics check me—and begin to rattle off my vitals in urgent tones. I close my eyes. They can't help me unless they can put my broken heart back together. The one that shattered into pieces when the vertical force of the ride pushed the door of our car open and sent us flying fifty-four feet to the ground. At least that's what I heard one of the firefighters say to a police officer at the scene. The large inflatable slide next door had partially broken my fall, most likely saving me. Why couldn't that damn slide have braced *her* fall?

"You need to try to breathe slowly, Mr. Suarez." The paramedic leans in and adjusts my oxygen mask. "We're almost to the hospital." Then he turns to his partner. "He's over twenty breaths a minute; let's give him a little more O_2."

This paramedic, with his gray hair and deeply lined face, has no idea that oxygen isn't what I need.

This man didn't see the woman who could make him whole literally slip through his fingers. I see Mia's face as our hands separated. Her scream echoes in my ears. My own cries magnified as she slipped away from me. She was terrified. I couldn't save her. And she knew it. Why was I able to save Amanda's life but not Mia's?

My heart starts to hammer again as I think about Mia. Dead. Alone. "Where is Mia?" I ask, the oxygen mask blunting the sound of my voice, and the paramedic doesn't understand me. "Where is Mia?" I try again, forcing the sound from my gut.

"Try to stay calm," is all he says.

"How?" I ask, but so quietly that he doesn't hear me.

I glance at his wedding band protruding through his latex glove, and it reminds me of Mia's engagement ring, long since returned to the small black box, which now lives in the back of my T-shirt drawer. Mia and I were never bound by vows. If only my grip had been tighter. If I hadn't let go, tonight or then. Those are my final thoughts before my eyes close.

~

When I come to, it's my mom's voice I hear first. She's asking the nurse what something means on a monitor.

"Mom?" I say. Then I remember Mia, and a cold chill takes hold of my body. I start to shake. I close my eyes, wanting sleep to take me again.

"Mijo. Oh my God." She turns and puts her hand on mine, pressing the IV line deeper into my skin. I open my eyes again and wince. "I'm sorry, did I hurt you?" She looks panicked.

"No," I say. The tight pain in my chest is far worse.

"You're shivering. Can we get him another blanket?" she asks the nurse. "You're okay. You're going to be fine." My mom's eyes are bloodshot. Her dark-brown hair is pulled into a low bun as always; a few errant strands have escaped and hang around her heart-shaped face. I can't remember the last time I saw her wearing it down. It would hit her waist if she did.

The nurse gently squeezes by my mom. "I'm Janet," she says. She looks to be in her sixties and has pale-green scrubs and short dark hair with streaks of gray running through it. She takes my vitals, and I struggle to keep my eyes open. "We have you on morphine, so that is likely making you drowsy." She checks a bag hanging above me, somehow sensing I'm more exhausted than I've ever been.

"You have a fractured shoulder. A broken leg. Several broken ribs." She pauses, readjusts something on my finger, and I hear beeping.

What about a broken heart? Did you diagnose that too? I bite back tears. Mia is gone. I'll never hear her laugh again. Or smell her sunflower scent. Or hold her soft hand. I'll never get that second chance.

She points to the thing on my finger. "This is taking your pulse. You didn't have any internal bleeding, which is a very good thing. We also did a CT scan and a chest x-ray, and everything looks good. When the doctor comes in, he will assess when you can go home. But it should be soon. You were very lucky."

I want to scream at this nurse that she's wrong. That I'm not lucky. Mia is dead and I'm alive, and there's nothing lucky about that. I let her take the seat by the cage door because I was a coward. I *am* a coward. I'm afraid of everything. Of fast rides. Of commitment. Of risk. Of the unknown. How do I tell this nurse that my only second chance with Mia is gone and how fucking unlucky that is? I will never feel the palm of her hand in mine. I will never kiss the nape of her neck. Never hear her voice. Never get a chance to tell her how much I love her. How I have never stopped loving her. Not for a minute.

"I'm so thankful you are alive," my mom says now, her eyes wet. "And I'm so sorry about Mia—I know what she meant to you." The truth is my mom doesn't know the depth of what Mia meant to me. No one does—Mia included. And now I'll never have the chance to tell her. My throat closes, the regret I'm feeling so intense that I can't speak. It feels as if life has lost all meaning. I hear a laugh from someone down the hall, and I'm struck how other people are living a normal Thursday night, having no clue that my entire world has ended.

When I don't respond, she keeps talking. "I can't imagine what her mother is going through right now." My mom presses her fingers into the corners of her eyes to keep the tears from falling.

"Son, we are so thankful you're still with us." My dad is suddenly standing over me. How long has he been here?

"I shouldn't be here," I snap, and my dad presses his lips together as if forcing himself not to respond.

"Don't say that," my mom says.

"Mia should still be alive," I say, ignoring her.

"Dom, we're so sorry about Mia," my dad says.

"No, you aren't. You didn't want me to go out with her."

"We were only trying to—"

"Protect me. I know. But I'm thirty-four years old," I snap.

"Dom, I—"

"Will you stop making excuses? You never liked her."

My mom recoils, and I fight the urge to apologize. I know it's a low blow, but the rage boiling inside me needs a target. Why did I agree to go on the ride? I was so intent on impressing Mia that I got her killed. And had I simply taken the outside seat—it would be Mia recovering in this bed instead of me.

She should have lived.

The hospital room is silent for several moments, save for the machines connected to my body. When I decide no one is going to speak, that we are going to chalk this up to Dom's grief, I hear my dad's voice: "We're sorry, son. We should have been more supportive."

"Thank you. I appreciate that." I look over at my mom, but she won't meet my eyes.

I see Mia's face in my mind again, her wide smile as she leads me to the Zipper. I suggested we get in line right then. What if we'd waited longer? Or if I hadn't stopped to play that stupid basketball game? Would she still be here? We cover terrible tragedies every day at the station, but they've always seemed out of reach. I think of the hundreds of people we've interviewed who've said, "I never thought it would happen to me." Now I understand what they mean. How the randomness of tragedy haunts you.

"Is that mine?" I ask, nodding in the direction of a cell phone resting on a table across the room.

My dad picks it up and turns it over in his palm as if he's never held a cell phone before.

"I don't know if it's yours," he finally says, and I hear it buzzing in his hand.

It can't be mine if it's still working.

"Can I see it?" I ask anyway. If it is my phone, I want to savor my last text messages with Mia. I hear my mom start to say something, and I know she's going to tell me to rest, that I don't need to worry about it. I shoot her a look, and she closes her mouth. I feel a pang when I see the sadness in her eyes, but I ignore it.

My dad holds the phone out to me, and I grab it with my good hand. It's mine.

The screen is covered in spiderweb cracks, and my heart lurches, the shattered phone reminding me of Mia's broken body on the dirty ground. I brush tears from my eyes as I squint and scroll down. Missed calls. Texts. Facebook notifications. They are all about the accident.

"Has this been on the news?" I ask my parents.

They look at each other. "We've been here the whole time," my dad says. "But Lance did call us, making sure you were okay and asking that we send updates. We didn't ask how he knew." He looks over at my mom, and she nods.

I check the messages from Lance. First asking if I'm okay, then saying that he's talked to my parents, who updated him, and he'll be at the hospital the second he's done with the eleven o'clock news. Apparently Alexis asked him to anchor that hour because I was the one who was injured. The gall of Alexis. Making my best friend anchor the news for ratings. I feel so angry at the exploitation that I have to stop myself from calling and telling her off.

I look at the time—it's 11:02 p.m. "Turn on the TV," I ask my dad. "Channel seven."

He grabs the remote and clicks awkwardly until Lance's concerned face fills the screen. There's something dead in his eyes. Most likely because he's reporting on the accident that killed his best friend's unrequited love. That should have killed his best friend.

Lance clears his throat, then begins speaking. "Tragedy strikes at the San Diego County Fair in Del Mar. And it involves one of our own here at the station." His voice breaks slightly, though it's probably only noticeable to me. "According to witnesses at the scene, the door on one of the cars on the Zipper opened while the ride was in operation, and its two passengers were catapulted nearly sixty feet to the ground. Our esteemed producer Dominic Suarez was one of them. He survived the fall, sustaining only minor injuries. But the woman with him, identified as Mia Bell, died upon impact. Our hearts go out to Mia's family, who had no comment for our Channel Seven producer. We will continue to follow this story as we investigate how this tragedy happened."

I cringe. How could they have called her family?

The line producer in me knows exactly how and why. I would have told someone on the assignment desk to do so if it were any other story. But this is different. It's about Mia. My heart begins to throb as I imagine her mom, Janice, answering the phone in Illinois, having to deal with some random person at a news station calling her about her dead daughter. They cut to footage of our car and the door hanging on only one hinge. I gag, and my mother grabs a bedpan and puts it under my nose. I wave her away and force myself to watch the footage of the moment my life fell apart.

On the television they're now showing a crowd of people gathered around the scene. An ambulance pulling away. Was Mia's body inside? My chest aches as I picture her lying on the concrete, her eyes open but her life already gone from them. *I* did this to her. She's dead because of me. If I hadn't been in that coffee shop, she'd still be alive. Why did I run into her? What was the point of us coming back together after so many years only to have her die? My body feels heavy. My heart heavier. My breathing intensifies, and suddenly I can't slow it down. I'm gasping for breath. I hear monitors start to beep in the distance. The room spins around me.

"Nurse! Somebody!" my mom screams.

The nurse runs in and checks me. "He's hyperventilating." She places an oxygen mask over my nose and mouth. "Breathe, Dominic," she says calmly. She fiddles with something on my IV bag. "Here's a little something that will help you calm down." My chest heaves, and I gasp until finally my breathing slows and a calmness washes over me. As my eyes are closing, I have one thought. One wish.

That I had been given the chance to save Mia's life.

CHAPTER SIX

JUNE 11, 7:00 A.M.
THURSDAY #2

Music plays. The notes are faded, hard to hear. My mind tries to latch on to the tune, to figure out where I've heard it before. It's familiar, the words slightly out of reach. Slowly the song becomes clearer. Closer. Louder. The melody begins to take shape, the chorus bursting into focus and the title coming to mind: "How to Save a Life."

I shoot up in bed. My arm flies out from my side, knocking the alarm clock over, and it falls to the floor, unplugging itself from the wall. I breathe in hard when the music stops, my foggy mind using the silence to make sense of why it is playing.

I rub my eyes. My mind is fuzzy around the edges, as if I'd taken a sleeping pill last night. Then I remember.

Mia is dead.

A horrid coincidence that our song would play on this morning of all mornings. A cruel reminder.

I see her lifeless body in my mind. I try to press away the horrible image, but I can't. Her empty eyes, the blood pooling around her on the concrete—every last detail is burned onto my brain. I feel like I'm going to vomit and start to dry heave over my trash can. When I'm done, I lie down on the floor and curl into a ball. I don't know how long I'm there before I finally gather the strength to sit up, feeling bleak. I've started to walk to the bathroom to splash cold water on my face when I realize:

I'm not in the hospital.

I'm in my bedroom. In the condo I share with Lance.

What is going on?

Am I dreaming? Hallucinating? Because there's no way I can be back home right now. "Mom?"

Lance materializes in the doorway in a white undershirt and khakis, brushing his teeth. He moves the toothbrush so he can talk. "Should I be concerned you're asking for your mommy right now?" He grins, exposing a mouthful of white toothpaste, then walks away before I can respond, his laugh still lingering behind him as I stare at the doorway, dumbfounded. I want to call after him, to ask him why I'm not at the hospital. When was I brought back here? My thoughts feel disjointed, like a fog has descended upon me. I push to break free of it. Why can't I get a grip on what's going on? I touch my shoulder, my leg. No broken bones. I squeeze my eyes shut, then open them and look around again. No hospital monitors. No IV. No nurse named Janet.

I grab my phone, which is sitting on the bedside table, to call my mom—ask her if she remembers anything about last night. I open my calendar app. The date is Thursday, June 11.

But *yesterday* was Thursday, June 11.

If I'm not in the hospital . . . if today isn't Friday . . . then that means it was all a dream. I breathe easy for the first time since waking.

Mia is alive!

I rush into the kitchen to find Lance.

Lance is pouring coffee into a mug. "You okay, man?"

"I had the most insane dream. About Mia."

Lance raises his eyebrows in that way he does. I hold up my hands. "No, dude. It was not sexual. I dreamed that we were at the fair and we both fell out of a ride—the Zipper—and she died." I run my hand over my mouth, still in minor disbelief.

"That's messed up," he says. "Sex would have been better."

"No shit," I say. "What day is today?" I ask, needing him to confirm. Because it felt so palpable, down to the taste of the deep-fried corn dog batter. I should have known it was a dream when I won that bear for Mia. I suck at basketball. But still. I've never experienced a vision where the physical pain I felt was so visceral. That searing heat that burned inside my chest when I heard she hadn't made it *felt* so real. The tears I cried hot on my cheeks, salty when they rolled into my mouth. The instant hole that formed inside of me like nothing I'd ever experienced.

"It's Thursday," Lance says, pulling open the fridge and grabbing a carton of eggs. I shake my head, feeling an overwhelming sense of déjà vu.

"The eleventh?" I ask, trying to forget the image of the IV attached to my hand.

"Yes. It's the eleventh." He stares at me for a beat. "Listen, this is psychology 101. You are stressed about seeing her tonight, so you had a dream where you couldn't control what happened. Because you, my friend, feel out of control," he says, pulling out a pan.

"When did you start watching Dr. Phil?" I deadpan.

He ignores my quip. "Or flying out of a ride is code for you being worried you won't be able to get it up." He smiles.

"Well, whatever it all means, thank God it wasn't real," I say, remembering the feeling of flying out of the Zipper, the paramedic's urgent voice as he pumped Mia's chest. His sympathetic eyes when he realized she wasn't going to make it. Was it my subconscious trying to tell me to hold on to Mia this time?

"I'm going to make some eggs and bacon. You want some?"

I shake my head, my stomach in knots.

"Here, this will help." He grabs a Channel Seven mug out of the cupboard and pours coffee into it. "Want me to spike it for you? Take the edge off?" He smiles, handing it to me.

"No. I'm already out of it," I say, taking the mug and heading down the hall.

"Hey, have you heard from that source that stood you up at the coffee shop?" Lance asks.

I turn around. "I already told you—no. I think he changed his mind about whatever it was he was going to tell me. We had a whole conversation about it yesterday."

"You talking to yourself again?"

"We discussed Devon and how you think Alexis is in love with him. I told you how badly I need that next big story. How Alexis is all over me because we're slipping in the ratings?"

Lance shakes his head. "Wasn't me, man."

I squint at him, trying to discern reality from my dream. "I'm losing it," I say.

"Clearly." Lance smirks, then grabs a bottle of Jack Daniel's from our bar cart. "You sure about not wanting a little spike of JD?"

"One hundred percent," I say and walk to my room. My hands are shaking as I grab my phone to text Mia. Although Lance has confirmed the date is June 11, and I realize it was most likely all a dream, there's still a part of me that's worried she won't respond. That she really is gone.

I stare at the screen for a long time. Finally I text: We still on for tonight?

I hold my breath. Nothing. No response.

I wait. Pace my room. I walk back to the phone and stare at the screen, willing her to respond. But still, nothing. My hands get clammy, and I feel like I'm going to puke. I decide I have to call her. I can't wait another second.

I finally see the three little dots. She's typing.

Yes!

"Mia's alive!" I yell.

"No shit!" Lance yells back.

8:00. The fair! I can't wait! Mia types and adds a heart emoji.

I laugh and pump my fist in the air and look up at the ceiling. "Thank you, God, for this second chance."

Thank you. Thank you. Thank you.

I practically skip to the bathroom. As I step under the stream of hot water, my smile fades. *The fair.* We are supposed to go to the fair. Because we haven't gone yet. It was all a dream. Or was it a premonition? I would never be able to live with myself if I took her there and something happened to her. I know she's looking forward to it, but it feels wrong.

I shut off the water and grab my phone.

I know we said the fair, but how about my place instead? I'll make you my mom's famous enchiladas. It will be easier for us to catch up and talk.

I see the three dots start, then stop, then start again. Finally, her text comes through.

Ok. But this had better not be a play to get me into your bed. Then she adds the emoji with the hand over its mouth.

That response I wasn't expecting. A little pushback about wanting to eat cotton candy and ride the Rave Wave, sure. But sexual innuendo? I stare at my phone, not sure how to play this. I bite my lip, my emotions swinging back and forth like an old tire hanging from a tree. Finally, I type.

Not me! I'm a gentleman all the way.

If you say so Lol!

Scout's honor. Nothing more than cheesy tortillas and conversation over here. And maybe some wine if you feel like living on the edge.

That's my favorite place to live. But this will be good. We can talk. See you tonight!

My stomach is doing flips, and I can't stop smiling. There's no better feeling than the one I have right now—a cross between joy and gratitude. I make a promise to myself to live in the moment with Mia tonight. To appreciate each and every second we are together. I text her my address, then let out a long breath. I cannot believe it wasn't real. It was so vivid, down to the fuzzy brown bear that I won for her by shooting a few hoops. What did she name him? I think for a minute. Then it comes to me, as familiar as the pink ribbon that was tied around its neck.

Beary.

CHAPTER SEVEN

June 11, 8:00 a.m.
Thursday #2

I hit the button for the lobby rather than the parking garage, deciding to walk for a while, then grab an Uber to the station. I'm too shaky to drive myself today. I confirmed that the love of my life isn't dead. She's alive and planning to go out with me tonight. I don't trust myself behind the wheel right now.

I walk out the glass doors and spy Chuck, the homeless guy. I pause and slide my wallet out of my back pocket. As I'm flipping it open, I lose my grip on it, and it falls to the ground. I bend over to grab it and pull out a five-dollar bill, and I feel another overwhelming sense of déjà vu as I make eye contact with Chuck. He was in my dream, too, I think.

I hold out the bill, and he grabs it. "You've never given me money before. Why now?" He coughs deeply after he speaks, and I wait until he stops.

"But I did give you—" I stop myself. I gave him cash in my dream, not in reality. "That cough sounds pretty nasty."

Chuck waves me off. "It's nothing." He glances at the money in his hand and back up at me.

"If you say so." I give him a once-over. His face is covered in a film of dirt, his clothes have probably never been washed, and his stench is . . . well, I can smell him from three feet away. There are things, like this hack, that he's obviously grown used to. "As for my change of heart, I have a friend who told me it's a good thing to give."

"Sounds like a good person."

"She is."

"She?" He lifts his eyebrows.

"Yeah, she's pretty great," I say.

"Well, don't take this the wrong way, but you've always been kind of a jerk, so I'm glad your girlfriend talked some sense into you," he says. "Not that I'm desperate or anything." He puffs his chest out slightly.

"Of course not," I agree and think back to the man outside the coffee shop. I guess homeless people have pride too.

"You okay, man?"

"If I had a dollar for every guy who's asked me that today."

"You'd have what? Two bucks? It's not even eight." Chuck laughs.

"The truth is, I'm not okay. You know the girl we were talking about? I had a nightmare that she died last night," I say, not sure what propels me to tell Chuck, of all people. "It's freaking me out."

Chuck smiles, exposing missing teeth on the left side of his mouth. "But she's still here, right? The love?"

"Yes. I'm seeing her tonight."

"Then you better make the most of it," Chuck says, then laughs, which turns into a deep cough and lasts for several seconds.

"That doesn't sound very good," I say after he catches his breath.

"It's part of the life," Chuck says, and I don't know how to respond. I simply give a final wave and head to work, but his words continue to sit with me.

He's right. I need to make the most of it. Not hold back like I did in my dream. Not be afraid to ask her the hard questions. Be in the moment with her.

I walk briskly to the corner of Seventh Avenue and K Street and scan the intersection. There are tourists standing at the corner. I notice a couple hovering over a map, two kids in matching San Diego Zoo hats dancing next to them. I do a double take. It can't be. The same family as in my dream, down to the orca T-shirts. A tingle runs up my spine, and I feel her before I see her—I turn, and there she is. The woman in the black bandage dress.

The woman I dreamed about. The one I saved from being hit. I try to make sense of it as the light turns from green to red. Our turn to cross. Every synapse in my body pulses with the same message: *Pull her back.*

She steps off the sidewalk. I hesitate. It can't be coming true. It was a dream. It's not real. But still, what if it was a premonition? And if I don't stop her, what will happen?

I need to pull her back.

I hear the car before I see it. But I already know it's the white Camry. The sound of the revving engine spurs me into action, and I throw myself off the curb, grabbing the woman and pushing her back to the sidewalk violently. We both land hard on the concrete as the car whizzes through the intersection and slams into a bus. She is dazed. And to be honest, so am I.

I stagger up and stumble backward, the realization hammering me. I hold my hand out and help the woman up. She thanks me profusely. Asks me how I knew. I shake my head. She holds out her hand. "My name is—"

"Amanda," I finish for her before I can stop myself.

"How did you know that car . . ." She trails off. Stunned. She looks like she might faint. I grab her gently by the elbow to steady her—or myself. "And how do you know my name?"

"I don't know," I answer honestly, my voice shaking. My body shaking harder. What is happening to me?

I glance into the street. The bus driver is helping the driver of the car out. His airbag is deployed. He looks dazed but fine. Which is a miracle because the front of the car resembles a crushed tin can. How is it possible I dreamed in that kind of detail?

I start to walk away. I have to get out of here. Figure this out.

"Wait! Can I get your email?" Amanda calls after me.

I turn around and hand her my card, then break into a jog.

"Thank you so much," Amanda yells.

"You're welcome," I say over my shoulder. After a few blocks I call an Uber, and it pulls up four minutes later.

It's a Subaru Outback.

I dreamed that too.

I shake my head and get inside. It could be a coincidence. Maybe I had this guy another day. After all, the same drivers cover the same areas. Don't they?

I close my eyes and lean into the leather seat, trying to figure out what's going on. Maybe the incident at the intersection means that my dream *was* a premonition. I could handle having psychic abilities. It couldn't hurt. Or maybe I'm still dreaming. The events looping in a circle in my mind. "Wake up!" I say.

"What?" My driver half looks over his shoulder at me.

"Oh, nothing, sorry," I mumble.

~

I walk into work, starting to feel normal again as I see the newsroom full of life. The interns hovering over the wires, the producers staring at their computer screens looking for stories. I ease into my chair and look around my cubicle. Everything appears normal. My favorite coffee cup that I use every day sits on top of a stack of papers. The photo of my mom and dad at their thirty-fifth wedding anniversary angled the way it always is. I head over to the assignment desk and scan the headlines.

I start to breathe easier. Nothing weird is happening at work. I didn't dream anything that's going on around me now. I'm okay until I see the story about the skateboarding bulldog. Then the shark attack in Pacific Beach. One by one, the same stories I read in my dream appear before me on the page. I squeeze my eyes closed for several seconds, then open them and look around the newsroom again. Is this a dream? Or did I dream the future, and now it's happening as it did in my subconscious?

Or am I losing my mind?

I grab my mug and stand up to get more coffee. As I start for the kitchen, I freeze in place. If my dream *was* a premonition, does that mean Mia will die tonight? I picture her freckled nose, her long red hair. Her megawatt smile. No, she won't, I decide. Because I've changed the plan. We won't be at the fair. So we won't fall out of the Zipper. She won't die.

As I'm about to enter the kitchen, Brian, one of our photogs who handles field shoots, approaches me. "Hey, man, how are you?"

"Good," I say, forcing a smile, trying not to look over his shoulder longingly at the half-empty Mr. Coffee carafe.

"Got a sec? I need to ask you something."

I nod in response, shaking off another sense of déjà vu. Like Brian and I had been standing here before in this very spot. And I'd wanted coffee.

"So, I caught Julie in a lie last night—"

"Right—didn't you see that flirty text from her to her trainer on her phone, and she denied it?"

"How did you know that?" Brian frowns.

"You told me," I say, starting to move around him toward the coffee.

"No. I was about to tell you. I haven't mentioned this to anyone."

"Oh, lucky guess?" I say, my heart beating faster.

Brian gets a call, and I take the opportunity to duck into the break room. Sweat forms on my brow, and I wipe it away. What the hell is going on? If Brian hadn't already told me that story, then how did I know it? How did I know about Duchess the bulldog? The accident at the intersection? Amanda's name before she told me? Will there be a plane crash later today? I lean over the sink and splash cold water on my face over and over.

I've never believed in psychics or ESP or any of that. Mia and I went to a psychic once—in the early months of our relationship, when I thought it would be cute to indulge her. We were on the boardwalk in Santa Monica, and there was a stand. We walked behind a curtain and sat across from a woman wearing long feather earrings and a kimono. She predicted we'd get married. Have three kids. Live in a small white house in California. None of that happened, obviously.

There's only one explanation: I'm losing it. I rush back to my cubicle and google *psychotic break*, because that has to be what's happening. I've lost all touch with reality.

According to the first answer, a "psychotic break with reality" means losing contact with reality, such as hearing, seeing, tasting, smelling, or feeling something that has no external correlate (i.e., hallucinations) or believing something to be true that is false, fixed, and fantastic (i.e., a delusion). But then it goes on to say I would need to have misused drugs or be suffering from a mental illness. I don't do drugs, but do I have a disorder that is only now showing itself?

I slump down in my chair and close my eyes, trying to think.

"You coming to the meeting?" Dan, one of my colleagues, asks, startling me.

"Shit, you scared me, man," I say.

"You okay?"

"Yeah," I lie. But I'm so far from okay right now. I walk by Lance's office and see that the door is closed, the lights off. Déjà vu hits again. I decide to try something. I text him the picture of Duchess the bulldog and the trainer to see if he will respond the same way he did in my dream. The three gray dots appear, and I hold my breath, praying it's different. Finally, a GIF appears. It's the Rock with a man bun. I drop my phone.

"You okay?" an intern asks.

"I'm fine!" I snap as I pick up my phone. "Sorry," I add quickly. "Bad day."

The meeting is an exact replica of the one in my dream. The only difference is that I pitch the shark attack instead of the bulldog. I don't need a lecture from Alexis about positivity. And not surprisingly, Alexis is happy and chooses the shark story.

Though I don't want to suffer through it again, I text my mom to have lunch. I need to see if this day keeps playing out the same way. She tells me my dad is coming too. *Shock.*

The conversation at Chiquita's is identical, down to my hasty departure. A part of me was hoping the outcome would be better. That my version of their reaction to Mia was only a nightmare, but in reality they would be supportive, excited. I keep looking for the one thing that will be different from my dream. So far, everything has been identical— unless I purposely make different choices, like choosing to pitch the shark story to Alexis, a change that worked in my favor.

That gives me hope that I can change other elements too—like Mia's dying. Although it was a dream, I'm not going anywhere near the fairgrounds. We'll be having enchiladas in the safety of my own home.

After lunch, I get back to the office and find Lance. I'm tempted to tell him how so many things in my dream have come true today. But I worry he'll think I'm insane. How could he not? I do. Instead I ask him if he can clear out of the apartment tonight because there's been a change of plans. Mia is coming over.

He gives me a funny look and doesn't respond for a moment. "You sure about this?"

"About what?"

"Bringing her to our place?"

"Yeah, why wouldn't I?"

Lance looks at me, and I'm sure he's going to explain. "Never mind, man. It's cool. I'm trying to get the weather girl to go out with me anyway."

I want to ask him more about his strange reaction, but then the assignment desk calls out that a plane crashed in Oceanside. My insides twist into knots. I could have called the airport. Warned them. Thankfully no one on the twin-engine Cessna died, like no one had died in my dream. But I still feel awful. And stranger that I'd predicted it.

"You okay, dude?" Lance asks. "You look peaked. It's only a plane crash. Everyone survived."

"Yeah, yeah, I'm fine," I say. But something occurs to me as I do.

The more things that happen like this, the more it feels like I'm reliving the same day all over again.

I push the thought away, because that would be more impossible than predicting an entire day in a dream. We get through the five o'clock and six o'clock hours of the news, and I Uber to the store to get what I need for enchiladas, then hurry home to get everything ready for Mia. I pray once she arrives, everything will go back to normal again.

CHAPTER EIGHT

Later, at home, I'm sliding the enchiladas into the oven when the doorbell rings. My heart starts hammering, and I take a quick drink of the cabernet blend before letting Mia in.

"Hi," she says, hugging me. She smells like sunflowers, like she did at the coffee shop. When she pulls back, her cheeks are flushing slightly. Her red hair is falling loosely around her makeup-free face. Tonight, she's wearing one of those one-piece things that women love—what's it called? A romper. It ties at her small waist, and she looks beautiful. She holds up a bottle of red wine. "The least I can do since you're making dinner." She walks past me into the condo. "Not too shabby," she adds as she puts her purse on one of the barstools in the kitchen. I realize I'm still standing there, staring at her, the front door wide open.

"Lance bought it a few years ago," I say as I pull the door closed, then regret it. Why did I offer that? I can afford my own place. I don't want her to think I'm not financially sound. She needs to know I can support her. Losing her in my dream last night has given me a sense of urgency—it's reminded me that nothing in life is guaranteed. It's funny—having Mia back in my life has made me imagine, for the first time, what my long-term future might look like.

I make a mental note to start looking for my own place. I could afford a small house in one of the nearby suburbs. White picket fence. Somewhere for our kids to play. Our kids! If she could read my mind, what would she think? My stomach starts doing that flip-flop thing again, and I can't help but grin. She's here. She's alive. Everything is fine. As I knew it would be once she arrived. We are going to have an amazing night. It's like a do-over. I can say all the things I was too afraid to say at the fair. That I've been thinking about for years. Years! I pull her toward me and hug her again.

"What was that for?" She smiles after I let go.

"It's so good to see you. I'm so glad you're here."

"Well, don't I feel special!"

"You should. And Mia?"

"Yeah?"

"You are. You are special. I should have told you every day when we dated. Every single day." I clear my throat, trying to find the words. Then I see the look in her eyes, and it makes me stop.

"Dom . . ." She gives me a look that I can't read.

"Am I coming in too hot?" I ask, stepping back from her.

"A little. Can we take this night slowly?" She offers me an apologetic smile. "Maybe tackle some easier subjects to begin with? Like the weather? At least until the wine kicks in?"

I mask my disappointment but understand from her perspective that I'm coming on strong; she has no idea that I thought I'd lost her. How that finality felt—how it pierced me so fiercely that I still lose a breath thinking of it. And I don't plan to tell her. It would only scare her off. I watch as she walks over to the glass doors that lead out to the balcony. She slides them open and steps out. "Wow," she says. "What a view."

I pour her a glass of wine, grab mine, and follow her out. It's a warm night, but there's a breeze blowing in off the Pacific Ocean that's only a few blocks away.

A plane flies overhead, and we watch.

"Did you hear about that plane crash today in Oceanside? It wasn't that far from Hailey's."

"Really?" A chill runs through me.

"Everyone lived—on the plane and ground—although it almost hit an apartment complex." She takes a drink. "It reminds you, you know. That life is random. We can't take it for granted."

If she only knew how true her words are ringing now. I think of Amanda from this morning. And I'm about to tell Mia about it, but she speaks first. "Anyway, I'm getting all serious and philosophical. Blah, blah, blah."

I decide to let it go. She's right. We don't need to discuss heavy topics right now.

We stare down at Petco Park. From the balcony you can see the entire stadium and the buildings from downtown San Diego to the coast. The Padres are away tonight, but the Dog Days of Summer event is in full force below. People and their pooches are spread out across the ballpark.

"Aww, I love dogs! I would love to get one," Mia says.

"What kind would you want?"

"Anything, really. I'd adopt for sure. Maybe an elderly dog—one that always gets overlooked at the shelter."

"I didn't know you were a dog person," I say, picturing the tabby cat she had when I first met her.

"There's a lot you don't know about me," she says, her expression even. Her eyes unblinking.

I can't hold her gaze, and I look at my feet, a pang in my stomach. She's right—there's a lot I don't know. And that's my fault. I force myself to meet her eyes again, and now she's smiling.

"Dom, I was only giving you a hard time. You looked so sad."

Because I am. Because I can barely look at the one who got away, though she's right in front of me.

"Don't you remember how sarcastic I can be?"

"I guess I forgot," I say, forcing a smile. But I can't help but wonder if there is some truth to what she said. If she's thinking what I'm thinking— all the things I *would* know if I hadn't ended our relationship.

"This wine is delicious," she says, draining her glass. "I needed this tonight."

"Hard day?" I ask.

"It's been weird being back, living with Hailey again. I didn't think I'd miss my parents as much as I do. My friends."

"Are you considering going back to the Midwest?"

"No. No way. I want to see this through."

"But if you miss all those people, why move away from them?" I ask, feeling a pit form in my stomach. I don't want her to leave. Not again.

"That's a longer answer than I can give you right now. Because I'm still processing what I'm doing back here. But I can tell you that my gut tells me this is where I should be." She looks at me for a while, and I wonder where I fit into her decision to return. An easier question to think than ask. Because a part of me worries I wasn't a factor. And if I wasn't, I want to prolong the not knowing.

"I get that."

"You know, Dom, I was going to reach out to you once I was settled and figured things out." Mia plays with a silver ring on her index finger as she speaks. "I wasn't sure what I was going to say after so many years. But then I ran into you in that coffee shop. I can't stop thinking about it. Like it was meant to be. Like the universe decided the right time for me. Do you believe in fate?" she asks, eyes wide.

I take in what she's said, and this time I look at her as if for the first time. She's so damn beautiful. Always was. But age has enhanced it. Her features more pronounced. Her eyes full of wisdom. Yesterday if she'd asked me about fate or signs, I would have laughed. But now, after my dream, there's something different—something I can't put my finger on. Maybe we were supposed to run into each other.

"I don't know. Maybe," I say truthfully.

"I do—always have," Mia says, looking back out at the horizon.

"I remember. You were always talking about signs. And fate. You loved that movie *Serendipity*."

"You still remember that?"

"I remember a lot, Mia," I say, letting the statement sit there. Hoping she'll open the door for me to say more.

She smiles, her arm brushing mine as she leans against the railing. I feel my entire body light up at her touch. When I think she isn't going to comment, she turns to me. "What else do you remember?"

I remember the way you looked when you woke up in the morning—your hair hiding most of your face until you groggily pushed it out of your eyes. I remember how you had a dozen different shampoos, conditioners, body washes, and face masks in the shower next to my lone bottle of Axe two-in-one. I remember your gentle kisses before we went to bed—how you always told me you loved me even if we were in a fight. I remember the look on your face after I ended things—how you fought back tears, your deep frown, your disappointment.

I want to say this, but I'm scared it's too much, too soon. Yet I woke up this morning thinking that I had lost her and regretted not telling her how I felt.

"Well?" Mia looks at me.

I decide to go for it—say what's in my heart. "I remember it all, Mia. The way you spent fifteen minutes methodically making a sandwich. Toasting the bread, then putting on the spread, then the meat, then the vegetables that you would always julienne, and lastly the two slices of cheese—always in that order. I have never forgotten the way you would dance while you cooked, when there was no music on. I'm not sure you knew you were doing it. I can still hear all of your different laughs—the deep belly one that I worked hard to get out of you. The fake one reserved for people you were appeasing. The short, light one you used when you were right and I was wrong about something." I stop and take a breath.

She gives me a strange look, and my stomach flutters. Did I come on too strong again?

"This one?" she says, then demonstrates the laugh.

I nod, flashing back to us so many years before. How much we still feel like a "we" tonight. How we are falling back into a familiar rhythm. Like no time has passed.

"I must have laughed like that a lot. I don't ever remember being wrong." She does the laugh again.

"That was going to be the next thing I told you—how I remember you were always right."

"And I was going to mention how you had a perfect memory." She laughs—the deep belly laugh—and I laugh with her.

The alarm on my phone starts ringing, interrupting the moment. "That's the enchiladas," I say and walk inside toward the oven. Mia follows.

"It smells wonderful," she says, grabbing the wine bottle and refilling her glass and mine.

"Let's hope it tastes wonderful too," I say, thinking of my mom, as this is her favorite dish. Her recipe I've had memorized since she taught me to make it when I was ten. She's texted me multiple times since lunch and left a voice mail, but I haven't responded. I know I acted immaturely—but I can't respond to her tonight. I need to focus on Mia. I grab an oven mitt and open the door; the cheese is bubbling as it should be.

I put the casserole dish on a towel on the counter and look over at Mia.

"I'm seriously impressed," she says, eyeing the enchiladas. "But you always were a great cook."

"Do you remember when I made the—" I start, but Mia jumps in.

"The chocolate soufflé? For my birthday?"

"How did you know I was going to say that?"

Mia shrugs.

"It was damn good, wasn't it? I'm still kind of amazed I pulled it off."

"I still think about it sometimes," she says. "No one else has ever been able to top it."

I know she's talking about a dessert I made, but I wish she were talking about me. I wait a beat before speaking. Let her compliment linger a moment longer.

I hold in what I'm really thinking. *I wish I hadn't let you go. That I'd been around to make it for you a hundred more times.* Instead, I say, "Let's hope these are as good." I cut into a corner of the tortilla filled with chicken and cheese and spoon out a bite. I blow on it and then touch it with my finger. I start to put the enchilada in my mouth.

"Ah, ah, ah. Ladies first!" Mia says, walking toward me and reaching for the spoon.

"Wait." I pull it back so she can't get it, some cheese dripping off the end. "What if by some fluke it's terrible?" I say.

"You've got to have faith." She grins at me.

"Okay, but if it's bad—"

"If it's bad, we'll DoorDash. No biggie."

She opens her mouth, and I guide the spoon into it. She closes her eyes and chews slowly. I watch her, waiting. Finally, her eyes pop open. "Oh my God, Dom, it's delicious. What's in this sauce?"

I grin. "A chef never divulges his secrets." I grab a spatula and spoon an enchilada onto her plate and then one onto mine. "But for you, I could be persuaded."

"I'll keep that in mind," Mia says, holding my gaze, and my heart speeds up. "Can we sit out there?" she asks, using her plate to point to the balcony.

I look at the teak table and matching chairs. I can't remember the last time I ate there. "Sure," I say but grab a paper towel and get it wet. "Let me clean it off first."

"Don't sit out here much?" she says as I wipe the table.

"I don't."

"If I had this view, I would be out here every night."

"I know. I should appreciate all the fine things that are right in front of me," I say, staring at her and not the view.

She gives me a look.

"What? Too much?" I ask.

"No. It's sweet, like you."

I grin like a dope, but I don't care. I love hearing that she thinks I'm sweet. I take my first bite, and while it's good, it deserves nowhere near the reaction Mia gave it. It makes me want to kiss her. "Mia," I say after swallowing.

She looks up. "Yeah?"

Now's the time for me to tell her. Bring out my full sappy cheeseball. Tell her I love her. I've always loved her. I've never stopped loving her. That she's the one. She's always been the one.

But I can't do it. The things I said earlier were already too much of a risk. And they were nowhere near the feelings of love sitting in my heart right now. I don't want to push her away.

"More wine?" I end up asking.

"Yes, please!" she says, and I hurry into the kitchen to uncork another bottle.

You're such a dumbass, Dom, I think as I pull out the cork. I lean against the counter, my back to the balcony, and take several deep breaths.

"You all right in there?" Mia asks.

No, I'm having a panic attack! I'm in love with you and can't tell you.

"Yep, on my way," I say, grabbing the bottle and tossing the cork and the foil in the trash. She's sitting on the railing when I come out, her back to me. Her legs dangling over the edge. I nearly drop the bottle of wine. It's eleven stories down. If she were to fall . . .

The sight of her perched there makes my heart start to pound. If she were to lose her balance . . . "Mia—" I start.

She turns her head. "Your face!" she says. "You look like you're going to have a heart attack. I'm holding on tight. I promise."

"Mia—"

I can hear my blood pumping in my ears. I want to run over and pull her down, but I don't want to accidentally send her sailing over the edge. Suddenly she swivels her head back again.

"Dom, what happened to us?" Mia asks. "Why didn't it work?" she adds, so softly I'm not sure I've heard her right.

"Why don't you come down from there and we can talk?" I ask, stepping a little closer. Could I grab her arm and pull her in?

"You're acting like I'm suicidal, Dom. It's the opposite. I'm living. It's so invigorating being up here. So high above everything."

"Mia, please," I say, panic rising, the memory of losing her in my dream flooding through me. The reminder of her old ways rushing to the surface. She loved to gamble with life. When I asked her why she wanted to bungee jump, she declared she *needed* that rush of defying gravity.

"Tell me why you ended things, and I'll get down."

"Mi, it wasn't about you. It was about me."

"Come on, don't give me that 'it's not you, it's me' crap. Of course it was me."

"No, it was me," I plead, not wanting her to harbor that blame for one more second.

"Bullshit!" She points at me for emphasis and starts to lose her balance, her arms flailing.

Oh God, no. Not again.

She tries to grab the railing but misses. She screams, the sound spiking my senses.

"Mia!" I run toward her, but I don't get there in time. My breath catches in my throat. My heart pounds so hard it could explode. My chest slams hard into the railing. I look over the edge and see her falling toward the ground, her eyes wild.

Just like when she fell from the Zipper in my dream.

CHAPTER NINE

"Mia!" I scream, a guttural cry, as I lean over the railing, squinting at the ground. I sprint out the door and down the hall and fling open the door to the stairs, running for my life. For Mia's. My heart banging so hard inside my chest it's hard to breathe. I dial 911 as I fly down flight after flight, panting, trying to explain what happened. I stammer through my name and address. The operator advises me to stay on the phone; I lose my balance but grip the phone tightly, refusing to lose my connection with the people coming for Mia. My leg twists under me as I hit the concrete steps. But I feel no pain. I have one focus.

Mia. I must get to her. Because maybe she's okay. Like I was in my dream. Maybe something broke her fall. *Please let her be okay. Or let this be another horrible nightmare.*

I heave myself up and continue down five more flights of stairs. I push open the exit door and see a semicircle of people has formed, and I know Mia must be on the other side of them. A man in a Padres jersey and worn ball cap peers up, as if wondering how a woman could fall out of the sky.

"Let me through," I say, forcing my way in. Past the gawkers. Why isn't anyone helping her? "Is someone a doctor?" I shout. "We need help over here."

"Someone called 911," I hear a woman say as I fall to my knees next to Mia's body. I gasp and suppress a wave of nausea when I see her up close. Dark blood pools around her head, and her body is twisted in directions that shouldn't be possible. It's exactly like in my vision. Her eyes are open, but she's not there. Oh my God, she's not there.

"Mia, please live. Please," I cry as I check her wrist for a pulse, already knowing I'm not going to find one. I begin to perform CPR. I've never done it before, never been trained. But I clearly remember the four rounds the firefighter performed on Mia in my dream last night as I watched her die, and I mimic his motions. Sirens roar in the distance, but all I can focus on is the absence of Mia's breath in my ear.

"How did she fall?" someone asks.

Another person's voice. "I was walking, and she landed right here—out of nowhere."

"Where is the ambulance?" Someone else.

"This poor girl."

I want everyone to stop talking. I lift my phone to my mouth. "Where are the paramedics?" I shout at the 911 operator. She tells me they are almost here. "She's dead. I think she's dead," I scream. "They need to get here!" And then I drop the phone again and grab Mia's hand. I take off my hoodie and put it under her head. "Everyone stop staring at her!" I scream.

A hand taps my shoulder. "There's nothing you can do." I glance back at an older woman with large eyeglasses. Her tone is kind, but her words feel like an affront. I'm not ready to let go of Mia. Again. I cannot lose her. I can't.

Someone starts praying.

"Mia!" I yell. I begin another round of chest compressions. We were laughing. We were drinking wine. How did we go from that to this?

"Please. Please don't leave me," I whisper over and over, though I know she's already gone. But hope still lingers. Maybe I'll wake up and this will all be a dream. Again.

∽

Somehow I end up back inside the condo. A detective with a black mustache and buzz cut is taking measurements of the balcony. I wonder how much time has passed since I was eleven stories down performing CPR on Mia. Since the paramedics declared her dead. Since they took her body to the hospital. Since they told me I couldn't go with her. That I needed to stay here and talk to the police. Time has lost its elasticity—shock has knocked me out of the clock's rhythm. Now seconds stretch, and minutes feel like hours. Maybe I've been sitting on this couch for thirty minutes. Or possibly two hours. Like it matters anyway. Because all I can contemplate are the milliseconds before she fell. What I could have done differently. Why didn't I force her down off the railing and back onto the safety of the balcony? Why did she have to be up there in the first place?

The detective on the balcony is trying to calculate how she fell. He's already questioned me at length, although I don't remember much of it. I know it's his job to make sure my story holds up. To determine that I didn't push her. Because why would Mia climb up on the guardrail that encloses my balcony? Eleven stories above the earth. Why? Why couldn't she play it safe? Keep her feet where they belong—on the ground?

I'm shivering on the couch despite the blanket draped over my shoulders. "Do I need a lawyer?" I ask the detective when he walks inside. My body is shaking, whether from the cold or the shock or the fear, I can't be sure.

"Why? Are you guilty of something?"

"No," I say, and he gives me a look like he doesn't believe me. My heart is slamming inside my chest. Mia is gone, and now they think I've killed her? I start shaking even harder and look around for my phone. I need to call my parents. A petite woman, with her hair pulled back in a severe ponytail and kind brown eyes, walks over.

"I'm Officer Stevens." She sits down in the chair across from me, then leans forward. "It's not standard procedure, but I prefer to use first names. Especially in times like this." She looks out toward the balcony, and I remember it all over again. Mia losing her balance. Falling. I start to cry. "I'm so sorry. Let me get you a tissue," she says, starting to stand.

"No, no. I'm fine." I wipe my eyes with the back of my arm.

She sits back down. "I'm Lynette." She nods toward her partner. "He's more old school. He won't tell you to call him Frank." She laughs quietly. "But he's a good cop."

"He thinks I pushed her." I bite my lip to keep myself from crying again.

"He's only doing his job," Lynette says.

"My . . ." I stop. What do I call Mia? Friend? But were we friends? After not being in touch for nine years and some odd months? Facebook friends might be more like it. Or ex-fiancée? But that sounds so awful and harsh. "Mia is dead, and I'm trying to process it, and I get that he's only doing his job, as you say, but I didn't push her. She fell."

She gives me a long look. "Okay," is all she says.

"She didn't have to fall," I mutter.

But I saw something in Mia's eyes when she was perched up on that railing. It was a flicker that I remember from when we were together—a speck of light in the bluest part of her irises that would appear right before she did something risky. She was always the one flying down the black diamond run on her snowboard on Mammoth Mountain, her long red hair carelessly splaying out from her knit cap (she refused to wear a helmet). I'd follow behind slowly, careful to stay away from the tree line, where the run ended and the steep drop over the side of the mountain began. I found it exciting back then that Mia effortlessly bobbed and weaved through the trees while I did everything in my power to avoid them. Her ability to face fear attracted me to her in a very real way. Mia was also the one who would sprint across the street before the walk sign lit up, pulling me along. It was as if she was daring life to take her. And now it has.

I try again to process what's happened. My dream about the carnival. How real it felt. Like now. So maybe this is all an illusion. Maybe I am dreaming right now. I feel a spark of hope and start to stand, but I feel light headed. I grip the edge of the sofa and ease myself back down. "Wake up," I say and pinch my arm. *Please let this be a dream. Please let Mia still be alive, like she was when I woke up this morning.*

"What did you say?" Lynette asks.

"He said, 'Wake up,'" Frank chimes in. He pulls up a chair from the kitchen table and sits across from me. Up close, he looks older; I see that there is gray in his mustache and deep lines in his forehead. "Mr. Suarez, I know you are understandably very upset right now, but we need to walk through what happened." He looks over at Lynette, and I do the same.

"It's okay," she says.

"You can call me Dominic," I say.

They both nod and wait for me to speak.

"I told you what happened, didn't I?" I squeeze my eyes shut and try to think. Everything is such a blur.

"You started to when we were down there." Frank points as if I need clarification. "But you said your head hurt, that you wanted to come up here and call your mom and Ms. Bell's mom and"—he flips open his notepad—"a guy named Lance."

"My roommate," I offer. Although I don't remember calling any of them.

"We need a statement, and then we'll get out of your way," Lynette says.

"She was sitting on the railing, lost her balance, and fell off." My voice cracks as I say the last words, the memory of being just a second too late to catch her etched in my mind. I see the panicked look in her eyes as she registered she was falling and what that meant. Her arms flapping wildly as she descended toward the ground, trying in vain to defy gravity. The image of her when I pushed through the crowd. Her contorted body, the blood pooling around her, her empty eyes. "I begged her to get down. It happened so fast. I should have tried harder to get her off the rail, I—"

Frank interrupts me. "Let's back up a bit. How do you know Ms. Bell?"

"She was my ex-fiancée," I say, leaving out that she was also the one who got away. The love of my life. The person who I'd compared every other woman to for the past decade. How can she be gone? I grab my chest. My lungs burn as I try to breathe. I put my head between my knees and try to stop my heart from hurting so much.

"Let me get you some water," Lynette says.

I rise to see Frank writing something in his notebook. "How long had you been broken up?"

"Ten years," I reply.

He raises his salt-and-pepper eyebrows slightly.

"She moved out of state almost immediately after I called things off. I ran into her earlier this week and asked her out." I remember her bright smile at the coffee shop. Her energy—so infectious. How she cooed at the baby. Did she want kids?

"That's random, you bumping into her after all these years," he says. But I can tell he doesn't think it's random at all. Mia didn't think it was either. She thought it meant something. A sign. Why didn't I sweep her into my arms at that moment and tell her I didn't want to live another second without her?

"It was," I say, more defensively than I'd like. "I had a work meeting in Oceanside, and she walked in while I was waiting for a colleague."

His stubby fingers jot this down, and then he looks up. "So tonight, did you get to talking about your breakup—maybe it turned into an argument?"

"What? No. What are you suggesting?" I look at Lynette, who drops her gaze from mine. Where are her kind eyes, her reassuring words now? My mind starts working in overdrive. What if I can't prove I *didn't* push her? What if nobody believes me and I go to prison for this?

I can't stop thinking about Mia's last words to me, her heartbreaking tone when she said them. She thought it was her. That *she* was to blame. She was still hanging on to what she might have done to send me away. I didn't get a chance to explain. To reassure her. To tell her how stupid I was.

"I'm not suggesting anything—*yet*," Frank says, his smug expression telling me otherwise. "I'm asking you if you had an argument. If maybe it got heated and it led to her falling off the balcony."

"No. We were getting along great!" I say, my anger bubbling. I want to knock this guy's face off. How dare he ask me this when Mia is dead?

"Well, you understand that we'll need to interview neighbors, find out if there are any eyewitnesses. Anyone who can corroborate your story."

I clench my teeth. Wanting to say so many things to him. Wanting to rip his stupid mustache off his face. But worried he'll arrest me for assaulting a police officer.

I hear Lance before I see him. He's arguing loudly with someone, insisting that he lives here. A second later his tall frame fills the doorway, my mother a step behind him, her eyes red rimmed, her lips in a tight line. My father following behind. My mom wraps her small arms around me tightly. I bury my head into her shoulder. I've never been so happy to see her. I start to sob, and she holds me as I shake. The feeling of loss is eerily similar to my dream—the disbelief as raw. The hopelessness still stabbing every breath. How can this be?

When my mom releases me, I notice Lance staring at the balcony, his eyes glassy. "I'm so sorry," he says when he turns back around. "I can't believe she's gone." He grabs glasses and a bottle of Maker's Mark from our bar cart, pours two drinks, then nods at my father, who shakes his head no.

Frank glares at Lance. "I'm not done with Mr. Suarez—Dominic—yet."

"Yes, you are." Lance hands me a glass, and I greedily drink from it. Lance walks toward him. Frank stands, and they are face to face. "He's clearly been through enough. Unless you are advising him to get an attorney?"

I snap my head up, wondering what Frank is going to say. My heart starts pounding. What if he arrests me? I start to shake again. My mom puts her arm around me.

"I'm not advising him of anything. But cooperation is what will help us conduct our investigation," Frank says as he shuts his notebook.

Lance throws me a questioning glance, and I feel the color drain from my face.

"We must determine *how* Mia Bell died. If she fell or if she was pushed. We have an obligation to her and to her family to make sure Dominic's account is accurate." Frank meets my eyes and won't look away.

I stand, my knees shaky as heat flushes through my body. I hold my arms above me to catch my breath, some of the bourbon spilling from the glass still in my hand. "Mia is dead. She's never coming back. I didn't push her, but it is my fault. I had a dream last night that she died, and then she did. I knew something bad could happen, and I didn't warn her. I should have never let her sit on the balcony. So fucking blame me. Take me away right now." I set my drink down and put my arms out so Frank can cuff them. But he doesn't walk toward me. No one does. "What are you waiting for? You think I'm so guilty, then arrest me." At this moment I don't give a shit if they haul me off to jail. Nothing will ever be the same again.

"Mijo, please sit," my mom says and tries to guide me to a chair, but I shake her off and cross my arms over my chest. I'm crying again. My knees start to buckle, and I'm sure I'm going to pass out. Lance rushes over and grabs me.

"Listen to your mom," he says under his breath.

"How dare you treat my son like this after what happened?" my mom scolds Frank. My dad guides her away, whispering something in her ear.

"Let's all calm down," Lance says, taking a drink of his bourbon.

"We have a few more questions," Frank says.

"No." Lance spits the word.

"No?" Frank challenges.

"Lance," I mutter, but he ignores me.

"Do you know who I am?"

"I do!" Lynette says brightly, but she quiets as soon as Frank flashes her an angry look.

"I do not," Frank says, like he's proud of it.

"I'm the anchor of the Channel Seven News here in San Diego. I don't think you want us reporting this story—that you harassed this man after he watched the love of his life die before his eyes."

I suck in a breath, feeling like I've been punched in the gut. She was the love of my life. Why didn't I make her get off that railing? Why didn't I catch her when she lost her balance?

"Well, I don't think you want it reported by Channel Nine, where I am very close with the assignment editor, that an anchor at Channel Seven threatened a police officer." Frank puffs his chest out. "In fact, I could arrest you right now."

Lance backs off.

My dad steps between them. "Okay. If you don't mind, my son is very upset," he says to the officers and nods to the front door. "We'll take your cards in case we think of anything else that might help. Would that be an acceptable resolution?"

Frank nods. They hand him their cards and silently walk out the door.

"Let's get you to bed," my mom says after they leave. She grabs my arm and leads me down the hallway. I feel exhaustion in every bone in my body and find myself leaning on her tiny shoulder again. "I'm so sorry we argued about Mia today. I—" My mom's voice cracks.

"It's okay. You couldn't have known," I tell her.

But maybe I knew?

Lance follows us into my bedroom with two more glasses of bourbon. He drinks his in one swig and winces. He hands me the other.

I sit on the edge of my neatly made bed and drain my glass. But I don't blanch; I barely taste the alcohol. "I could use another." I look at Lance.

"Mrs. Suarez, would you mind refilling these?"

She flashes him a look of concern.

"He'll be fine," he says. "And I need to talk with Dom alone for a second." He hands her our empties.

As soon as she leaves the room, Lance sits next to me. "How are you doing?" he asks.

"I don't know," I say, trying not to lose it again.

"I'm so sorry. I can't believe it." He runs his hand over his jaw. "And then there's your dream last night. The Zipper. You said Mia fell out of it and died. And now—"

"Am I dreaming now?" I ask. "Hallucinating?"

"I don't think so, man." Lance gives me a sad look. "I wish you were."

"I have to tell you something—I predicted this entire day in my dream last night. Except for how Mia died. What do you think it means?"

Lance runs his hands through his hair. "Really? More than the fair?"

I reel off all the things I dreamed. Then I repeat my question. "What do you think it means?"

"I don't know. But that's insane."

"Or I am," I say, hoping he'll correct me. But he doesn't. And I don't blame him. I'm sure I sound mad. A shiver runs through me. What if I'm losing my mind? Because what other explanation is there?

My mom comes to the doorway with two full glasses of bourbon. Lance grabs them. "We'll be right out here if you need us." She nods toward the living room.

I down my bourbon and set the glass on the table by my bed. "I think I need to go to bed," I tell Lance.

"Things will be better tomorrow."

"Will they?" I lie back on my pillow.

Lance frowns. He knows they won't. "I'm sorry. Mia. I can't believe it. Let me know if you need anything." He closes the door behind him.

I stare at the door for a while, willing Lance to come back and tell me it was all a big mistake. That I was sleeping and Mia is fine. I start to cry again, because that's not going to happen. Mia is gone. She'll never get a chance to marry anyone. She'll never have a child. She'll never adopt a senior dog. And it's my fault. I may not have pushed her like that cop thinks, but I'm responsible. She would never have been here if it weren't for me. After I dreamed she died and predicted my entire day, I should have warned her—told her not to meet me at all.

She wouldn't be dead. I could have saved her life.

CHAPTER TEN

JUNE 11, 6:59 A.M.
THURSDAY #3

I wake with a start. My sheet is soaked and twisted around my body. I tug at it until my legs break free. The time on the digital clock shifts from 6:59 to 7:00. "How to Save a Life" bursts from the speakers.

The memory of what happened is like a blow to the gut. The kind where you get the wind knocked out of you and it feels like you'll never catch your breath.

Mia is dead.

I would do anything to rewind my life one minute to before I remembered. To the tangled sheets being the worst thing that had happened to me.

And our song is playing.

Suddenly I'm back there again. On the balcony. Mia sitting on the edge. Telling me she's fine. Holding on tight. She was one hundred feet above the ground. Why was she being so reckless up there? Why was that how she wanted to "live," as she said? It was foolish and stupid. But even worse, I didn't force her to get down. Why didn't I yank her off to the safety of the right side of the railing?

I will never forgive myself.

The song is playing again. Like yesterday. But I never set the alarm. Or maybe I did. Or maybe it's not actually playing right now. I'm imagining it. I don't trust myself anymore. I bite back my tears. Mia's life is over, and as far as I'm concerned, mine is too. "Mom?" I call, hoping she's still here. That she slept on the couch under the burgundy throw blanket that is draped across the arm. The one that was on my shoulders when I was shaking last night.

"Should I be concerned you're asking for your mommy right now?" Lance appears in the doorway. He's wearing khakis and a white T-shirt, and he's brushing his teeth. He grins, and I see the toothpaste in his mouth. He doesn't wait for my answer, and I hear him laughing as he walks away.

What the fuck?

This exact exchange between us happened yesterday.

I'm frozen in place, trying to make sense of what's going on. I breathe in and out and try to steady my mind, because this can't be real. I hurry into the kitchen. "Is Mia dead?" I ask Lance frantically.

Lance is pouring himself a cup of coffee and looks at me as if I've spoken to him in Japanese. I rub my eyes and try again. "Did Mia fall off our balcony last night and die?"

"What? No. Why would you ask me that?" Lance stares at me like he's seeing a ghost. Does he feel the echo too?

I am suddenly dizzy and grab the edge of one of the barstools pushed up against our counter. Mia died two different nights in my dreams. But were they dreams?

"Because she died last night—again," I stammer. "Didn't she?" The room is spinning. I train my eyes on one spot on the ceiling, worried I'm going to pass out.

"What's going on with you?"

"I'm freaking out, Lance." I remember my Google search from yesterday. "I think I'm having a psychotic break."

"Sit down," he says, pointing at the barstool I'm clinging to.

I oblige and rest my elbows on the counter, the weight of my feelings crashing down on me. "Let me see your phone," I ask, holding out my hand. He hands it to me, and I check the date—Thursday, June 11. "This doesn't make any sense."

"You're not having a psychotic break. You're hungover."

"Do you remember our conversation from last night? When we were drinking bourbon in my bedroom?" I ask, but I already know the answer.

"We didn't drink bourbon in your bedroom, bro." He attempts a laugh, but his face loses some of its color. "We were at Barleymash, *remember*?"

"I do, but it wasn't last night!" I say, and then when he frowns at me, I add, "Or maybe it was. I don't know anymore."

"Okay, man, *now* you're worrying me," Lance says.

I close my eyes and lean my head back, trying to make logic out of what I'm going through. To discern dream from reality. Do I know the difference anymore?

"I need you to listen to me," I finally say, staring him directly in the eyes. "I dreamed what happened on Thursday, June eleventh, twice. Both times, I went to sleep, and when I woke up, it was June eleventh again. I don't know what's happening to me." I take a deep breath. "What's today?"

"June eleventh," Lance says slowly, eyeing me like I'm the chemicals in a science experiment and he's waiting for me to combust. He's never been good with seriousness. He tends to make a joke when something is going down a road he can't handle. I see the look on his face. And I already know what crack is coming.

"Did you have some kind—"

"—of sexual anxiety dream about Mia? Her falling off the balcony means I'm worried about getting it up with her after all these years? No, I did not."

Lance pulls his head back, his eyes bulging. "How did you know I was going to say that?"

Am I going mad? Because the alternative is that I'm now living Thursday for the *third* time. Not dreaming it. And that can't be possible. No fucking way.

"Because we've had this conversation before."

"No, we haven't."

But we have. At least in my version of reality. Which is something I can't explain.

"So you don't feel like you're having déjà vu right now?"

He frowns and shakes his head.

I get off the barstool. "I know, you don't have to say it. I'm losing it," I say as I walk away, already knowing that he's pulling eggs out of the fridge.

"Hey, dude, I'm making—"

"Eggs and bacon, I know. And thanks, but I don't want any." I shake my head as I walk down the hall, trying to sort out how I know what I know about this day. How I feel in every bone that I've been here before, and not just in a vision. But the idea is still unfathomable.

~

I need to clear my head and step into the shower, not bothering to twist the knob to hot. Instead I let the ice-cold water hit me for several minutes, hoping it will knock out whatever craziness is inside of me. Mia isn't dead. I should be ecstatic. And I am so relieved. I am. But this time I can't celebrate. Because although she's still alive, something is seriously wrong with me.

I shut off the water, half dry my body, grab my phone, and pull up my text thread with Mia. Our last exchange is from Wednesday night. June 10, and my phone confirms what I already know. It's the eleventh. So have I lived this day before, or did I dream it? Why is time passing differently for me? Because, according to the date on my phone, last night I wasn't with her eating enchiladas on my balcony. I was at Barleymash like Lance said. I sent Mia a picture of the crowded dance floor and texted, Bet you can't guess where I am, knowing that she'd instantly recognize the mahogany walls and weathered DJ stand. She wrote back right away. Our old stomping grounds! I can almost smell the stale beer and cheap cologne. That's where the thread ends. Missing is the exchange from the first Thursday about the fair and the second Thursday about changing the plan to the condo. But how? How is today the eleventh—*again*? I think of a movie I once saw where a guy was in a coma. He woke up thinking all of his dreams had been his reality. Maybe I'm in a coma now? Because on what planet would I need to suffer through seeing Mia's bloodied body and her lifeless eyes—twice? Go through her dying two times only to keep finding out she's alive? Is she alive now? I know Lance said she is, but how would he know?

My hands tremble as I type, and it takes several attempts to get the words right.

Can we change the plan for tonight? Not meet at my place?

I stare at the screen, waiting, my heart racing. What if she doesn't respond? I let out a breath when I see the gray dots appear.

I thought we were going to the fair?

I drop the phone and stumble backward, steadying myself against the bathroom wall. How the hell is this happening? I wipe away the fog on the mirror. My eyes are bloodshot, and there are deep bags and lines beneath them. I look like I haven't slept in days. And maybe I haven't.

My phone pings. I pick it up. It's Mia again.

Hello? Anybody home? Too scared to take me there? Afraid I'll make you go on all the fast rides?

I put my head between my knees and breathe in and out through my nose, but I can't hold the bile back, and I rush to the toilet and throw up. That is *exactly* why I don't want to go. How do I explain that we cannot set foot inside the county fairgrounds? And that she can't come over here either?

A sickening thought comes to mind.

If the day is repeating itself, will the events keep repeating as well? Mia died on the Zipper, so I changed the location of our date. Then Mia died at my condo. So how do I stop Mia from dying again? I'll start by keeping her on solid ground. And by stifling her daredevil ways. She cannot do *anything* risky, even if it means I have to tie her down. I want to take you to dinner at Rustic Root—one of my favorite restaurants. It will be easier for us to talk and catch up. Is that okay?

I see the dots form, then stop, then form again. Finally she responds. Sounds good. I'll meet you there. 6? And let's hit up the rooftop at the Andaz after? I want to check it out.

Why does she want to go up there? So she can swing her legs over the wrong side of the edge again? Perch up there like she's a bird? She is not going to be a risk-taker tonight. I can't let her. I have to show her that life can be as exhilarating on ground level. Of course I can't say any of that to her because she'll think I'm batshit—and maybe I am. The Andaz is overrated—I have somewhere else in mind you'll love.

I'll take her to Parq afterward—a quirky club with vaulted ceilings and indoor trees with twinkling lights curled around the branches. There's a seven-foot robot who takes selfies with guests. That will excite her!

It better be somewhere good!

It will be. We'll have a great time. Promise.

Of course I have no idea if we'll have a great time. Have no clue if she'll leave the club alive. I wonder if I could be reliving Thursday again, which so far seems to be the case. But that's impossible. Isn't it? Could I be living my own *Groundhog Day*? I look around, half expecting to see Bill Murray. The time on my phone says it's almost seven thirty. I have to hurry if I'm going to save Amanda.

There's a knock at the door. I wrap a towel around my waist and open it.

"You all right?" Lance asks. His eyes are narrowed with concern.

"Yeah. I think you were right—I'm hungover. The shower helped," I lie, trying to weigh whether or not to tell Lance.

"Oh, good. Because you were freaking me out back there. But I get it: I've had some strange dreams and woke up thinking they were real. Like the one when I did the news naked. And I realized it midway through the broadcast, and Alexis would not give me my pants."

I grimace, trying not to picture it. And not telling him how his nightmare is nowhere near the same as this.

"On that note, I do have a work question."

I tighten my towel. "I know—no, I haven't heard from the source. But you'll be the first to know when I do. And I know Devon is freaking you out and that Alexis is giving him a lot of attention right now. The ratings are down. And you're feeling the heat." I say the words without thinking and instantly regret them.

"How did you know I was going to ask you about all that?"

I shake my head and make a snap decision. I'm going to tell him and see how he reacts. Screw it. "Because we've already had this conversation, or I predicted this conversation, or I'm having déjà vu. No idea which it is. But here's what I do know. You need to stop making bacon and eggs every morning and get your ass to work *before* Devon. Because he is going to attend the nine a.m. morning meeting. And you should be there too."

"What? Did he tell you he was going today?"

"Trust me. He'll be there. We'll end up going with a story about another shark attack in PB." Although I questioned telling Lance, it feels good to confide in him. Makes me feel like I'm not alone in all this. Even if he doesn't fully believe me.

"There's been another attack? I need to stop surfing," he says, then seems to put something together in his head. "Wait, I didn't see anything about that when I scanned the headlines this morning."

"Probably hasn't happened yet."

"You dreamed that too?"

"Yes," I say, even though I'm quite sure it was more than a vision—I've already lived it.

"All right, I'll head into the station now—even though you're tripping me out," he says. "And put on some pants, will you?" He smirks as he walks away.

"You came to me! I'm in the bathroom!" I call after him, but he doesn't respond. I stare at my reflection in the mirror. My eyes are a little bloodshot, my jaw tight. But other than that, you would never guess what's going on inside of me. That I'm possibly having a mental breakdown. Or living the same day over and over. Or both.

I need answers—but how? Where do I start? The magnitude of this freaky experience is taking hold—squeezing me hard from the inside out. My body temperature starts to rise as I consider that there might not be a solution. That I've simply snapped. I stare into my own eyes, searching for a sign that I'm not right. That I'm not to be trusted. I splash cold water on my face over and over and look at myself again. I can't accept that. There has to be a *logical* explanation.

Think, Dom, think.

Grabbing my laptop, I sit down at the kitchen island and google time loops. After dismissing a few tongue-in-cheek articles, I click on one that recounts stories of people who have claimed to be in a loop. It explains that light can bend space and time. A black hole can too. Or more recently, it's been theorized that laser beams can also bend the space-time fabric. A story from the *Telegraph* pops up about a British kid who swore he was in a time loop. He claimed to have had severe déjà vu for eight years with no scientific explanation; it went on to say that many scientists theorized he was caught in a time loop. But it was also clear from the article that many others thought he was a nut.

I recall covering it on the six p.m. news. We interviewed a local doctor for some context—who seemed to believe him. I need to look him up as soon as I get to work. Ask him if that's what's happening to me. At the time, I thought the kid was nuts. Now I'm not so sure. Not even close to being sure.

I only have a few minutes before I need to get out the door, but I'm feeling antsy for information. I keep going. I type *alternate universes* into the search window and am met with all kinds of theories. One that catches my eye is the "daughter universe," which suggests that for every outcome that can come from one of your decisions, there is a range of universes—each of which sees one of those outcomes come to be. Could I be living out different outcomes of my choices each day? No, I reason. I wouldn't be repeating the same things over and over.

I click on the string theory next. It suggests alternate universes are layers above and below our own and that if we explore far enough in our own universe, we'll end up meeting the alternate versions of ourselves. I sit back and consider it. Have I slipped through some sort of wormhole and started living an alternate version of my life each day? It feels like a stretch.

I rush out of our building ten minutes later. Right away I spot Chuck. Same worn flannel jacket. Same toothless smile. Same sheen of filth.

I fish a twenty out of my wallet and hand it to him without explanation. I also give him a package of Mucinex I grabbed from my medicine cabinet. I'm sure he thinks I've lost my mind, because in his world I've never given him money before, let alone cold medicine. Hardly given him the time of day. It's a little after eight, so I break into a run. I can hear Chuck hacking as I speed down the street. If this day is going to repeat itself, the Camry will be coming soon. I don't see Amanda up ahead on the sidewalk and start to worry it's already happened. I quicken my pace. *Please let me find her.* I can't let another person get hurt or worse. I let out a long breath when I spot her on the next block, her high heels dangling from her hand. She's nearing the edge of the sidewalk. Why have I been able to save her each day but not Mia?

"Hey!" I call to her. "Amanda!"

She turns and gives me a funny look. "Do I know you?"

"Yes," I start. "I mean, no, you don't. But listen, this is going to sound absurd, but I need you to wait with me here. Don't cross the street yet."

Amanda sighs. "Look, buddy, I've had a super long night, so if you're some kind of stalker or something, I'm not interested. Cool?" She starts walking again. She's almost to the curb. I can see the light about to change. It will be her turn to cross.

"No, wait, please." I run up to her and grab her arm.

She tries to break free, but I tighten my grip. "Let go of me," she yells.

The couple I've seen the past two Thursdays hovering over the map looks over. Their children in the San Diego Zoo hats stop dancing. "You okay over there, miss?" the man asks.

"No, I'm—" Amanda starts to answer him as the white Toyota Camry comes careening around the corner, through the crosswalk where Amanda would have been walking had I not held her back. It crashes into the bus. The airbag in the Camry deploys. I know the driver will be fine.

"Oh my God. How did you know?"

"I wish I could explain, but here's my card if you ever need anything," I say, then grimace. "Promise I'm not a stalker."

She takes it, staring at me in disbelief. "Thank you so much," she says.

"By the way, you made the right call sneaking out of that snoring douchebag's house. Maybe lay off Tinder for a while—the guys on there aren't good enough for you."

Her mouth falls open.

I hurry down the sidewalk, clicking my Uber app, not surprised at all when Joel in a black Outback accepts my ride.

～

I get to the station, and instead of going to the assignment desk to scan the news, because I already know what's going to happen, I find the name of the doctor who vouched for the British student. Dr. Shirash. I find the link to the segment and pull it up on my computer. The piece starts to come back to me as I watch it. The doctor sounds smart and knowledgeable and at this point might be my only hope. I shoot him an email saying that I'm doing a follow-up story and can I meet him? I don't want to put anything in writing about what I'm going through—just in case. I run into Brian in the kitchen but tune out while he tells me about his flirtatious girlfriend. Lance makes it to the morning meeting and raises his eyebrows at me after I pitch the shark attack and Alexis picks it to lead the hour. He also comes with a story of his own and pitches it, which impresses Alexis. Lance gives me a quick look, both surprised and pleased I was right. Devon scowls from across the table. From there, the morning is a blur. I use my knowledge to get through it as quickly as possible. As in I don't tell anyone I already know things that are going to happen. I don't need to answer questions about whether I'm all right. I decide to skip having lunch with my mom and dad.

Midmorning, Dr. Shirash gets back to me and says he's available early afternoon, bragging that he's retired. He invites me to his home in La Jolla, and I accept. And later I tell a very annoyed Alexis that I need to leave early and that Scott, the second producer, said he'd cover for me during our tapings tonight. (He wasn't happy about it, and I owe him a six-pack of Spotted Cow, which apparently you can only buy in Wisconsin, but he's doing it.)

As I'm heading out, I hear Lance. "Hey," he says. "Still hungover?"

"Nope. Feeling much better," I say, wishing it were true. Although I do have a tiny spark of hope that Dr. Shirash will help me.

"Super weird about the morning meeting. I don't know how you knew all that, but thanks for the tip. Alexis is very happy with me."

I nod. "Good."

"Where are you going, anyway? Scott's panties are all in a wad over covering for you."

I roll my eyes. "He'll get his damn beer. He'll be fine."

"But seriously. You *never* leave early. I can't remember the last time you missed one taping, let alone two."

"I promise I'll tell you after. It has to do with all the weird dreams I've been having."

"You checking yourself into the loony bin?" Lance laughs.

I don't respond, but his comment hits home. "By the way, that new weather girl you have your eye on? She'll say yes, if you ask her."

"How did you—" Lance stops himself. "The dreams again?"

I nod and feel a twinge of hope because Lance isn't hauling me off to the psych ward. He's listening. Being a friend. And it's what I need right now. I head out the door, praying Dr. Shirash can help me. That when I see Mia tonight, I'll have the answer to how to save her life.

CHAPTER ELEVEN

I grab my car from home and drive thirty minutes north to the La Jolla Cove, where Shirash lives. As I weave higher and higher into the hills of La Jolla, the sweeping views of the Pacific Ocean leave me breathless. I hope he isn't upset when I get there that I didn't tell him my real reason for wanting to see him: that I'm the latest version of the British student. I finally reach his drive and press a button at his gate, letting him know I'm here. He buzzes me in. My chest is tight as I approach his large black front door.

"Hello," Dr. Shirash greets me. "Come in, come in." He smiles warmly, his dark eyes lighting up.

He beckons me inside, and I follow, his small frame looking tinier in his huge entryway, the vaulted ceiling higher than I've ever seen in a house. His living room opens into a large patio, and we walk outside, the view of the ocean below like nothing I've ever seen. "Would you like coffee? Tea? Water?" he asks.

"No, I'm fine, thanks."

"Sit, sit." He motions to a large, inviting chair. He takes the other.

"Thank you for seeing me so quickly," I say.

"It's my pleasure. Like I said, retirement affords me a lot of time."

"So I have a confession. This isn't exactly a follow-up interview for the British-student story." My words spill out rapidly. My hands tremble slightly, and I tuck them under my knees so Shirash doesn't notice. I'm so close to finding answers.

Shirash raises an eyebrow. "Oh?"

I lean forward and wipe my sweaty palms on my pants. "I need to talk to you about me."

"You?"

"I think I'm in the same predicament as the British student."

Shirash's eyes widen. "Tell me more."

I walk him through the past two Thursdays and today. How I feel they've been repeating. I give him the examples. Amanda. Mia. To my surprise, I'm crying when I finish.

He pulls a handkerchief out of his pocket and hands it to me. I wipe my eyes.

"I'm sorry for what you're going through."

"Do you believe me? Am I crazy? Can you help me save Mia?"

Dr. Shirash holds his hands up. "I do believe you."

My shoulders relax slightly. "Great, so what do we do to fix this?"

"I do believe you, but I'm not sure I can help you." The tension immediately returns, my neck tightening.

"Why not?"

"Please, listen."

I nod, biting my tongue, and he continues.

"We have theories, as you know from when you interviewed me about the British boy who claimed to be in a time loop for eight years. He, like you, thought he was reliving the same day over and over. He eventually stopped doing simple things like reading the paper and watching TV—he said he had already seen it all."

"I can relate," I interject.

Dr. Shirash offers me a sympathetic smile. "What that British boy was experiencing wasn't as most of us have experienced on occasion. It was ultimately diagnosed as persistent psychogenic déjà vu. Usually this is in relation to epileptic seizures or dementia. A neurological assessment didn't indicate any abnormalities. He was tested the way a patient with dementia would have been—often those with dementia lack the awareness that what they are saying is false. They found no memory deficit. They ultimately determined he was suffering from severe anxiety. That it had been triggered by the anxiety rather than a neurological condition."

"So I'm either severely depressed or I've lost my mind?" I ask, suddenly finding it hard to breathe. My hopes crushed right along with my lungs.

Dr. Shirash barely blinks at my outburst. "The best advice I can give you is to get tested for a few things so we can figure out what's causing this."

I slump in my chair. I could be mentally unsound. Need to check into a loony bin, as Lance joked. "So I'm insane?"

"Not likely, no."

"Not likely but possible?" I ask, touching my temples and closing my eyes, wondering what else I may have imagined.

Dr. Shirash waits a moment, clearly trying to choose his words carefully. "We'll need to rule out a few things. So let's not get ahead of ourselves."

"But listen, Dr. Shirash: I don't have a lot of time here. My date with Mia is"—I check my watch—"in seven hours. I can't watch her die again. I can't." My lip starts trembling. I don't want to break down again. I need to keep it together.

"Okay, okay, I understand," he says. "Tell me, have you been through anything traumatic lately?"

"Besides this?" I laugh.

Dr. Shirash doesn't respond.

"Mia died twice. But she died in the loop."

"Before that."

I think for a moment. "Mia came back into my life after a decade. But I'd hardly call that traumatic. It was a good thing."

"But you said this started happening to you after that first date. After she first died."

"Well, yes, but that doesn't mean Mia caused this."

"You must understand I'm not accusing Mia of anything. I'm trying to help you see things the way you might not be seeing them."

"Okay, I'm listening."

"You also mentioned you broke off an engagement to Mia. But never stopped loving her or thinking of her. Couldn't this 'time loop' be a way of you trying to make up for lost time? Hence, you *think* you're reliving the same day."

"You said you believed me." I sound like a child when I say this.

"I believe that you believe you are going through this—as did the Brit—and I'm as curious as you as to what is causing it. But that doesn't mean I know a way to fix what you're going through, aside from medication."

"So are you saying you don't believe in time loops? Because when we interviewed you, it sounded like you did." I know it seems like I'm accusing him of something. "Sorry, I don't mean to seem harsh. I'm—"

"Stressed?" Dr. Shirash offers.

"That doesn't begin to cover what this is." Hopelessness engulfs me. If he can't help, what the hell will I do? I put my head in my hands and breathe.

"I'll get you some water," Shirash says, heading into the house before I can respond, then returning moments later. "Here, drink."

I look up and take the glass, sipping slowly.

"Let me explain. Time loops haven't been proven. There have been theories. Scientists have *claimed* there are two kinds of time loops or time travel. One is a predestination paradox, which occurs when events in the future trigger certain events in the past. The second is the onto-logical paradox, in which an object or information creates its past self or becomes its past self."

My head starts to pound, and I massage my temples. "What does that mean?"

"In layman's terms, both are time travel theories. In one, the future self creates itself, and in the other, the future self becomes involved in its own past. Does that make sense?"

"Not really," I say as my temple throbs harder. "Am I the time traveler in this scenario?"

"It's entirely possible," he says, and a spark of optimism ignites inside of me. "Or it may be a fiction of your own mind," he adds, and the flame burns out.

My heart races. What if I'm truly ill? Will I be able to continue my job? Live with Lance? Will my parents have to take care of me? And Mia—does this mean we'll never be together? I deflect the thoughts. "Let's assume I'm not losing it. Which of those scenarios would best apply to me?"

"It's hard to say." Dr. Shirash stands and starts to pace. "When this is going on, no one knows if the body or the spirit or the conscious is looping. Some think our dreams could be from another lifetime."

"So if scientists are making these claims, it must be based on some-thing concrete? Something that could help me? I thought *you* studied this," I say, trying to keep the accusatory tone out of my voice, but it's impossible. The more he speaks, the less hope I have.

Shirash doesn't blanch. "Not time loops, per se. Quantum mechan-ics. But I would be thrilled to study you. And I know many scientists who would as well."

I stand up and walk toward the edge of his patio, feeling the urge to scream at the top of my lungs. Could it be true that I only *think* this is happening to me? I don't have time for testing. If this day keeps repeating itself, I will have to reexplain and remeet Dr. Shirash every Thursday, and to set up those tests in one day will be impossible.

But how would any of those diagnoses explain how I know what's going to happen before it does?

I turn around. "What about Amanda? The plane crash?"

"Predictions and time loops are two very different things." Shirash sits again and folds his hands in his lap.

"So . . . this could be all in my head?" I ask, fear absorbing me. What if I'm not sitting here across from this man? He's a figment of my imagination? This whole interaction conjured by my psyche? I rub my arms, suddenly cold.

"Yes, it could. You could be having short-term memory loss."

I blanch. Shirash seems to be throwing out a ton of theories to see what sticks. I slowly shake my head as the disappointment sets in. I'm no closer to answers and only have more questions. "Why would I be losing it now? After all this time of being fine?" Unless I wasn't as fine as I thought I was. Teetering on the edge of crazy, only one thing needed to push me over the edge.

Was that *thing* Mia?

"I can only attribute it to the tremendous stress you feel you are under. Self-imposed or not. So getting tested will be the way to rule out a lot of neurological conditions," Shirash says smoothly, and I wonder if he's always this calm.

"Or confirm them."

Shirash nods.

If I am insane, that means Mia is safe. That she isn't going to die. And while that brings me some semblance of hope, it would also mean that I'm not well. Panic rises in my chest as I consider being trapped inside this world for perpetuity, and I force myself to breathe normally, in and out, in and out. "The thing is, I don't have time for tests. If I'm not nuts and this *is* happening, then tomorrow you won't remember this. I will have to come here—explain this all to you again. And then you will tell me the same thing. This is so frustrating." My voice shakes as I speak. I came here for help and now feel more lost than before.

"I understand. And you have my number now. Please call me when you're ready for testing. Once we get those results—"

Something occurs to me, and I cut him off. "If you were stuck in a time loop, how would you get yourself out of it?"

Dr. Shirash looks at me for a few moments before answering, and I can't decide if he pities me or sees me as an exciting test case. "I would go to the source of my anxiety that most likely brought this on, and I would try to fix that."

"Mia."

"Yes, Mia. That's the psychologist in me talking. The quantum physics professor would get the testing."

"There is no time to get tested," I remind him.

I can tell he disagrees, but he doesn't say so. "Okay, but will you at least consider seeing a therapist? That I could arrange quickly."

I nod, sick with the thought of what a therapist might say. But I have to know. Not only to save Mia but for my own sanity, or lack thereof.

"Come with me."

I follow him into his kitchen, and he jots down a name. "This is a colleague. She's the best. Tell her I sent you and it's important, and she will fit you in same day."

I take the piece of paper and notice a framed picture of Shirash and Mr. T on the bookcase. They have gold chains wrapped around their necks and are both gesturing a thumbs-up.

Maybe I made a mistake coming here. Maybe Shirash is a quack. I look around his grand kitchen. A quack who made himself a lot of money? Not likely.

"*A-Team* fan?"

"Huge!" Shirash says. "You?"

"I'm more of a *MacGyver* guy," I say, my voice flat, deflated from this visit and the reality that I may be sick.

Shirash laughs, oblivious to my pain. "All I need is a wire and a piece of bubble gum, and I can get us out of here."

I stare at him, at a loss for words.

"Listen, Dom. Call my friend. Trust me—she will help lead you in the right direction. What have you got to lose?"

Time.

"I have a son about your age. It's all going to be okay." He pats me on the shoulder. It feels more comforting than I would have expected.

"Thanks for your time. I appreciate it," I say, and I decide to call the doctor. Because I won't be able to solve this until I'm sure it's not all in my own mind.

CHAPTER TWELVE

When I get inside my car, I dial Dr. Jane Turner's number. She answers on the first ring and tells me she got a text from Dr. Shirash, and she suggests I come right over.

That was fast, Shirash.

On my way to Dr. Turner's office, I notice the time and call Palomar Airport to warn them about the plane crash, blocking my number so they can't trace it back. I get sent through an automated system and can't reach an actual person. Finally, I'm forced to leave a message that I hope somebody listens to and takes seriously. But I'm not holding my breath. I take some solace knowing that everyone lives.

Twenty minutes later I'm reluctantly sitting across from Dr. Turner. She's in her sixties, I'd guess, with deep-brown skin, long dark hair, and huge eyes. As I observe her, I can feel the profound ridge of conflict inside myself. Both wanting her help and not wanting to *need* it.

"So, Dominic," she starts, then stops. "May I call you that?"

"Yes."

"I've spoken briefly to Dr. Shirash, but I'd like to hear from you why you are here."

"Dr. Shirash suggested I see you because *I believe* I'm living in a time loop."

She doesn't bat an eyelash. "Could you be more specific?"

"I've repeated Thursday, June eleventh, three times." I rush the words out, as if saying them quickly will take the sting off, not sure if letting a medical professional document them is in my best interest. But I have to know if this has been fabricated by my mind.

She nods and writes something down. I swallow hard.

"Do you mean that you've had chronic déjà vu?"

"Shirash brought that up as a possibility . . ." My head starts to feel heavy with the thought that this is all a case of bad déjà vu. My voice cracks when I speak again. "I think it's more than that. After Mia, my ex-fiancée, came back into my life, this started happening." I wonder if it could be possible that seeing Mia upended my psyche so much that it's created its own fantasy world as a result. The thought is terrifying.

"Okay, before we talk about Mia. Have you ever been diagnosed with depression or anxiety? Ever had a panic attack? Do you take any medication—maybe an SSRI like Lexapro or Prozac?"

"No diagnosis. And no meds—ever. I tried a sleeping pill once and hated it," I answer. But now, I wonder if signs were missed. If my perpetual all-nighters in college were a result of being manic rather than driven. I'd go thirty-six hours sometimes without so much as closing my eyes. I'd push myself to the brink of a drunk exhaustion before I'd ultimately collapse. Or was my inability to move on after Mia symptomatic of some deeper-rooted psychological disease? It has been ten years, and while I've functioned, I haven't emotionally healed. Not even close.

"Have you ever been suicidal?"

"No. Absolutely not," I say with conviction, leaving out that there were some dark nights after Mia when I doubted life would ever get better. If life was worth living without her.

She writes this down.

"Tell me about Mia."

I start to tell her the details of what happened since she walked into the coffee shop—how I'd felt frozen in time until seeing her started the clock moving again, heightened all of my senses, jolted my emotions. As I say the words, I study Dr. Turner's face. Is she considering the same possibility that I am? That Mia was a trauma, and now I'm having a type of posttraumatic stress reaction to her return? As if reading my mind, she stops me.

"Why do you think her return affected you so much?"

"I think maybe I've never gotten over losing her. That I've been stuck in some kind of Mia quicksand, unable to move." My voice trembles as I say the words, acknowledging the truth I've been afraid to admit. I turn away from Dr. Turner, as the realization hits hard. The decision to let her go and my inability to win her back have haunted me for years.

"Why? What makes her so special?"

"She's beautiful. Smart. Kind. Independent. She takes risks." I lean back in my chair.

"Risks," she repeats and writes something down. "What do you mean?"

"It's like she doesn't have fear. She's always pushing boundaries. When we were engaged, she would . . . do things."

"Like what?"

I think back to the time she danced on the table at a bar in Ensenada. It was wobbly, and I stood below, bracing for impact. Wanting her both to come down and to stay up at the same time. Her thrill seeking simultaneously excited and terrified me. "Like stand up in a crowded room and call attention to herself."

"How did that make you feel?"

"Well, it was Mia. It's what she would do. Her odd way of thinking. Like standing in line for four hours to audition for *Survivor* or scaling a wall at the Sleep Train Amphitheatre so she could see Maroon 5 do their sound check. Or insisting on skydiving solo when everyone else was going tandem with an instructor."

"This risk-taking, or 'crazy' behavior, as you call it—were you on board with that too?"

I shake my head. "I would worry. Tell her what could go wrong. Warn her to be careful. It felt like a burden sometimes."

"I imagine it would."

Now I'm on a roll. Remembering more things. "Like, she was the kind of person who *wanted* to get on the jumbotron at sporting events—once we were at a Lakers game, and they played Kiss Me, and if you're caught on camera, you kiss. And it came to us, and I didn't kiss her. We had one of our biggest fights after that."

"Why, do you think?"

"She was upset. Why hadn't I kissed her? The truth was I was stunned. I froze. And it felt, I don't know, silly."

"Did you think Mia was silly?"

I think about this for a moment. "No, but I didn't feel like she took things seriously."

"And that bothered you?"

"Yeah, I guess it did."

"Did you ever talk to her about it, before the engagement ended?"

I ponder this for a moment. I didn't. Why? I don't know. I guess she scared me. And I wondered if I could keep up. If I wanted to keep up.

"No," I say. "But I was young. I didn't understand myself or her."

"And you do now?" she asks pointedly.

I laugh nervously. "I guess not."

"What's she been like since you've reconnected?"

"Older, but still Mia."

Dr. Turner squints at me. "When did you say you reconnected?"

"It's been two days or four days, whichever way you want to look at it," I say and try my best to explain my situation.

"And you saw Dr. Shirash, and he referred you to me?" She takes off her glasses and puts them in her lap. Her face is unreadable, which I take as an occupational hazard.

I nod.

"Dr. Shirash gave me a little backstory, said that you told him Mia died on your first date, and then she died again. That you can't save her." I try to read her expression. Does she believe me? Does she think I'm as crazy as I feel?

"This is true. We were thrown from the Zipper ride, and I lived and she died. And then she fell from my balcony—" A bubble of grief rises in my throat, surprising me, the image of her falling, wide eyed, still haunting.

She interrupts me. "I think you are experiencing a trauma that we should explore."

"Like PTSD?" I ask, flinching slightly as I remember my earlier thought—that Mia's return has triggered deep wounds inside of me.

"I'm not offering you a formal diagnosis right now. But I do think Mia coming back into your life has created a deep anxiety that you will fail her again; therefore, your subconscious is creating this time loop so you can finally redeem yourself. And until you do, you may feel trapped within it."

"Did Shirash tell you to say that?" I snap, feeling defensive.

"No, he offered his opinion, but from speaking with you—"

"And that's your opinion after speaking with me for—" I glance at my watch.

"For twenty-five minutes," she interjects. "Yes, that's my initial reaction, but we need to explore your relationship with her to make true progress."

"Did he tell you I don't have that kind of time?"

"He did mention you feel you don't have the time for the testing, which I agree with him you should get." She looks pointedly at me. "We also need to rule out other causes, like a tumor or other neurological disorders. A brain scan would be the best way to determine a differential diagnosis, indication of where to start, what medications would be best to try."

"So Dr. Shirash thinks I might be crazy. And now you're saying I might have a brain tumor?" My hands feel clammy, and I blink rapidly, recalling a story I worked on last year about a woman who, after developing a benign brain tumor, thought she was from Australia and would only speak in an Australian accent until it was safely removed. Is that happening to me? Is something inside me altering my own reality?

"We need to rule a tumor out before we can know anything."

I look over her shoulder at her framed degrees. Undergrad at UCLA. Masters and doctorate at USC. No sign of any pictures with an actor from a bad eighties TV show. Maybe she's right. Maybe I need to find out if something medical is causing this. "How soon can I get a brain scan? It would need to be today, and I'd also need the results immediately." I look at the clock—it's nearly two thirty.

Her eyes light up. "I can make a call. I'm sure I could get you at UCSD this afternoon. I have a colleague who owes me a favor. And I must say—I'm intensely curious to see the results."

That makes two of us.

"Thank you," I say as she picks up the phone and makes the call that may hold all the answers I seek. I lean back in my chair, overwhelmed by either possibility—that I'm sick and may need medication and hospitalization to find reality again, or that I may have a mass in my head causing hallucinations. One thing I know for sure: no matter what the answers are, life as I know it will never be the same.

CHAPTER THIRTEEN

JUNE 11, 3:30 P.M.
THURSDAY #3

I swallow hard as my body slides into the small cylindrical chamber of the MRI machine. I feel claustrophobic when there are too many people in an elevator with me, so the thought of spending a half hour inside this pseudocoffin does not excite me. Not to mention I'm worried about Mia. Is she looking both ways when crossing the street? Keeping her feet on the ground? Wearing her seat belt?

"Lie still!" The tech's voice booms through the large headphones she placed over my ears to protect me from the loud clicking noises she warned I would hear. "It will sound like someone is hitting a radiator with a metal pipe," she adds.

"Lovely," I answer, trying to force down the crippling anxiety that is filling my gut: That these dates with Mia were only in my mind. That the truths I've discovered about her, about myself, are all false memories. "So glad I came."

My twenty minutes in the MRI feel like hours as I wait to be released from this prison. Wondering if Mia is okay. If I'm okay. I keep trying to get comfortable, the tech scolding me each time I move an inch. Finally I feel the plank below me give way and begin to move.

The tech is waiting for me when I come out. "It took longer because you wouldn't lie still," she says, her brows furrowed in judgment.

I kick my legs over the side. "Am I good to go?" I ask, blinking rapidly, anxious for the results.

"Dr. Finn wants to see you first."

I look toward the door. "Who's that?"

"The neurologist." She gives me a bewildered look. "Isn't that why you're here? To see him? He moved things around to fit you in."

"Right. Of course," I say quickly.

After I change back into my clothes, the tech leads me down a hallway and into a small room. She points to a chair. "He'll be with you as soon as the report comes in from the radiologist. But I must warn you, it can take a while." She looks at me quizzically. "It's unusual for them to turn it around the same day. You must have friends in high places. Or be someone special."

Is that what I am? Special? I give her a wan smile as I sink into the seat and wait to hear if something is wrong with my brain. I watch the second hand moving on the clock on the wall. Not even a full minute has passed when I hear a male voice. "Hello, I'm Dr. Finn."

I look up and see a lanky man standing in front of me. He has thick black hair and a large nose that stands out on his otherwise uninteresting face. He smiles and holds out his hand. "I'm a neurologist here." He nods to a framed photo of himself next to several other doctors hanging on the wall. "Radiology sent me your scan." He frowns. Or at least I think he does.

"Already?"

"Let's talk in my office," the doctor says, ignoring my question.

My knees feel like they might give out as I follow him. What if I have an aggressive tumor and that's why he already has the report? The radiologist shocked by how large it is, wanting to get it into the neurologist's hands as soon as possible. In his small room down the hall, he steps around his messy desk and taps his mouse. He turns the monitor toward me, then pulls up a black-and-gray image of what I assume is my brain. I study the image, wondering where my tumor is.

Dr. Finn slides a pair of black-rimmed glasses onto the bridge of his nose and gives me a long look. "Your scan appears totally normal."

"Really?" I ask and let out the breath I was holding.

He nods and points to a dark-gray patch on the screen. "See this area? This would be where we would see abnormal activity that may result in memory loss or a tumor in a case like yours. But there's none."

"So I'm not paranoid?" I laugh nervously, realizing that ruling out a tumor isn't necessarily a positive. Because it means I may have a psychological disorder.

He clears his throat. "Here's what I can tell you. Based on this scan, you do not have a tumor, dementia, or any other neurological disorders. But what it cannot tell me is how to interpret your thoughts, your beliefs." He reads something in what must be my file. "It says here you think you're living the same day over and over? Today—Thursday, June eleventh. You believe you are in a time loop?"

"Yes," I say slowly, not loving the look on his face. Hearing the words read aloud to me is unsettling. Because they do sound absurd. I can't believe I've been telling people this and hoping they'll buy it. I must sound like a total loon when I plead my case. My palms start to sweat, and I wipe them on my pants as Finn studies me, probably waiting for me to go into some long-winded rant about it so he can hear it for himself—what's already in the file: that I'm one step away from being institutionalized. *Sorry, buddy, not going to happen.* "But hey, I think I only said that because I was exhausted. I need more sleep. That's all. Thanks for your time." I start to stand.

"Hold on," he says, knitting his brow. "I wouldn't be doing you any favors if I let you walk out of here right now. My colleague said this was of the utmost urgency, and I want to make sure I'm helping you in all the ways I can."

I half sit and half stand, hovering over the chair. "I will tell Dr. Turner you were incredibly thorough and helpful, but I should go. I'm needed at the station. I'm a producer down at Channel Seven News," I add, to give him *and myself* some validity as to who I am. "Thanks so much for fitting me in, Doc—"

"Wait," Dr. Finn says. "Protocol requires an inpatient psych evaluation as well."

That last one does it. I stand fully upright and head for the door. I picture myself in a stark white room wearing a straitjacket, psychiatrists forcing me to take my meds so I don't act out. "No thanks. I'm good," I say over my shoulder, speed walking down the hall.

Dr. Finn calls after me. "Mr. Suarez. I'm afraid it's not up for discussion. The delusions you're having are quite serious. We need answers so you don't hurt yourself or someone else."

Delusions.

I'm in a full sprint now, my lungs burning as I race down a corridor, dodging a group of doctors in blue scrubs, narrowly missing a medical supply cart. I trip but regain my balance as I hear an announcement over the PA about detaining a man who meets my description. I race around a corner and open the first door I see and duck inside. My heart hammers inside of me as I lean against the wall, realizing I'm in a linen closet. I hear the sound of strained voices outside the door, loud footsteps coming closer. Did they see me enter this room? Sweat is running down my face and my back. I scan the closet—shelves piled high with sheets and towels. There's nowhere to hide in here. Another voice comes over the loudspeaker: to please detain the man meeting my description. *Oh God.*

I hear the doorknob rattling. My heart is about to burst out of my chest. There's a brief exchange about a patient in 517, and the person on the other side of the closet is called away. I wait a beat, then open the door only a sliver and look out. The hallway is empty save for one man in a hospital gown who is pushing a walker. I dart toward the door at the end of the hall marked Exit.

"Hey! Hey, you!" the man calls after me. "You're that guy they're looking for!" I keep running as fast as I can until I reach the door. I push through it with my shoulder and fly down the stairs, praying when I reach the bottom there isn't a team of people waiting to lock me up. I see the final door and decide to go for it. I push it open and run for my life. I look over my shoulder, and there are two security officers. They point at me and start rushing in my direction. I can see my car up ahead, and I push myself to go faster, my lungs burning. I reach in my pocket, fumble for my key, and open the door. My mind is spinning as I jump inside the car and start it, pushing the gas pedal to the floor. I gun it out of the parking lot, the guards in my rearview mirror still tearing across the parking lot in my direction.

As I'm pulling onto the 5 freeway, I wonder how far Dr. Finn and the hospital security staff will go. Will they send the police after me? I cringe as I remember putting my address, employer, and phone number on the medical forms. Will they pound on my door tonight and demand I go with them because I'm a danger to myself or to others? And if I am locked up in some room at a mental hospital, how will I save Mia from dying tonight?

How could I have been so stupid as to involve medical professionals in this? How could I ever have expected them to believe me? They're scientists. They need proof of everything. And this is becoming increasingly difficult to prove—especially to myself. Because how could a time loop be real? I shake my head. I don't blame them for thinking I'm delusional. For wanting to commit me.

I press the gas pedal harder, biting down on my lip so hard I draw blood, and squeeze the steering wheel until my knuckles are white. My eyes darting to the rearview mirror every two seconds. I am sure as hell not going down without a fight. So . . . change of plans: I'm not going home.

CHAPTER FOURTEEN

When I'm certain no one is following me, I pull into a parking garage off Eighth, find a space in the back, and cut the engine. I lean the driver's seat back and try to get a grip on how this day has gone. My mind whirls, playing back the doctors' blank stares, pitying looks, pointed questions. The hospital chase. Because I'm apparently delusional. A danger. I need a psych evaluation.

I stare at the ceiling of the car. I'm at a total loss. No one believes me, and I only sound crazier with each person I tell. So what do I do? Is there anyone who can help me?

I think back to the night of my second Thursday, when I drank bourbon with Lance. He didn't completely laugh at me when I confessed the premonition I'd had about Mia's dying. And this morning he seemed somewhat open to the idea that I could be psychic. And I hadn't tried to prove anything to him. I'd simply been telling him how I felt. Maybe I can convince him—somehow *show* him—why I think I've been reliving Thursday. Then he can help me somehow. He is my best friend. I've known him for fifteen years. If anyone is going to be in my corner, it's him.

I hope.

But first I have to meet Mia. And hope I can save her life tonight.

I keep my head down and walk briskly over to Rustic Root. I hover near the entrance in a doorway back from the street. Sweat rings are forming under my arms as I wait. Part of me hopes Mia won't show up. That she'll text and tell me she's sick or simply changed her mind. That we'll both go to bed tonight and wake up tomorrow and somehow it will be Friday. My phone buzzes. My heart leaps. Did I predict her cancellation text? But it's not Mia. It's an email. The subject line says: Thank you. It's from Amanda. She thanks me profusely—as in types the words *thank you* dozens of times. Then she makes a joke about deleting Tinder from her phone, and at this point someone couldn't convince her to so much as join eHarmony. She is looking into nunneries. She says she's grateful that her life was saved and not to take this the wrong way, but she's also a little freaked out about the details I knew—down to the douchebag's snoring. Could I enlighten her a bit?

I wish I could, Amanda. I wish I could.

"Dom!"

I look up and see Mia waving to me from the other side of Fifth, and my stomach tightens into a hard ball. As I lift my arm to wave back, she doesn't head for the crosswalk; she steps into the street and jaywalks toward me.

"Mia, wait!" I yell, but she doesn't hear. A band playing in a nearby restaurant drowns out my call. My heartbeat thunders, everything moving in slow motion. Mia smiling as she runs toward me, her purse bouncing on her hip, the cars on the street heading in her direction, a gaggle of women in a bridal party getting into a limo. Mia is still coming; she's almost to me. I'm frozen in place, nothing I can do but wait. Hope. Pray.

Please, God, let her be okay.

Mia makes it safely to my side of the street, and I feel like a thousand-pound weight has been lifted off my chest. She propels herself into my arms. I inhale her sunflower smell. I'm so relieved to be holding her, but still, I'm angry. She's always taking risks. I pull back from her. "You should use the crosswalk! You could have been killed!"

"Dom, I'm not eight years old. What the hell? That's a super uptight thing to say—even for you!" Her nostrils flare. She was always passionate—in love and in war. She could love hard but fight hard too. I won so few battles with her that this one is unlikely. Plus, she has no idea why her action petrified me. She has no clue what I've been through. What *she's* been through.

"Sorry, I've had a rough day," I say, and this seems to appease her. I feel like I've been running since this all began—running to save Amanda, to try and fail to save Mia, and to escape my own demons earlier today. My blood pressure spikes as I think where I'd be now if the hospital security guards had caught up with me.

"Let's get you a cocktail, then, and you can tell me all about it."

That's the thing. I can't tell you a damn thing about it.

"Find it okay?" I ask as we walk to the hostess stand on the sidewalk. She nods.

The hostess asks if we want to sit on the rooftop or downstairs in the restaurant.

"Let's sit up there!" Mia says. And I know I can't put up a fight. Not after my crosswalk rant. We are directed to a high table near the bar, and I glance over Mia's shoulder, assessing how far we are from the edge of the balcony. "So what's going on?" Mia asks once the server walks away. "You seem tense." She puts her hand on top of mine, and I feel a jolt of electricity run up my arm.

I don't move my hand, hoping she'll keep hers right where it is. Her warm touch makes me feel safe for the first time all day. How could I have wished her not to come when she's the very person I need? I take in the way the light hits her face. She is real. This is real.

"I don't want to bore you with my bad day. I'm sorry I freaked out back there."

"It's okay," she says, moving her hand away and grabbing a menu. She looks at it but then back at me. "You sure you're all right? You can tell me anything."

"I always could," I say, reminiscing. "You were seriously the world's best listener. And gave the best advice. If it weren't for you, I wouldn't be at Channel Seven!" I balked after receiving an offer years ago. The salary was lower than I'd expected, and a buddy told me he could get me a more lucrative gig as a financial advisor. Mia reminded me that I needed to take a chance. That there was no way she'd let me walk away from my TV aspirations over a few dollars.

"True." She smiles.

I debate telling her what's going on. Would she believe me? But then again, how do I tell her and leave out the part about her dying?

I force a smile.

She gives me another glance but seems to decide to let me off the hook.

She points to the menu. "They have mini margarita shots!" she squeals, and my smile quickly becomes genuine. I love that she finds joy in things like mini margarita shots.

"They're known for them," I say and order two when our server, a leggy woman in a skintight black dress, swings by to introduce herself. She reminds me of Amanda, or maybe the dress does, and I remember her email to me. I should write her back, if only to say *you're welcome*.

The shots arrive, and we take them and order another round, laughing at how ridiculous it is that we both didn't order regular-size margaritas in the first place. "But they are so cute! I love them!" Mia declares. Her happiness fuels me, and I start to feel slightly relaxed, wanting to push away the thought of her dying but also scared to not have it on my mind. Because will it happen when I'm not paying attention? When I get too comfortable? I rub my head. I'm in a total lose-lose situation.

"Dom? Do you have a headache?" She rummages through her bag. "I might have some Advil in here."

"No, no, I'm fine. Was thinking."

"About all the bad stuff from today you won't tell me about?"

"Yeah, that. Okay, so I lied that it was boring stuff that happened to me today," I confess, deciding there are parts of my day I *can* tell her about. "I saved someone from getting hit by a car this morning, and she emailed right before you walked up to say thank you."

"Isn't that a good thing? That you saved her?"

"Yes and no."

"Why not? You're not making sense."

"It freaked me out. I knew the car was going to run the light before it did. I saw it in a dream," I say, wishing I could tell her the rest.

"Wow, a lot has changed since we were together. There was a time you would have told me having a vision was total BS." She laughs.

"I know. I was too skeptical. I'm more open minded now."

"Like when it comes to jaywalking?" She arches an eyebrow.

"You got me. I'm still pretty cautious when it comes to safety."

"No shit." She laughs. "We need to loosen you up. Maybe start by unbuttoning the top button of your shirt. Can you breathe?" she teases.

I do as she says, and we start laughing.

The server drops off two more shots, and we take them.

"Hey, for what it's worth," Mia says, "I know you're freaked out, but it's a good thing what you did. I'm glad the woman is okay. And that you are too. Did you hear about that plane crash in Oceanside earlier?"

I nod, looking down to avoid eye contact. They ignored my warning.

"Did you know it barely missed an apartment complex? Everyone lived on the plane and the ground, thank God, but it shows that life is fleeting. Time is fleeting." She reaches across the table and gives me her hand. I take it and make myself breathe normally. Hold myself back from blurting that yes, I know all about the plane crash. That I've known about it for days.

We stay like that for a few moments. I'm struck by every minuscule movement she makes, the way she plays with the heart-shaped silver ring on her right finger. How she chews on her pinkie nail when she thinks I'm not looking. The way the breeze keeps pushing one lone strand of hair into her mouth. These are not things I would notice if I were dreaming. If it were an illusion. We are here, now. And I want to tell her how much I love her. How I've never stopped loving her. "What are you thinking about?" she asks. We're still holding hands. I don't ever want to let go.

"You. Us. The old days."

"Ah, the old days," she repeats. "What do you remember?"

"Everything," I say.

"Like what?" Mia tilts her head playfully. "What do you remember about me?"

I decide to go with the rest of the speech I didn't give her last night. The one that sat on the tip of my tongue but seemed like it would be too much. I tell her about her hair in the morning—the way it hid most of her face. Her never-ending pile of shampoo and conditioners. She stares at me, eyes wide, as I confess how I still think of her gentle kisses before bed. How she'd tell me she loved me, even when we fought. And I end on the laughs and which one was my favorite.

Mia blinks several times when I finish. "Wow."

"Too much?" I ask, not sure I want to know the answer.

"No, it was perfect. Absolutely perfect." She looks down for a moment, then back up at me. "But I do think you're wearing rose-colored glasses."

"No way. I was walking around blind before. Not paying enough attention to all the wonderful things about you. I took you for granted. And Mia?" I pause, remembering her question to me before she fell off the balcony.

"Yeah?"

"In case you've ever wondered or second-guessed things, you didn't do anything wrong. You aren't the reason I broke things off. I was stupid and young and uptight and so many things. It was all me."

Mia cocks her head, her eyes searching mine.

The server walks up, interrupting. We scan the menus quickly and place our order. My stomach is twisting, so I order something small—the pork belly appetizer. Mia gets the fried chicken after seeing it delivered to the table next to ours.

After the server leaves, Mia gives me a dubious look. "You're giving me the 'it's not you, it's me' speech right now?"

"I am. Because it's true. I wish I could have articulated it better when I came to your parents' house. I should have sat out on that lawn until you believed me or I froze to death—whichever came first."

This gets a laugh out of her. That deep one that I crave. Then the waiter delivers our food, causing us to pause the conversation for a moment. When he walks away, she begins speaking again.

"I appreciate you saying that, because I did wonder. I still wondered . . ." She trails off. "We should eat this food before it gets cold." She removes her hand from mine. I try not to fall apart when she does. Were my overtures too much? Or is she simply processing?

I decide to let her off the hook the way she did me earlier and change the subject, filling her in on what Lance has been up to. I force myself to act normal, but internally I'm scanning for any hint of trouble, any ominous sign that Mia may be in danger again.

"This is delicious," she says, lifting another bite of chicken into her mouth.

"My favorite thing here." When she looks suspiciously at my pork belly, I add, "I'm not super hungry tonight."

"How's your family?" she asks. "Your mom?" She looks down, and I wonder what she's thinking. If she's remembering my introducing her for the first time. My mom wrapping her into a giant hug. Mia later telling me she couldn't remember her own mother ever embracing her that way. Or if she's thinking about what she said almost immediately after I popped the question. "Now your mom will be my mom too," she said, then paused. "I hope that's what she wants."

"She loves you," I said a little too enthusiastically.

"She loves *you*, so she's begrudgingly accepting me. Don't think I can't feel her disapproval. She might not say it, but it's in her eyes when she watches us."

"She's great," I say now. "You know. Like before."

"Oh, Dom, I hardly remember her. It was so long ago," she says, and I feel a sting in my chest. She notices my face. "I didn't mean it like that."

"It's okay. How are your parents?" I ask, wishing I'd tried harder to get to know George and Janice. I had a tough time connecting with her dad, who took me ice fishing up in Wisconsin the first time I ever visited their home in northern Illinois during the holidays. Not only did I freeze my balls off in the very impractical coat I'd brought and not catch a single fish, but I had to suffer through eight hours of one- and two-word answers to my questions. Thank God he'd brought a twelve-pack of beer. Her mom was always cordial to me but a bit standoffish. The first time I met her, I put my arms out to hug her, and she shook my hand instead. Mia later told me her mom wasn't like her—Mia was a hugger and a cheek kisser, but her mom had never shown much emotion, not even to Mia or her sister.

"Good. They retired a few years ago." If I remember correctly, Mia's dad owned his own plumbing company, and her mom taught at the local high school. She laughs softly. "But I think they're driving each other a little bit crazy being together twenty-four seven."

"Or not—is your dad still a man of very few words?" I ask.

"Yep. If anything, he talks even less now! Although he texts. And he's on Facebook and Instagram." She laughs.

"No way!"

"I swear. He loves it. Communication without talking! I can barely get him on the phone. He's like a teenager. If I call, he won't answer. But if I text him or DM him on Instagram, he responds in a hot minute."

I laugh and scoop the last bite of pork belly off my plate. When I look up, Mia's eyes grow wide. At first I don't register what's happening. Then she pats her neck furiously, and her face reddens.

She's choking. I feel my own throat tighten as I realize death has come for her once more.

Adrenaline makes me shoot up out of my seat. "She's choking—we need help," I yell to everyone sitting around us, then dart to Mia's side of the table and reach around her chair awkwardly to grab her abdomen and heave my arms under her rib cage. I thrust several times, but nothing happens. I crane my neck to see her face. It's beginning to turn blue.

Blood pumps furiously into my veins. Sweat drips down my face. It's happening again. As soon as we got comfortable. Were laughing. Talking. Connecting. And now she could die—again. Right in front of me.

"I don't know if I'm doing this right! Does anyone know the Heimlich?" I scream, searching the crowded rooftop. A crowd has gathered, but no one is offering up their help. How is that possible? "Please. Somebody," I cry out. My chest tightens. I pound my hand on the table. "Stop staring and help me!"

"Here, let me." Our server pushes me aside and expertly grabs Mia's torso, forcing her fist against her stomach. "Come on!" she says in exasperation, her own face reddening as Mia's loses more color. She looks at Mia's plate. "Might be a chicken bone. Fuck! Somebody call 911!"

A man rushes over from the stairs. "I'm an EMT—I was downstairs in the restaurant." He tries for what feels like hours to dislodge whatever is blocking Mia's airway. There is a palpable desperation in the air. Mia's eyes go from wild to empty in what seems like mere moments.

I'm both shocked and not surprised at all that I've lost her again. I fall to the ground and wrap my arms over my head, horrified, but sure of three things.

I am not crazy.

This is not a dream.

I have no idea how to stop it.

CHAPTER FIFTEEN

I wake to *my fourth* Thursday, the screen on my iPhone taunting me with the date: June 11. The clock radio turns on, and the opening notes of the song that is now officially my personal ghost starts playing. I throw the clock radio against the wall, shattering it, the plastic shards shooting across the room. I spew victorious profanities that the Fray song has been stopped, though I'm painfully aware that the radio could again be in one piece, mocking me from my bedside table, tomorrow morning. *If I don't make it to Friday. And at this rate, it isn't looking good.*

Last night, after the paramedics had left Rustic Root, after people had hugged me, cried with me, and touched my shoulder and told me how sorry they were, I stumbled out of the restaurant and walked in a daze to Little Italy. I had no idea if it was safe to go home or if, when I did, Dr. Finn and hospital security would be waiting. I found a dive bar that smelled like stale beer and body odor and ordered double bourbons until closing. Then I got a room at the Holiday Inn Express, praying I'd wake to another Thursday at home. I lie in my bed now, staring at the ceiling, taking inventory.

1. Mia isn't dead.
2. I am trapped in a time loop (because I'm not willing to accept that I'm crazy).

The juxtaposition of those two feelings sends me running to the toilet. Lance must hear me because he knocks on the door, asking if I'm hungover from last night. "Worst one of my life," I say honestly.

"I've got the cure for that."

"Coffee spiked with Jack Daniel's, and bacon and eggs. I know," I say, my tone sharp.

"Only trying to help, man." Then two seconds later, "And how did you know that was what I was going to say, anyway?"

"Can't talk right now."

When I feel like I can finally stand up, I stagger to my room, thinking about how to use my time today to save Mia and break out of this time loop. I couldn't perform the Heimlich on her correctly, and maybe if I'd known what I was doing, she'd still be alive. Maybe the key to saving her is that *I* have to be the one to do it, literally. I decide I need to research and learn all of the possible techniques I can to be able to save someone's life. I also want to try to convince Lance of what's happening so he can help me. Two people working on this will be a hell of a lot better than one. I check the time on my phone. It's 7:15 a.m.—I have less than an hour to save Amanda.

I decide to start with Lance. I get dressed and find him in the kitchen, pouring coffee.

"Sorry about before," I say.

"No worries. Too many shots last night?" he asks.

"No."

"Morning sickness, then?" He laughs, and I roll my eyes. He grabs the carafe of coffee, and I nod. He pours me a cup. "But no Jack." I smirk.

"Hair of the dog, though."

He hands me the mug, and I breathe in the deep aroma and take a drink. "I need to talk to you about something."

"Oooh, mysterious," Lance says, fluttering his fingers at me.

"I'm being serious here."

Lance gives me a strange look. "Is this about Mia?"

"No, why?"

"No reason," he says, but his face tells me there is one.

"Why, Lance?" I press.

"I thought since you were going out with her tonight, you wanted to discuss it. My bad. I forgot our rule—that we don't discuss her."

I don't completely buy it, but I don't have a lot of time, so I press forward.

"I need you to hear me out on what I'm about to say. It's going to sound impossible. And your inclination might be *not* to believe me, but I need you to. I need your help."

"You have my attention."

I explain everything that's happened over the past three Thursdays and end with this morning. I pause when I get to the part where I was almost involuntarily committed, worried it may dampen my credibility. But then I shove it out anyway, wanting everything on the table. Lance's mouth falls open, and my eye twitches slightly as I describe Mia's death in detail, my voice breaking as I recall the way she choked last night. How the helplessness I felt nearly broke me.

Lance doesn't speak when I'm finished. He takes a deep breath. I watch him, hoping he won't make a joke but knowing he probably will. I try to put myself in his shoes. If I were hearing this nutty-sounding story from him, what would my reaction be? Before this started happening, I didn't so much as believe in fate. Now I'm researching alternate universes and visiting quantum physics professors.

"This probably isn't the time to make a *Groundhog Day* joke? Ask where Bill Murray is?"

I shake my head. "Look, before you say anything, I've seen a therapist, I've had an MRI, I've ruled out that this is all in my head."

"You did this all after we got home from Barleymash last night?"

I swallow my frustration. Of course this is hard to follow. For him last night was shots at a bar a few blocks away. He hasn't lived four days in one.

"No, I did this yesterday—on my third Thursday."

Lance runs his hands over his face.

"This is a lot. You're not fucking with me?" He looks around. For what, I don't know. Probably the hidden cameras. I guess I can't blame him. I would probably say the same thing.

"Look, I have to go."

"To save that girl?"

"Yeah." I make a face because I know how ridiculous it all sounds. Then I have a thought. "Come with me. Will that help you believe? Seeing that I know the car is coming before it does? That I can describe the girl before I see her? Know her name? And then you'll see that she won't know who I am. That she has never met me."

Lance stares at me a beat before answering. "Okay. I'm in," he says, but his voice isn't as confident as his words. He's afraid we'll get down there and it won't happen. Then he'll have to face that his best friend is losing it. Or maybe he's afraid it *will* happen. And he'll have to face that too. As for me, I'm looking for an ally. Someone to help me make sense of this mess without putting me in the mental ward.

I need someone to believe in me.

As we head outside, I fish a twenty out of my wallet and hand it to Chuck, who looks at me with surprise, then looks at the money like it's not real. Lance's face is equally shocked. Chuck nods at me and breaks into a coughing fit. His hack is thick, and I take a beat to assess him—I haven't ever noticed how pale he is or his glassy eyes. Or maybe I assumed he was high? Now I wonder if it's because he's ill.

I pause. "You okay?"

Chuck continues to cough but nods at me. I hesitate, wanting to ascertain whether he's okay but also needing to prove to Lance that I'm not insane. Although by the way he's looking at me right now, that ship might have sailed.

"What?" I say to Lance when we are a few steps down the sidewalk.

"I thought you had a policy against that? That you'd only be feeding their drug habit or alcoholism?"

"Let's just say I've had a change of heart," I say. "Come on, we need to hurry. There she is." I point out Amanda, then call her name. I pull her out of the way. I make sure the driver is okay. I give Amanda my card. I tell her to stay away from douchebags on Tinder. She gives me a funny look. Asks me how I knew. Thanks me profusely. I introduce Lance. They look at each other in disbelief, both confused about how I knew. I tell Amanda I have to go and pull Lance's arm so he'll come with me.

We walk several blocks in silence. Finally, Lance speaks. "I don't know what to say. I mean, how could you—"

"I told you how," I say, feeling impatient, but I have to remember I've been at this for three and a half days, and he's playing catch-up.

"But that can't be—"

"It is," I interrupt again as we head back into our building. I look around but don't see Chuck. His things are gone too. I punch the button for the elevator. The doors open, and we silently ride up with an elderly woman and her teacup Yorkie, who growls at us the entire time. Almost as if he can sense the weirdness going on between us. I'm anxious as we step off on the eleventh floor, and once we are inside the condo, I turn to Lance. "Listen, I get that it seems unbelievable. But it is happening to me."

Lance chews his fingernail, thinking. "I want to help you, but this is all like out of some sci-fi movie."

"I thought the exact same thing. Like, where's Neo in his black trench coat, you know?"

"Exactly!" Lance shouts, like he's happy to be agreeing on *something* with me. Then he gives me a long look. "Are you sure? There's no other explanation?"

I throw my hands up. "At this point, after I proved to you I could predict the car crash, Amanda, you either believe me or you don't. And I need you to believe me. I've got nowhere else to turn." I hunch my shoulders in disappointment, Lance's disbelief sucking the wind out of my sails.

"Okay. I believe you. But if you're screwing with me . . . if this is some kind of prank . . ."

I stare at him, waiting.

"You couldn't have staged that car crash," he says, looking down at the floor.

"I know."

"Okay. What can I do to help?"

I feel a swoosh of relief blast through me. "Really?"

Lance laughs nervously. "Really."

The sincere expression on his face coupled with my intense relief makes me throw my arms around him. "Thank you," I say, still clinging to him.

"You're welcome," he says, pulling away from me. "We're man hugging now, are we?"

"Yes, well . . . you have no idea how good it feels that you believe me. That I'm not crazy."

"Well, the jury's still out on that one. Always has been," he laughs.

I frown at him. "No jokes about my sanity, please."

"Fine, okay. But you've got to know there are like a hundred one-liners in this."

"Believe me, I do. But maybe let's save them for another day."

"Friday?"

"Yes! God willing!"

"Okay, so what can I do to help?"

"I need you to make some calls for me."

Lance nods.

"First, call Alexis and tell her we're both sick, but pitch her a shark-attack story that happens in Pacific Beach as the lead story." I look at my phone. "It should have just happened."

"Okay," he says and grabs his phone.

"And call Scott and ask him to produce for me—"

Lance cuts me off. "He won't go for it."

"Yes, he will. Tell him I'll get him a case of Spotted Cow."

"Anything else?"

I tell him to block his number, call Palomar Airport, and warn them that there might be a plane that's not up to par mechanically. I give him all the details I know.

He salutes me and heads to get his phone. I breathe out. Finally, someone to help me. It makes me feel as if I can accomplish it all—and save Mia too.

I text Mia.

I need to see you earlier than we talked about

Ok When?

I look at the time. Can you do 11:00 a.m.?

Wow that's a lot earlier! What's up? She adds the monocle-wearing emoji.

I'll tell you in person

Ok . . . you're in luck. My lunch plans just canceled. So I'll be at Hailey's.

Text me the address?

She sends it, then types: Any hints?

Only that I'm going to save your life, I think.

Nope! But do me a favor—don't leave the house! Please.

WTF?

Trust me, ok?

Is everything ok?

I hope so, I think.

Yes! is what I type.

I want to go on to tell her to eat only soft foods and not blow-dry her hair anywhere near water, but I stop myself and type: See you soon!

Lance walks over, shaking his head in disbelief. "Okay, I'm more on board with you knowing the future. Alexis was thrilled and checked the story while we were on the phone. She saw it on the police scanner, not online. She was impressed I knew about it! And Scott? He was thrilled when I mentioned that beer. I couldn't get a live person at the airport, so I left a message. Told them there was a plane that needed to be checked out and gave them the type of plane and the number. I'm not sure they'll do anything. At least no one dies, right?"

"Right."

"What's next?" Lance rolls up the sleeves of his oxford button-down. I resist the urge to hug him again. That will be one man hug too many—he'll really think I've lost it.

"We teach me how to save a life. And we need to do it in two hours. I'm seeing Mia at eleven a.m. I'm hoping if I change the time, it will stop the pattern. And if it doesn't, I'll be prepared to save her."

We grab our laptops and sit side by side on the couch. "I'll start with the Heimlich," I say. "You look up what to do if someone is electrocuted." He looks at me sideways.

We also research head trauma, CPR if there's a drowning—although I have no intention of taking her anywhere near deep water—seizures, and heart attacks. We make index cards with the basics on what to do in each scenario while we wait for 911. I also decide to bring the first aid kit we keep in the house. It's ten fifteen when we finish. "I have to go."

"What do I do now?" Lance asks.

"You've got the day off now. So make some bacon and eggs and wait for me to call." I start for the door. "Oh, and Lance?"

"Yeah?"

"Wish me luck!"

CHAPTER SIXTEEN

I pull up to Hailey's house five minutes early. It's a tiny sky-blue bungalow. Two red Adirondack chairs sit on a cozy porch. I park, grab my backpack with the first aid kit and index cards, and knock.

"Dom," Hailey says coolly when she answers, her lithe frame blocking my view inside. She doesn't invite me in.

"It's good to see you," I say, trying to break the ice. Trying to recall the last time I saw her. She would have still been in high school.

"I wish I could say the same." Hailey frowns, then recovers slightly. "Sorry, protective sister over here."

"I get it."

"Do you?" she asks, not unkindly. "I mean, I hope you do."

"I do," I say, meaning it more than she could ever know. I had a great relationship with Hailey—she was like a little sister to me. And in many ways I let her down too. "I promise you, Hailey, I'm a different person than I was then. I know I screwed up royally. I know how much I hurt her. And for what it's worth, I'm sorry I hurt her. I was a stupid kid."

"You can say that again." She smiles for the first time.

"I was a stupid kid," I repeat and return her grin.

"Thank you for saying all that. Mia's been through a lot. And she's getting settled in. She doesn't need any drama in her life right now."

I pause. What has Mia been through? A bad job? Breakup? Both? "I hear you. I'm on your side."

This seems to satisfy her, and she opens the door wider. "Now you may come inside."

I take in the tiny living room, a small blue sofa against the wall and a TV opposite. The coffee table is covered with novels. I wonder if they're hers or Mia's. Mia used to be a big reader. Is she still?

I follow her in and see Mia sitting on a worn couch across the room, holding a mug.

"Hey, Dom." She smiles. "Coffee?"

"Please."

"I'm off to work." Hailey walks to the door and glances back. "See you later."

"Bye, Hay," Mia says.

My phone buzzes with a text from Lance.

Is she still alive?

I text him a quick thumbs-up as I walk into the galley kitchen. Mia hands me a mug. She's not wearing one of her rompers. Instead, she has on a pair of sweatpants and a white tank top. Her hair is pulled up into a bun on top of her head.

"I like your hair." It's the way she used to wear it on lazy Sunday mornings, while she was studying, or when she went to the beach.

She touches it. "It's a topknot. Which is fancy for 'I didn't feel like doing my hair.'"

"I remember you always wore it like that."

"You do?" She looks surprised.

"Yes. It was how I liked you best. When you weren't worried about how you looked was when you were the most beautiful. Like right now." I smile, walk over, and touch a strand that has come loose. It's strange.

I'm so worried about what may happen to Mia but also immersed in this moment. Soaking each one in like a sponge. Desperate to create something beautiful to replace the ugliness of her many deaths.

She looks at me funny and doesn't say anything, so I move away. I must be coming on too strong. I have to remind myself she doesn't remember the last three Thursdays like I do. In her mind, our only conversation has been at the coffee shop.

But then she surprises me. "That was sweet of you to say, Dom."

"I meant it. You're so beautiful inside and out."

She blushes. "Thanks."

I take a sip of the coffee. It's strong—a little too strong for me. "Do you have any cream?" I ask.

Mia gives me a look as if to say, *Wimp*. She opens the fridge and pulls out a carton of almond milk. "This is the best I can do."

"I don't think I've ever had this before." I pour it into my coffee.

She laughs. "Is Lance aware of this travesty? I can see him now, puffing his chest out and reading the—what do you call that thing?"

"The teleprompter."

"Right." Then she deepens her voice. "A born-and-raised Southern California boy who has never drunk almond milk! Tonight at five," she says, then laughs.

"You've watched him?" I ask. Her impersonation is perfect.

Mia's face registers something, but it vanishes like a puff of smoke. Before I can comment, she asks me a question. "What are you doing here, Dom? I thought we were going to the fair tonight? Your text kind of freaked me out." She pauses. "Hailey thinks I should have made you wait."

"I'm glad you didn't."

"I guess you could say curiosity got the best of me."

"Good!"

"So what's up? I feel like you're stalling."

It's because I am. I spent so much time researching how to save a life that I didn't think through what I was going to say to her to explain the urgency.

"I needed to see you."

"So you said. But we were going to see each other tonight."

I don't have a good answer for this, or at least one that won't sound insane, so I take a sip of my coffee and look down at the scratched wood floor.

She holds my gaze. "Dom, what's going on?"

I pause for a moment. I can't tell her I'm worried she might die and I am here to prevent it. So I make a choice to tell her what's in my heart.

"After so many years, I couldn't wait another minute to be with you. I have so many regrets, Mia. About how I ended things. About breaking your heart. I'm so sorry."

She stares at me, eyes wide, unblinking.

My heart begins to race, but I take a deep breath and continue. "You didn't deserve to go through any of that. I want you to know that you didn't do anything. It was all me and my stupidity."

"I heard you talking to Hay," she says. "That you were a stupid kid. Maybe we were both stupid kids." She sighs heavily.

I shake my head. "No." I step toward her. I want to pull her into my arms, but I hold back. I don't want to push her too fast. "It wasn't you. You were amazing. You *are* amazing."

"Then why call it off?" She wrinkles her nose.

My therapy session with Dr. Turner comes to mind. Sure, I thought she was silly and attention seeking at times and way too much of a risk-taker, but those qualities weren't enough to make me question marrying her. Were they?

"Dom?"

I don't tell her what I was thinking, because Dr. Turner only recently helped me put together that those things bothered me. I hadn't been actively thinking about them then. "Because I was overthinking everything. You know how I was. Always worrying. And I was young. And I was stupid. And I should have trusted my heart. There's never been anyone who's come close since. It's always been you."

This is true. Sure, I've dated plenty of intelligent and attractive women, but none of them held the same spark Mia does. I always felt they were similar in personality to me. And it turns out I'm pretty damn boring.

She blushes slightly. "I think you're romanticizing what we had. Who we were."

"Nope!" I say. Although maybe there is a little truth to that. After so many years of distance, it's possible I put her on a small pedestal. That sometimes I'd play our relationship back like a movie in my head, late at night, after another mediocre date. Rewind the story of our time together. My favorite parts. Like when she convinced me to drive us four hours to the Nevada state line so she could place a one-hundred-dollar bet on the number three. I watched as the ball bounced haphazardly, then gasped when it dived into the slot. Mia grabbed my face and kissed me hard, right there, in front of everyone at the roulette table. And then she high-fived the elderly couple next to us, nearly knocking the fragile man over. I remember thinking how lucky she was that night. How things often seemed to go her way. Later, years after we broke up, I would still long for the light that trailed her. I'd ache for the sliver of warmth from it I'd feel when I stood close.

"Thank you for saying it wasn't me, because I have wondered. I still wonder . . ."

Time seems to freeze. This is the point of the conversation at which she choked last night. My heart starts to pound, and I look around for anything that could harm Mia. A live wire. A loose ceiling fan. I sniff the air. A gas leak?

"I still think about you too, Dom," she continues. "I wonder what would have happened if I'd given you another chance when you came to see me. I mean, you flew out to the Midwest wearing only shorts and a T-shirt. And it was forty-degree weather, and I was so cruel to you. Didn't let you come inside. Didn't so much as offer you a blanket to wrap around your shoulders while we talked. I'm sorry for that."

"I'm a big boy. It was fine. And anyway, *you* do not need to be sorry."

"I came after you, you know." She laughs nervously. "I've never told anyone this, not even Hailey."

My stomach does a flip. "What?"

"I couldn't sleep that night. I woke up early and drove to the hotel you said you'd be at, but you were already gone."

"Had you changed your mind?" I ask, the regret of what could have been if I'd still been at the hotel overwhelming me.

"I don't know," Mia says softly. "I knew I didn't want you to leave yet. And when you were gone, I figured it was the universe's way of saving me from myself."

"Wow," is all I can say. I cover my face with my hands, trying to imagine what our lives might have looked like had we connected, the regret of years lost punching me in the gut. But there's something else too—hope. She came back for me then. And maybe she's back for me now too.

"Want to take a walk?" she asks.

I hesitate. We are safe inside this bungalow. If we venture out, I lose a lot of control over my ability to protect her.

"Only if we use the crosswalk and abide by all pedestrian rules."

But she only laughs. She thinks I'm joking.

"I'm going to change into some shorts. It's already seventy-five degrees out there. You got other clothes in there?" She points to my backpack.

"No," I say, patting my jeans. "But I'll be fine."

"Better hot than freezing, right?" she calls from the other room. She's referencing the incident in her parents' front yard. I love that we're having playful banter again.

"Right."

When she comes back out, her hair is in a ponytail, and she has a pair of white shorts on and the same tank as before. She's slathering on sunscreen. She catches me watching her. "The curse of the redhead."

"I remember," I say, thinking back to college. "The river."

She knows exactly to what weekend I'm referring. "That horrible sunburn I got. Oh my God, I was delirious."

"We went to the only convenience store that was open, and they were out of aloe."

"My skin was on fire. I was seeing things. How did I get so burned?"

"Alcohol."

She frowns at me. "I didn't drink for like two months after that."

"I remember that too," I say. I took her back to the hotel that day, helped her strip off all her clothes, and put cool washcloths on her forehead as she moaned in pain. After about an hour, she finally fell asleep, and I sat on the other side of the bed and watched her sleep, her breath making a low whistle sound. I had recently turned twenty-one, and taking care of Mia had created a swirl of conflicted feelings in my gut. I knew that I loved her at that point and of course wanted to be there for her, but I also felt my first prick of fear—that this was a segue to the next level of our relationship. And as much as I cared for her, there was a part of me that wasn't sure I was ready.

"Ready?" she asks after rubbing the last of the lotion into her cheeks and forehead, having no idea how ironic her question is.

"You have a little right here." I am wiping it off before I realize what I'm doing. "Sorry," I say reflexively.

"It's okay. Old habits, right?"

"I'm sorry for all of it, Mia," I say again, needing it to hit home. For her to understand.

"It's okay. We already settled this. You were a stupid kid."

I think back to my younger self in the hotel room, what an idiot he was. How that guy couldn't wait until Mia fell asleep so he could go meet his buddies for more beer.

"But since you've brought it up again, it was more than being young and stupid, right?" She arches an eyebrow. "I mean, what goes through your mind when you decide to reverse a decision like that? To take something like that back?"

The question slams me in the gut. "Mia, I don't know. I freaked out. The idea of setting a date and finding a venue and all that stuff, it kept me up all night. But I need you to know it wasn't because of you. It was never because of you. It was always me. My weakness."

"You say that. And you make a strong case. But you can understand why it's still hard to believe." Her eyes glisten, and I can almost reach out and touch the scar tissue from what I did to her.

"It's the truth," I say, stepping closer to her, wanting to close the physical—and emotional—distance between us.

"Why tell me this now? You've had years to say these things. To try again. It's not like you couldn't find me."

I contemplate her question, trying to settle on the words to explain what was going on inside me, which is hard when I don't completely understand. "I wish it were an easy answer. Because you're right. Why not pick up the phone? Or hell, send a chickenshit Facebook message? I didn't do those things because you'd become an enigma. And I'd convinced myself I didn't deserve you after what I did. That there was no way you'd ever consider us again." I pause and look at her, hoping I'm getting through. Her eyes are trained on mine. At least I have her attention. "But then you showed up at the coffee shop. You thought it might be fate that we were both there. Remember?" At the time, I dismissed her theory, reasoning it was simply luck. But now, I understand otherwise—something has brought us together.

"I do," she admits, her face inches from mine, her lips slightly parted and her chin tilted as if she's absorbing every detail of my words. "But you've never believed in things like that."

"Things change. People change. I took you for granted. I realize that now. I'm sorry it took so long for me to tell you, but it's true."

"We were probably too young anyway," she says, her eyes conveying far more than her words. "We wouldn't have made it."

Does she feel that way, or is she justifying what happened?

"We were young, yes. But your parents were—"

"Twenty-one," she says.

"And mine were—"

"Twenty," she confirms.

It was one of many things we discovered we had in common when we first met—both sets of our parents had married young and had managed to keep their unions intact. But it's so much more complicated than that. Because being together and being *happy together* are two totally different things. For instance, Mia's parents' relationship seemed bleak to me, and it caused me to wonder if her dad, the ice fisherman with a ten-word vocabulary, and her mom, the female equivalent of the Tin Man, had once been like us—deliriously in love. I worried it might be impossible to escape the wear of time, no matter how amazing the starting point. And my parents aren't any more of an example of making it work. They once separated for a year, my first year of college. Neither of them moved out, but they lived separate lives. They eventually decided to get back together and seem happyish now, at least for a couple that has spent more than thirty years together.

We both drink our coffee without talking. Finally, Mia speaks. "Life is so much shorter than we realize. I mean, think about it—ten years passed by in a flash." She snaps her fingers to make her point.

I wish I could tell her that I understand perfectly. That we may have only hours together.

The realization launches me out of my seat. I take her mug out of her hand and set it on the counter. I tip her chin up toward me. And I kiss her, feeling completely like myself for the first time in days when I feel her lips accept mine, when she presses the angles of her body into mine. I smell those sunflowers, glide my fingers through her ponytail, a fireworks show of emotions exploding in my chest. She puts her hands under my shirt and runs them over my abdomen. After so many years, I still remember how it feels to kiss her. No one else has ever felt like this. And I've spent a ton of effort searching for the feeling. To my surprise, it's better than I remember.

As I begin to relax into her, she pulls back. My stomach drops. I could have sat here all day, kissing her. Is the connection lopsided? Am I imagining the shared connection because of all the other things going on?

"Let's take that walk," is all she says.

I'm breathing hard, and my heart falls to my feet. I want to ask her why she stopped. But I don't. I don't want to push too hard. Scare her off. Not after we've finally kissed. Instead I straighten my shirt and murmur, "Of course." I grab my backpack and follow her to the front door.

"Let's go down to the beach," she says, twirling as she moves down the sidewalk. I look for any sign of regret about our kiss, and I see none. Maybe she simply didn't want things to go any further? Or maybe she wants to take things slow. Build back to what we were. Or hell, build something new. We have ten years to catch up on. Hope rises in my chest. It's possible we've been stuck in this loop so we can move forward the right way. If so, our conversation, our kiss, could be the antidote to the curse.

I trail behind her at first. I love the way she moves. I always have. She was a dancer well into her teens, and she still has that gracefulness about her. She's up ahead on the sidewalk and turns around to make sure I'm behind her. "Coming?"

I nod and quicken my step, although staying behind her makes me feel like I'm in control. I can see what's coming.

She starts to step into the street.

"Mia!" I yell. I know I sound panicked.

She turns and puts her hand on her heart. "What?"

"I was going to tell you to look both ways," I say, forcing a smile.

"You scared me. I thought a car was coming or something."

I see her visibly exhale. And I do too. She's safe. "Nope, only being cautious."

"Whatever, Dad!" she says.

"Now I get a comparison to 'I speak ten words a day' George?"

"You're treating me like a child, so yeah," she laughs, but she waits for me to cross the street.

I survey the road and don't see any cars coming. Hailey lives on what seems to be a quiet side street. The beach will be nice. We can sit safely on the sand and talk. Maybe kiss again. My shoelace is untied. "Wait for me," I say.

"You're being weird, but fine," she says.

I bend over to tie it. As I'm pulling the lace through the loop, I hear the sound of screeching brakes.

My heart stops. *No. Please.*

A large SUV is hurtling toward Mia on the sidewalk, the oversize tires making skid marks on the pavement as it flies into her small body, sending her soaring into the air. I scream her name and nearly gag— physically ill at the thought that I'll lose her again. She lands several feet away. I run, but my legs feel like cement blocks. The driver is already out of his car, kneeling next to her. "Oh God. I only looked down for a second to check my phone. I didn't see her."

"Call 911!" I order as I expertly feel her pulse and begin chest compressions. I work hard to conjure the instructions from the YouTube video I watched. Panic strangles me, but I force myself to compartmentalize. *I must save Mia. I must save Mia.* I say this again and again as my hands pump her chest in vain. If you don't know me, if you don't understand the information I have, I probably look like a man who believes he can save a life. This life.

But the truth is that I've lost all hope that I can bring her back.

CHAPTER SEVENTEEN

Another Thursday has joylessly arrived. Today, I observe Hailey slam the front door of her bungalow and stride toward her ancient Land Cruiser parked in the driveway.

She stops and stares out at the patch of sidewalk where Mia was struck and killed yesterday, and a chill runs through me. Does she carry a memory of what happened to Mia—even if in her world, which is Thursday, June 11, it didn't happen? Even though Mia is still inside her house, alive and well? I know this because I texted her this morning. To check in. To be sure. But Mia told me she was leaving at eleven. That she had lunch plans. As I watch Hailey get into her truck and drive away, I flash to the memory of seeing her at the hospital yesterday after Mia was fatally hit right where I'm parked now. Hailey surged toward me in the hallway outside of Mia's room in the trauma unit and pounded her fists against my chest, screaming that it was all my fault. That Mia wouldn't have been crossing the street at the exact moment the SUV had sped down the block if *I* hadn't insisted on coming by. That Mia should have listened to her—made me wait. Or better yet, not seen me at all. I stood there and let her hit me over and over, the nurse busying herself on the computer next to us, pretending she didn't notice.

Tears streamed down Hailey's freckled cheeks, and she looked so much like Mia in that moment that I had to turn away. And although intellectually I knew Mia would most likely wake up to another Thursday tomorrow, the ache in my heart was palpable. I pulled Hailey close to me and said I was sorry. That she was right: I was to blame. And I wasn't merely placating her. Hailey yanked herself out of my grasp and pointed at me. "You broke her heart ten years ago, and then you came back into her life, and now she's dead. Why did you have to come back?" She paused, looking at me. I stumbled, the truth in her accusations sending me off balance. My reconnection with Mia had killed her. "Did you find out she was in Oceanside, stake out the coffee shop you knew she'd be in?"

"How would I have known she was back?"

Hailey looked like she was going to say something but must have thought better of it. "Forget it. It's not like yelling at you is going to bring her back."

But she will be back, I wanted to say. *Tomorrow.*

She stormed away, and I stood in the doorway to Mia's room, her lifeless body lying there, waiting to be taken away. I walked over and held her hand. "I'm so sorry, Mi. I'm going to figure out why this is happening, and I'm going to fix this." I leaned down and kissed her on the top of her head and could smell the remnants of sunflowers.

∼

The clock hits 11:15 a.m. as a very alive Mia finally emerges from Hailey's house and climbs into the white Chevrolet Malibu she told me she rented. I asked her why she hadn't brought her own car out, but she was evasive. And I didn't want to push. I don't know how many Thursdays we have together, but I plan to use each one to get closer to her. To get her to trust me again. To make up for hurting her. It's possible that's the entire point—that to escape the loop, I will need to make amends for what I did.

Lance texts me: **I handled all the phone calls.**

Thanks! I type. And exhale, because I was able to convince him again this morning and get him to agree to help me. He told me that something felt familiar. He didn't remember the conversation, but he recalled us positioned in the kitchen as we were. I told him it was likely he felt something because we'd done it for five Thursday mornings now. That maybe somehow he was subconsciously aware.

That made me hopeful.

I told him to go into the office this morning and attend the editorial meeting. He did and updated me that Alexis had praised him to the group when he'd pitched the shark-attack story, impressed that he'd known about it before it had hit the wires. Devon had sulked in the corner because he hadn't brought any ideas with him.

Today I decided not to tell Lance about Mia's dying on my repeated Thursdays. He'd freaked out when I'd called him from the hospital yesterday to tell him Mia was dead. He'd blamed himself. Argued that he should have come with me. Yelled at me for not warning her. Started crying in a way that surprised me. He'd known Mia in college, but they had drifted apart when we'd broken up. I decided I couldn't put him through that again today. So I told him I had some important things to take care of and that I'd see him later.

I've decided to follow Mia today without engaging her, hoping it will yield answers. That I will be able to gain some insight into her life, into the parts she's not telling me. That it may possibly help me save her. I know it's stalkerish, but I tell myself it's for Mia's own good. If I learn anything, I'll involve Lance, and we'll come up with a plan.

I follow a few car lengths behind Mia's sedan and am surprised when she turns right onto South Coast Highway and merges onto the southbound 5 freeway. She accelerates into the fast lane and is going well above the speed limit. I cringe, wanting her to slow down. What if she gets into an accident and dies with me helpless four cars behind? I have to floor it to eighty miles an hour to keep up with her, and I stay in the neighboring lane, hoping she won't notice me. And also praying she will slow down. Why does she have to be such a daredevil? I still struggle with that part of her that obviously hasn't changed. And there doesn't seem to be a part of her that wants to change it. It's who she is. I accept that now. We start to slow once we pass through Carlsbad, and I struggle to stay with her. I almost lose her behind a semitruck but am able to catch her again.

We stay on the 5 south for a long time, and as I start thinking she might be headed to the Mexican border, she puts on her blinker and takes the Front Street/Civic Center exit. Why is she headed to the Gaslamp Quarter? My heart surges. Could it be that she pretended she had a lunch but is coming to see me? I told her I was working from home today.

She heads down Front Street and turns on Market, blowing through a yellow light. The light turns red, and I slam on my brakes and pound my fists against the steering wheel. "Dammit, Mia!" I'm stuck at the red and keep my eye on her as she continues forward. Why is she driving so fast? My condo isn't far from here—is she in a hurry to see me? I keep my eye trained on her car and watch as she turns on Fifth. My light changes, and I speed up to catch her. She whips into a space a block later. I slow my car and park at the corner of Market and Fifth as a gaggle of people with San Diego Convention Center lanyards around their necks cross the street. Mia crosses at the same time (on the cross-walk, thankfully) and heads into Rustic Root. What the hell?

She's been to the restaurant before? She gave no indication when we went out two Thursdays ago. Why didn't she tell me? Was she trying to spare my feelings because I'd made a big deal about taking her there? Mia tucks her hair behind her ears as she speaks to the hostess at the stand on the sidewalk. I hover behind a streetlamp and watch as she walks toward the middle of the restaurant on the lower level. Is that why she wanted to sit upstairs with me? To not give away that she'd been to the restaurant on the main floor? She's seated at a table for two facing the sidewalk. Who is she meeting? She scans a menu and checks her phone several times. Whoever it is, is clearly late. Then she smiles, and I follow her gaze to see who she's grinning at.

My heart does a nosedive when I see Lance striding into the restaurant.

As they hug and Lance takes the seat across from her, I feel like I've been punched. He never once mentioned to me he was still in touch with her, let alone currently making lunch plans with her. After I ran into her at the coffee shop and called him to tell him, he was stilted, blaming it on some snafu at work. I thought he was masking his concern about my getting involved with her again. Is that because he already is? And then there was his concern that I wanted to talk to him about Mia when I said I had something important to discuss. So this was why. He thought I'd found out they'd been in touch and were planning lunch. To think when I convinced him about the loop this morning, I spared him the critical detail about Mia's fate to protect him. And here he is, lying to me. My best friend and the woman I'm in love with are having lunch. And neither of them has so much as hinted they still know each other. My chest burns with jealousy, with the embarrassment of being so incredibly clueless. I am obsessed with saving Mia. Intent on Lance understanding and helping make that happen. And they both clearly have no respect for me. The thought consumes me, replaying like a broken record as I stand there, staring.

As if Mia and Lance can hear my thoughts, they glance in my direction. I move behind the thick concrete of the light post, my heart racing. I poke my head out again a few moments later. Lance is leaning in as Mia speaks. She's playing with her hair, something she used to do when she was nervous. Or flirting. She used to do it when she was talking *to me*. Lance says something, and she laughs—that deep laugh that *I* crave. That laugh is mine, not his. I ball my hands into fists at my sides, wanting to punch something hard. Their interaction is intimate. This is not the first time they've seen each other in a decade.

I'm not sure whether to storm into the restaurant and sucker punch Lance or walk away and give up on everything. I've never felt so defeated in my life. When I thought my best friend was going to help me out of this, he stabs me in the back. What else am I in the dark about? Mia died several times over, and Lance did not mention *one time* that he'd seen her earlier in the day. Not when she fell out of the Zipper. Not when she fell off our balcony. Not even on the fourth Thursday, when I first convinced him about the loop and told him she'd been dying. That was the time—that was the damn time! What is so important between them that they need to hide it from me?

Lance reaches over and grabs Mia's hand. Mia bows her head at something he says. It feels like a knife to my gut, and I bend over to recover.

This is out of character for Lance. Yes, he is popular with the ladies. All types, all nationalities, all shapes and sizes. They sidle up to him at the Tipsy Crow. Send over drinks at Altitude, saying they love watching him on the news. Maybe they've seen the billboard off the 163 freeway—the one with Lance and his coanchors, Melinda, Terry, and Claudia. I gave him shit for weeks for that one. You could practically see up his nostrils.

We are like brothers, both of us only children. When his mom died of breast cancer four years ago, he was such a wreck he couldn't get out of bed for a week. Who took care of him? I did! And when our ratings were the lowest they've ever been, Alexis was threatening my job, and I'd lost out on another huge story to Erik at Channel Nine, and I decided to quit the business, be done. Who talked me off the ledge? Reminded me why I love what I do? He did. Anger spikes inside my chest. I can almost understand Mia's side of it—she hasn't had a relationship with me in ten years, so maybe she doesn't feel bad. But Lance. He is breaking man code, best friend code, every damn code right now.

But Lance has always respected the bro code. In fact, he is the consummate wingman. He is loyal. So this thing with Mia doesn't make sense to me. I breathe out hard, refusing to accept the scenario. There has to be an explanation. But as I watch them holding hands, it becomes harder to give him the benefit of the doubt. The way he's looking at her makes me want to punch him. I could walk across the street right now and confront them—find out what the hell they are doing. Are they meeting to discuss how to break the news that she came back to be with Lance? Because they are meant to be together? Or are they simply having a lovers' lunch, oblivious to my feelings? Or have they decided they aren't going to tell me at all? Keep up this charade and hope I never figure it out? We were at this exact restaurant, and she could have mentioned, *Not only have I been here before, but I was here today with your best friend, Lance*! A burn rises in my chest as I realize she may have pretended to be surprised by the mini margaritas, the pork belly. Was it all a charade—our conversation about us, the holding hands?

And then at Hailey's house yesterday, Mia imitated Lance's reporting as if she'd watched him hundreds of times. When I asked her about it, she changed the subject. And when we were at the condo, what better place to tell me? In his *house*. I continue to watch them, the earlier seed of anger growing with each minute—their cozy interactions the fuel. They're eating something, and Lance takes a bite off her fork. We haven't shared a fork! I feel bile rising in the back of my throat and look around for a trash can. I grab onto the light post and breathe slowly through my nose to settle the nausea. I can't confront them now. I need to wait. Give Lance—or Mia—the opportunity to tell me the truth first. Ask one—or both—of them about it and see if they lie.

If they do, I'll storm into that restaurant on tomorrow's Thursday and go all Real Housewives on their asses. Maybe I'll flip a table. What will I have to lose?

A man with a mullet hanging out of the back of his weathered trucker hat pulls up behind me in a pedicab. He has music blaring out of a speaker taped to his handlebars. "Want a ride?" he calls out, and I cringe as Lance and Mia look over. I duck behind his bike. "What are you doing?" he asks, and I put my pointer finger over my lips as my ears pound.

I peek around the wheelbase and see they are still looking over. Lance is probably telling a story about one of the many times we climbed into one of these late on a Saturday night. We have some great pedicab stories. I cringe as I imagine them discussing me. Like I'm a fool.

I wave the driver to turn his bike toward the street and jump into the back, the canvas cover shielding the view from the restaurant. "Head that way!" I point away from Rustic Root and don't pick my head up until we turn back onto Market Street.

"I'm Bobby," he yells over the street noise.

"Bobby, head down to the marina," I say, staring at his mullet blowing in the breeze. Bobby creates more distance between us and the restaurant—and Mia and Lance—and my eyes fill with tears. If they are in love, then why is my relationship with Mia the obvious catalyst of this loop? To save her so she can live happily ever after with my best friend? My heart throbs at the thought of losing her again—right when I thought I was getting her back. Yesterday we kissed for the first time. And I thought that meant something. But when she pulled away and suggested the walk, she must have been thinking of Lance. The betrayal feels like a weight sitting on my chest, crushing my heart. Tearing down every single notion I've ever had about the people I care about.

Unfortunately, the only thing I've learned from following Mia today is that I now have many more questions than answers.

CHAPTER EIGHTEEN

"Buzz it," I say to George, the guy who regularly cuts my hair at Monarch Barber Shop on Tenth. He's holding the clippers and cocking his head at me in the gold-framed mirror. "What?" I ask. My perspective has vastly changed in the last twenty minutes. Now I want my appearance to match.

"You sure, man?" George sets the clippers down on the wood shelf and rolls up his sleeves, and I catch sight of the dragon tattoo on his arm. He once told me it had taken an entire day for the tattoo artist to create the image that George drew from scratch.

Maybe I should get a tattoo. What would I want? I think for a moment and catch George's eyes in the mirror. I avert my gaze to the black-and-white photos hanging on the striped wall. I'll get an infinity loop. To represent my life.

"I'm sure," I say and smile for the first time all day. Maybe I've been going about this all wrong. I can do whatever I want—anything—and I'll still get a fresh start in the morning. I have seen it as a curse, and maybe it is. But what if there is another reason? Maybe it's the universe's way of telling me to let go. To not be so afraid. To be more like Mia. Stop pushing against her wild side. Clearly she likes it in Lance.

"But you always get the one inch. Not the two and never the three. The one. Like, you never waver." George raises an eyebrow. "What's changed?"

"So much," I say, then point to my head. "I'm ready."

George shrugs. "If you don't like it, I guess it will grow back," he says and starts slicing the clippers through my hair.

"Tomorrow," I say.

"Well, probably not that fast. A few weeks, maybe," George says as chunks of my hair fall to the floor.

"No. It will grow back tomorrow, which will actually be today. Because there is no tomorrow for me. Just today."

"That's deep, man."

I leave it at that. There's no sense in explaining it. The one person I told because I thought he could help is currently betraying me. I'm back to navigating this time loop alone. George finishes up, and I take in my new hair—or lack of it. I run my hand over my smooth scalp. It feels so soft. And I look kind of cool.

"Hot-towel shave today?"

I check my watch. "No, there's something I need to do. Can I get the name of the guy who did your dragon?" I point to his arm.

George studies me before answering. "Some chick really did a number on you, huh, man?"

"Yep," I say truthfully. Because Mia is at the epicenter of this earthquake that has crumbled the foundation of my life. Am I stupid to think she came back here for me? Was it only dumb luck that I ran into her that morning in the coffee shop? I'm not so sure. The universe clearly has a plan for me. For her. The question is, What are those plans? What is the lesson I need to learn in order to make it to Friday? Is it that Mia is in love with Lance and I need to accept that? Is this some insane metaphor to show me that I need to move on with my life?

Or is this a punishment? A penance? I'm not perfect; that's for sure. Sometimes the things I've had to do for my job—exploiting others to make headlines—don't sit well. I think about the fifteen-year-old girl Alexis demanded we interview because she was the lone survivor in a car crash on the 8 freeway that killed her entire family. That one haunted me for a while. We blurred her face, but it still felt wrong. The field producer, a new mother, almost quit over it. But I talked her into staying. Promised there wouldn't be more like it. But of course there were.

George makes a call, and his guy says he'll get me in if I can arrive within a half hour. And then I need to meet Mia.

Mia.

She lied to me—well, omitted information when talking to me—about Lance. And Lance has done the same. Beyond that, I don't know jack shit. I need to start by finding out what else she and Lance are hiding.

I could cancel on her, but I want to see her. And I'm hoping she'll explain the lunch. Maybe she will if I hint around it. Ask the right questions. Flash my edgy tattoo. Where can we go that she won't die a tragic death? I'd prefer something peaceful this time. I know I sound callous, but I've lost faith that I can save her tonight. I won't be able to change her fate until I figure out *why* she's dying. I'm an investigative journalist and producer—if anyone can solve this mystery, it's me. I've been nominated for a Daytime Emmy! I think about the information I've gleaned so far.

Maybe if I can get her to trust me again.

But how?

After giving it some thought, I text Mia and suggest we go to Dog Days of Summer at Petco Park. After seeing her response to the puppies as she watched them from my balcony two Thursdays ago, I decide it's a good plan. Maybe she'll find an elderly dog to adopt. To my relief, she responds with a yes and several dog emojis. We agree to meet there at six thirty. If she asks to head up to my place afterward, I'll have to deflect. I can't take her there again, have her ask to go out on the balcony. Relive that horrible memory.

~

Getting the tattoo hurt like a mother, but I didn't cry, so I consider it a win.

I arrive at the gates of Petco exactly on time.

"What's with the bandage? Oh my God, you shaved your head!" I hear Mia before I see her. "Wow, Dom!"

She hugs me, and I inhale the sunflowers as if for the first time. Or the last. Depending on how you look at it. I take her in, trying to glean what's going on. In her mind, nothing has changed. But my world has been upended.

"Guilty," I say. "And it's a tattoo." I pull back the bandage on my arm and show her the infinity symbol now etched there—two never-ending loops. It felt right.

She steps back and surveys me. "Interesting choice."

"What?" I shrug.

"It's . . . well, never mind," she says as a woman with a Maltese wearing a tuxedo walks by.

"Tell me."

"The old Dom, the one I knew ten years ago, he would never have gotten a tattoo or—"

"Shaved his head."

"Exactly."

"Well, consider me a new and improved Dom," I assert, pleased she likes the change.

"Is that a promise?"

"It is."

"I like this Dom, one who's willing to take a couple risks," she says, looping her arm through mine.

I like him too.

I put my hand on top of her arm and wonder how she can act like she's not hiding anything from me. Like she didn't secretly have lunch with my best friend today. The thought makes my stomach twist into a hard knot, but I try to ignore it. Especially because I'm not revealing that I followed her today, that I know.

I buy us two tickets, and we walk into the park, surrounded by dogs of all shapes and sizes. Mia must stop to pet each and every one. I am enjoying watching her so much that I almost forget about Lance. Almost. The pain from the lies I've uncovered tries to break the surface again, but I shove it down. "So how was your day?" I ask as we walk up to a concession stand, praying she tells me about her lunch. Explains it so it all makes sense.

"Fine," she says, not meeting my eyes. "Oh, Red Vines! We have to get some!"

I bite my tongue, wanting to scream, *Only fine? I saw you holding hands with my best friend!* But I still have hope she'll tell me. Maybe she's waiting until we're alone.

I order us two beers and a package of licorice, and we walk over to the grassy hill to sit down.

I hold my beer up to hers, and we toast and sip.

"What did you do today?" I ask once we are situated. Then, deciding I need to be specific, I add, "You had lunch plans, right? With whom?" I search her face.

"An old friend. No one you know," she says, and if I didn't know better, I'd believe her. But I *do* know better. How in the hell can she sit here and lie right to my face? My blood boils, and I force myself to take another drink of my beer so I don't say the words. I don't want a confrontation. I want an explanation. And I sure as hell won't get one if I attack her. But still, how *and why* did that lie slip so easily off her tongue?

She sips her beer. "What about you? Worked from home?"

I shake my head. "But I rode a pedicab. And did this." I point to my head and my arm.

"Why did you choose an infinity loop?"

I didn't think about what I'd tell her when she asked. Obviously it can't be the truth. Or can it? What if I tell her right now what I've been going through? There's a chance she might believe me. Then we can work together to save her life. But why burden her with it now when I don't have enough information? I don't know how to stop it. And I'm not sure I trust her.

"It's a strong symbol," I finally say. "It speaks to me."

"Why? Why does it speak to you?" she probes.

I shrug, not wanting to explain. "If you think about it, all of life is a loop, isn't it?"

She gives me a curious look. "I suppose."

Mia heads to the restroom, and I offer to walk her there. But she laughs and points to it. It's about fifteen feet from where we're sitting. I watch her until she disappears through the entrance, still struck by the lie she so easily told me. I scroll through my emails and stop when I see the one I realize I was searching for. On the past four Thursdays I've failed to reply to Amanda's thank-you email. I decide that tonight I will. Mia's not the only one who can have a secret.

I count her thank-yous. There are twenty. I match it with as many you're-welcomes. Then I send her a link to a dating-app-addiction support group. I can't believe I found one. I think it's probably a sex-addict group in disguise, but I want the laugh factor and know I'll get it. Something about making Amanda laugh makes me feel a little better. I hit send, Mia walks up, and I put my phone away. "How did it go?" I ask.

"Oh, you know, toilet, sink, hand dryer—a regular party in there." Mia laughs and picks up her beer.

I don't laugh. I can't. Seeing Mia's face again brings the lie right back and my anger along with it. It hurts that she went so far as to say that I didn't know the old friend she had lunch with. Not only do I know him, I live with him. He's my best friend. I glance at my watch. I probably have little time left to get the truth from Mia.

"So after you and I stopped talking, who did you keep in touch with?"

"Of our friends from college?"

I nod.

Mia takes a minute before responding. Is she deciding how many lies she's willing to tell? How to spin her continuous correspondence with Lance? "Nobody, really. A couple of people." She pets a Chihuahua that walks in front of us on the grass.

"Like who?" I press, draining my beer.

"No one special," she says, looking out toward the baseball field. I follow her gaze up to the empty seats in the ballpark.

So Lance isn't special? I want to say, but I force the words back inside. Unless she didn't keep in contact with Lance and they only resumed their friendship today? It doesn't seem likely based on what I witnessed. Plus, if that were the case, wouldn't she tell me she saw him?

"Tell me more about your time in the Midwest," I probe, hoping this will open the door to her telling me why she's back. "I feel like I missed out on so much."

"You did," she says evenly, and a pang of jealousy hits me.

"Were you happy?" I ask.

"Not at first." She pauses for a few moments as a couple walking four white poodles passes. "I was a mess for a long time."

I cringe at the thought of this. That I screwed her up. "I tried to get you to come back," I say, thinking of her confession yesterday that she had thought about giving me a second chance. That she'd come to my hotel, not quite ready to let go.

"I know, but it wasn't that simple." She pulls a Red Vine from the package but doesn't move it toward her mouth. "I lived with my parents at first. Which was *not* fun. And very humbling. But many of my friends from high school were back, and we reconnected. Eventually I got a great job teaching kindergarten. I found my own place, and eventually I was happy again."

"You wouldn't return my calls," I say, the reality of that harder to deal with now that I know she was open to giving it another shot.

"I couldn't," she says, fidgeting with the end of her necklace.

"Why not?"

"For so many reasons, Dom. I had made a choice to go it without you, and I had to stick with that. I didn't want my feelings to get muddled by hearing your voice. You know?"

I shrug. Because I don't know. Maybe that's exactly what we needed—to talk.

"I'm sorry, Mi."

I take a Red Vine from the package and chew, debating what to say next. I visualize Mia and Lance holding hands at the restaurant again, and my heart throbs, the pain of witnessing them radiating through me. If they are planning to be together, then I have to tell her what's in my heart. Because maybe if she hears it, she'll want to give *me* another chance. But before I can, she speaks again. "For what it's worth, I forgave you a long time ago."

"You did?"

"I had to. Being mad at you took too much energy. And you did what you thought you needed to do, so I finally had to accept that."

"That's true. It's what I thought I needed to do. But I was wrong. It was the exact opposite of what I needed to do. I shouldn't have ended things."

"But you did," she says, not harshly.

"I did."

"And here we are," she says, a light smile playing on her lips.

"But Mia, it wasn't about you."

"Of course it was." Mia frowns.

"No, what I mean is you didn't do anything wrong." My voice comes out shrill, and I clear my throat, not wanting to sound as desperate as I feel.

"It's in the past, Dom," she says too quickly.

"But Mia, I still think about it. About you. Us. What could have been."

"Let's leave it in the past." She finishes her beer and leans back on her hands. "Focus on the now," she says dismissively.

Her words sink my resolve. What has changed today? On the other Thursdays, Mia has had this conversation with me. Hasn't shut it down. A thought occurs to me suddenly and smacks me in the face. What if Lance told her about my time loop today? And that's why they met? Because he was worried about my sanity? She obviously never made it to lunch yesterday. But today she did. And what if when he told her, she not only talked him out of believing me but now thinks I need to be in an asylum? And only showed up because she feels sorry for me? I want to convince her I'm not insane, I'm still me, but how?

"Okay, let's talk about the *now*," I blurt.

"All right . . . ," she says tentatively, not sure where I'm going with this.

"Let's talk about *today*."

"Okay . . ."

"Is there anything you'd like to say to me about today?"

"There is," she says, surprising me. She squints at me. "Is something going on with you? I've never known you to do something so drastic like a tattoo—knowing it's irreversible. Why—and why now?"

"Why do you ask?" I question. This is the moment when she can tell me she knows what I told Lance. And ask me about it.

"It's out of character for you. You know people sometimes do drastic things when their lives are in chaos." She looks away.

"What makes you think my life is in chaos, Mia?" I hold my voice steady, but her assessment gives me pause.

"I'm talking in generalities."

My face pinches, and I smooth it out. *Tell me, Mia. Tell me the truth.* "We just finished discussing how much time has passed since we've seen or talked to each other. For all you know, I do drastic things all the time."

She looks away and tucks a strand of hair behind her ear. "You're right. I shouldn't be making presumptions," she says softly, as if she's placating me.

Is that what they are? Or did my best friend tell you I've always been like that? Did he share intimate details about me when he was sharing your fork? Like how I'm trapped in Thursday, June eleventh? And now you're trying to decide how loony I am?

"Why are you back, Mia? Really?" I push. I'm tired of tiptoeing around this topic. Especially now that my best friend is involved. *Tell me the truth!*

"Dom," she begins, a sad smile forming on her face. I brace myself for the impact of her answer. And that it will involve Lance. She becomes distracted by a passing dog. "Oh my God, look at that Siberian husky! He has gray hair around his face. I want to adopt one of my own one day." Mia is on her feet and petting the white-and-gray dog within seconds.

I sigh, exhausted by all of her deflecting. "I know. You want an elderly dog because they get overlooked at the pound."

"How did you know that?" Mia's eyes bore into mine.

"Lucky guess?" I cover.

"A lucky guess, that's all?" She puts her hands on her hips. Is she waiting for me to tell her what's really going on?

I'll show you mine when you show me yours. Her refusal to level with me worries me. I've opened the door too many times for her not to walk through it. Unless she's too scared to tell me the truth because she thinks I'm crazy.

She turns her attention to the husky again, who is staring at me, his piercing blue eyes boring into mine. Mia is asking his owner how old he is. "Almost ten," the woman says.

I watch Mia. Like us. Almost ten years since we last saw each other.

"Do you think I did this because I'm crazy?" I ask her, trying to keep my voice calm. But I don't feel calm at all. The woman and the husky take that as their cue to leave.

"What? No. Not at all."

"So your *old friend* didn't tell you what's going on with me?"

"Dom . . ."

"No, listen. Here's the thing. I know you saw Lance. And he told you about the time loop, right?"

"Time loop?" she says, her nose wrinkling, confused. "No, he didn't," she says, and by the look on her face, I can tell she's telling the truth.

"Then what? What were you talking about with him?"

Mia's eyes get glassy. She turns away from me.

"Why did you lie to me?" I press, the urge to know taking over.

She doesn't answer, starts picking at the grass in front of her.

"I still regret calling things off. So if you have plans to be with him, I want you to have all the information *about me* first," I say, wanting her to correct me. That no, she doesn't have plans with him. But she glosses over that part of my statement.

"If you had so many regrets, then why didn't you try harder to reach me? Call me more times? Email? You could have sent a letter, for God's sake." Mia's eyes blaze.

"I should have, okay? But I was a chickenshit," I mutter. "And anyway, you said you didn't want things to get muddled, so it sounds like you wouldn't have talked to me anyway."

"That's not the point," she says, and I see it on her face. The pain of what I did to her. How she blamed herself.

"But I did jump on a plane. I tried my Hail Mary with you, and it didn't work."

"So it's my fault?" she snaps.

"No. That's not what I meant," I say, suddenly worried that confronting her about Lance has now shifted our reconnection. Now we're arguing, something we've never done before. Saying things that haven't been said. Facing the underlying resentments we feel toward the other.

"What do you want? A medal for flying out there that day?" Her accusation startles me.

"No, of course not," I say, my look imploring her to believe me. "But I tried to make it right. To make us right."

"It was too late," she says, shaking her head.

"Was it?" I say. "You didn't have *any* second thoughts? Not one?" I know my tone is snarky, but she's lying to me—again. Why?

"No," she says, her face stoic. There's no chance she's going to come clean.

We sit there for a few minutes without speaking, both of us processing what's been said.

"I'm not lying to you. And it isn't what you think with Lance," she finally says, her face strained. "Please give me more time to explain things. It's only been a few days since we ran into each other. And an hour tonight."

I don't have time, and neither do you! I want to say, but she won't understand that because she's right. For her, we've been in touch for only a short amount of time. I need to remember that. Not force an explanation, as much as I desire one. Because what if I do that and she refuses to tell me anything?

"Okay," I finally say, albeit reluctantly.

"Thank you," she says, a look of relief washing over her face. "And here's the thing, Dom. About us. We can rehash it and analyze what could have been. But I think maybe both of us eventually decided it was for the best. Right?" she says, her tone soft. "Or else we'd have gotten back together."

"Maybe. I don't know." I think for a moment, because I hadn't considered that before. "If you're asking me if I gave up, the answer is yes. But if you're asking me if I decided that my decision to break things off was a good one because you didn't take me back and if I got over you, then the answer is no." I pause, thinking about my dating life after Mia. How most encounters felt off, like a seam that didn't quite match up. How that eventually made me gun shy. And lonely, if I'm being totally honest. "Also," I start, "you were pretty clear how you felt. I wanted to respect that after I'd already hurt you so much. Because, believe me, I thought about it. A lot." The confession releases something deep inside, the sharp edge of my regret rounding out slightly.

"I get that," she says, and I think I detect sadness in her eyes.

She's on her feet before I can say another word, taking off to pet one of those huge dogs that looks like a horse. I watch her talk to its owner, smoothing her hand over the dog's fur, the dog leaning its head into her body. She turns and walks back toward me but stops suddenly.

"Ow." She swipes at her arm.

"What is it?" I ask, jumping up.

Mia grabs her arm, and she looks like she's having trouble breathing. "Mia?"

She falls to the ground, her eyes bulging. Her face reddening by the second.

"Oh my God," I cry. "Somebody help! Please!"

"Is she okay?" a woman with a chocolate Lab stops to ask me.

"I don't know. I don't know." I kneel down next to Mia and grab her hand. "I think she was stung. Are you allergic to bees?" I ask Mia.

Mia shakes her head, tries to speak, and can't. Her face is swelling. She grabs at her throat.

"She can't breathe!" I scream, my heart racing. "We need help!"

"She's going into anaphylactic shock," the woman says, her voice frantic. "Does anyone have an EpiPen?" she calls out and palms her phone. "I'm calling 911."

I start running toward a group of people, asking if they have one. People shake their heads. Someone suggests going to the medical center. "I don't know where that is!" I cry. I run back toward Mia and unzip my backpack, but I already know I don't have what she needs in my first aid kit. In my research, I didn't think to consider allergic reactions. "Dammit!" I scream, falling to the ground next to her again. I start to cry and hold Mia in my arms until I hear her last breath.

CHAPTER NINETEEN

JUNE 11, 7:00 A.M.
THURSDAY #6

Thursday finds me once more. I keep my eyes squeezed shut as "How to Save a Life" plays loudly, blocking out not only the musical notes but any memory of the night before. All that matters is that I was unable to save Mia. Again.

But today I have a plan. I'm determined to get answers. From Lance. From Mia. And if I'm lucky, from the universe. Today I'm going to use this loop to my advantage.

I turn off the Fray, get dressed, and find Lance in the kitchen.

"Hey, man," I say.

"Hey! You look a lot better than I thought you would after all those shots last night." He pours some coffee in a mug. "Want some? I can spike it with—"

"Jack Daniel's, I know."

Lance looks at me funny.

"I need you to come with me. I need to show you something. It's important. So spare me the sex jokes, and any jokes, please."

"Right now?"

"Yes, right now," I snap.

On our way out of the condo, I give Chuck a hundred-dollar bill and the package of Mucinex. I wince at the sound of his hack. "Is there somewhere you can get that checked out?" I ask.

Lance looks at me curiously. And Chuck waves me off as he has before. To him, I'm simply some guy who is patting himself on the back for doing a small good deed. But what he doesn't realize is that repeating this day has forced me to look at the people, like him, that I pass each day. Really *see* them. And now that I've seen Chuck, it's getting harder and harder to look away. I narrow my eyes at Lance. "Before you say anything, I give to the homeless now. Okay?"

"Got it," Lance says. He's brought his coffee with him and is sipping it as we walk, glancing at me every few feet, trying to figure out what's going on with me. He'll see shortly.

I think about Mia's many deaths. How, dare I say, I'm used to them now. It's a strange thing to become accustomed to seeing a person die. I've often marveled at how police officers and firefighters are able to compartmentalize the tragedy they witness while on the job. Our news crew and I have often shown up on the site of a horrific catastrophe—terrible shit that has never left me, like a murder-suicide of an entire family in El Cajon or a drunk driver who plowed into a pregnant woman on the 163 freeway—and the first responders are always calm, cool, and collected. As if they understand that death is inevitable. That not all lives are meant to be saved.

But I believe Mia's is.

That it's my destiny to save her.

Why else do I keep reliving the day she dies? Why else do I get a new chance each morning? I refuse to consider that maybe I am in some sort of purgatory. Every nerve ending in my body tells me there is a reason for this madness. That Mia and I (and probably Lance, although it kills me to admit it) are linked somehow. And I'm hoping by showing Lance today and sharing what I'm going through—again—I will be able to get a confession out of him about Mia. Why they are in contact and why they haven't told me.

"Where are we going?" he asks.

I stop walking and look over at him. And tell him what's about to happen, down to the color of Amanda's nail polish—burgundy.

He starts to protest, ask questions, his face a mixture of expressions. He doesn't know if I'm joking or being serious.

"I'm not messing with you. Please, follow me. You'll see," I say.

After he watches me save Amanda, we walk back toward the condo. As we pace along Fifth Street, I confide in him all the other things that are going to happen today. I tell him how I know—that I'm living the same day. Lance shoves his hands deep in his pockets and listens, no longer protesting. No longer questioning. We stop in front of the entrance to the condo. I look over, and Chuck is still there, watching us. He offers me a gap-toothed smile.

"But I'm most interested in telling you what's going to happen in the noon hour," I say as we take the elevator up to our floor.

"At the station?" he asks as we push through our front door, his face slightly pale as he processes everything I've said.

"No, the hour from twelve to one. You know, when a majority of people have that meal called *lunch*," I say sharply, my anger toward him fighting its way to the surface.

Lance recoils at my tone. "Look, I believe you, okay? You don't need to keep trying to prove it. I searched the shark attack while we were walking back. It's there. I emailed Alexis." He stops. "Well, I guess you know how this ends."

"You're right—I do—" I pause, searching for the right words. "But this conversation we're about to have, this one is new. And I have no idea how it will end."

"What are you trying to say?"

"That I saw you and Mia having lunch."

"What?" he says, his eyes widening. Surprised that I know? Shocked that I've found out?

"You heard me. You had lunch at Rustic Root. You held her hand across the table. Shared a fork." I take a deep breath, picturing them enjoying the same bite of food.

"This happened on one of your Thursdays?" he says, narrowing his eyes.

I nod.

He looks at his phone. "At noon?"

"Right again."

"Well, it's eight thirty a.m., and you're accusing me of something that I haven't done yet. In *my* world, anyway," he says, and I wonder if he's mocking me now.

"Yes," I say. Then I add, "Is this the part where you tell me you *don't* have lunch plans with Mia today at Rustic Root?"

"Yes, it is," he says firmly. "Because I don't." His face is reddening.

"Seriously, Lance, you're going to lie to me right now?" I recoil. Why won't he own up to this lunch with Mia?

"I'm not lying. I don't have lunch plans with her."

"*Not anymore* is what you aren't saying." I shake my head and throw up my hands.

"I don't, period," he says, then frowns. "I'm worried about you."

"Don't change the subject!" I yell.

He ignores me. "You're too invested in this date. In her return."

"I don't want your armchair analysis of me," I sputter. *Of course* I'm invested. I've watched Mia slip from me, both literally and figuratively. I've had my heart smashed into pieces. I've found hope and lost it. Every single emotion has passed through me in the course of the past six days. So yes, you could say I'm invested. But I don't say this, because right now there is a more pressing question on my mind. "I want to know what's going on with Mia."

"Then ask *her*."

"I have. And now I'm asking *you*." I ball my hands into fists, my frustration about to fire out of me.

"And my answer is this: Mia is consuming you. She's all you've talked about, which is fine. But I'm concerned that if things don't go as planned this evening, you won't be able to recover."

"I already know how things are going to go!"

"Right, the time loop." I think I see a slight eye roll.

"I thought you believed me," I say, curling my arms over my head.

"I do, but Dom—"

"'But.' Are you just placating me?"

"Listen, please," he says, his eyes locked on mine. "Whether you're spending six Thursday nights with her or six hundred, you've needed her in a way that isn't healthy."

"You sound like my mom!" I hiss, but his observation worms its way into a crevice of doubt.

"Well, if we're both saying it to you . . ." He lets it sit there for a moment, most likely trying to measure his words so this doesn't escalate. I try to match his effort and withhold my defensive comments. But they are pushing to get out. To be heard.

"It's been a decade, Dom. It's concerning. And now that she's back, you think it's some kind of sign. And maybe she does too."

"Not maybe! She told me it was." The anger fires to the surface again.

"Fine. But I think you need to slow your roll here. Don't get ahead of yourself."

"What does that mean, don't get ahead of yourself?"

"You're being obsessive. You're telling me you've literally stopped time because of her. And you've watched her die how many times? It's morbid, Dom."

"Well, it is death, Lance," I spit.

"Wake up, man. You've been in a holding pattern since it ended. Calling other women Mia's name in bed. Having one, maybe two relationships since that lasted even six weeks?"

"Madison was eight weeks, almost nine."

Lance claps. "Well, congratulations."

"What's the big deal that no one has held a candle to Mia?" His accusation pushes me back on my heels. What's wrong with having high standards? I say as much to him.

"It's not healthy. And you're clearly not healthy either. Mentally, anyway."

I roll my eyes. "Why don't you tell me how you really feel?" I ask as I try to push away the sting of his words. The way he accessed some of my biggest fears—that I'm stuck because I've never moved on from Mia, and that I could be unstable. I look down, deflated.

Lance may sense this, because his tone softens. "Trust me on this."

"Trust you? The guy who is lying to me about a lunch with Mia."

"There is no lunch," he says, holding my gaze, his face open. If I didn't know better, I'd believe him.

"Maybe not anymore," I snap. "But let me ask you this: Have you been in touch with her?"

"Since she's been back?" Lance asks.

"At all, in the past ten years."

"Why don't *you* tell *me*? You're the guy who knows everything, right? Why don't you look into your little time loop crystal ball and tell me!"

My stomach twists at the undercurrent of his words. That it's possible he doesn't have as much faith in my story as he says.

"I wish I'd had a crystal ball when you told me not to marry Mia. When you told me ending the engagement was the right thing to do. Because I wouldn't have broken up with her if—"

Lance puts his hand up. "Don't. You came to me in a panic. Terrified."

"Maybe I needed my best friend to calm me down—not confirm my fears. Did you ever think of that?"

Lance sighs heavily and leans against the counter.

"But I guess now I know why you did that," I continue. "Because you wanted her all to yourself!" The accusation flies out before I can truly process the insinuation. That all those years ago, Lance may have had his own agenda. The realization smacks me hard, and I take a step back to recover.

Lance's face reddens. "You have no idea what you're talking about. None." He storms out of the condo before I can say another word.

I stare at the door for a long time after Lance leaves, rewinding the last ten years in my mind, looking for any other evidence to support what I said. Were there secret calls or texts that I missed? Clandestine trips? I search the data banks of my memory but come up empty. But if their relationship was innocent, then why refuse to come clean?

I need answers. Not only about why Mia is back but about how large a role Lance has played in her life. An idea strikes me. In order to get the information I seek, I need to be where Mia has lived the past decade. I look at my watch. I don't have much time. I send Mia a text and cancel, making up an excuse about work. She takes it in stride and mentions she's free early next week, which stings like hell. Here I am, trying to save her, and she doesn't seem to care. She's probably already texting Lance, asking him to meet up. I feel sick at the thought. At their betrayal. Yet I still text back, Sure, and add a plea for her to stay home tonight. To be safe. Because regardless of how I'm feeling, my first instinct is to protect her.

~

There's one first-class seat left on a United Airlines flight that leaves San Diego at 11:00 a.m. and gets into O'Hare at 5:45. That's not going to give me very much time to interrogate the people closest to Mia for information, but I suppose I can always fly back again tomorrow if needed. I purchase the expensive fare, knowing I'll wake up back here in the morning and won't have spent a dime. I have to take full advantage of the benefits of my time loop—free booze, free food, and a wide leather seat that reclines without causing World War III with the person behind me. I also book an Uber Black from my condo to the airport, because why the hell not? And a penthouse suite at the Four Seasons in Chicago. Because I can.

On the plane, I make a list of everyone I need to visit and where they live. I'll start with Mia's parents. She's been evasive when I've asked why she's back in California. I know I won't get anywhere with Hailey, who clearly still has reservations about me. I'm hoping her mom can shed some light on why Mia has picked up and abandoned her life in Chicago. She did live with them and then near them for the past decade, so maybe they became closer. And one other thought crosses my mind—that I may need her parents to understand how sorry I am for what I did to their daughter. That making amends not only with Mia but with those who were affected by my actions might propel me forward. It certainly can't hurt.

After Janice and George, I'll visit her former roommate. She seems closest to Mia based on what I've been able to glean from her Facebook page. Her name is Tami James, and according to this morning's status update, she's working tonight at a bar in the city. (I'll try to stop myself from lecturing her about her page's privacy settings.) And then I will find the dark-haired man who often tagged Mia in posts—frequently checking her into Sunday brunch at JoJo's Milk Bar in Chicago—and who had his arm draped over her shoulder in a picture she posted days before moving here. Who I've learned, after a deep social media dive, is Rob Wilson, a graphic designer who lives in Lincoln Square. I need to understand who he was, or *is*, to her. I jot down all of the addresses I've found and have a plan by the time the flight is over.

I bound off the plane, order my Uber, and am on my way to Glencoe within fifteen minutes. Being luggage-free is certainly paying off. As we speed up the 294, I dial the number for Mia's parents I dug up online. They still have a landline! I hold my breath as the phone rings.

"Janice?" I say when she answers.

"Yes, who is this?" she asks. I hear running water and the clanking of dishes.

"It's Dom. Dominic Suarez, Mia's—"

The sounds stop, and I hear her take a ragged breath. "Is it Mia? Is she okay?"

The question strikes me as odd. "Yes, yes, she's fine," I say and hear Janice exhale. "I'm sorry, I didn't mean to worry you."

"It's okay. I shouldn't have panicked. But no matter how old the girls get, I still worry."

"I'm calling because I'm in town and was hoping you were home. That I could come by and talk with you and George."

There's a long pause, and then I hear her clear her throat. "Sure, okay," she says unconvincingly.

"Great, I'll be there in about twenty-five minutes," I say and hang up before she can change her mind.

I check the time. It's four p.m. in San Diego. I wonder how Lance and Mia's lunch went. My jaw clenches as I picture them together, sharing bites of pork belly and kale salad. I open my mouth wide to release the tension.

My email pings, and it's Amanda. She thanks me again for saving her and affirms that was her last walk of shame—she's a changed woman. I can't help but smile. I write back with the link to the dating support group. She immediately responds with a GIF about douchebags. I write with a link to antisnoring chin straps on Amazon. We go back and forth for a while, and then she presses me more on how I knew so much about her, how I knew that car was going to run the light, how I was able to save her life. I stare at her questions and am struck with one of my own: Why is it that I can save her life every day but not Mia's? Is it because I know exactly how she could die? Or because I'm not emotionally attached to Amanda? I rub my chin, trying to discern how I can apply these lessons to Mia. But it feels impossible—I have no clue how she'll meet her fate each day. And I have no idea how I could disentangle my heart from hers. I love her too much.

The Uber pulls up to Mia's parents' Victorian house on Madison Avenue, breaking my concentration. I quickly type back to Amanda that I have no idea how I knew those things but I'm glad I did.

As I step out of the car, I take in the front lawn. Remembering Mia and me standing here nine and a half years ago like it was yesterday. I'm flooded with feelings of disappointment, pain, and regret. It was before Uber, so after she went back inside, I had to call a cab, and I waited for what felt like forever for it to arrive. I sat despondent on the curb in front of the house, hoping the entire time that Mia would fling open the front door and tell me she'd made a mistake, that she *did* want to give me another chance. It's hard knowing that she did come to that conclusion the next morning but that I had left. Thinking of the missed opportunity makes my head hurt.

I head up the brick walkway, and Janice opens the door before I reach it. "Dominic," she says, her polite smile not reaching her eyes. Clearly puzzled as to why I'm here. I think of my own mom. How we've barely spoken. To her, it's been less than twenty-fours, but for me, it's five days, which is a lifetime for us. But I don't know how to explain what's going on, how to make her understand. She's never been one for leaps of faith, and this would require an enormous one.

"Hi," I say, walking up to the door slowly. Do we hug? Shake hands? Nod?

Mia's mom extends her hand, and I shake it.

"It's good to see you," I say, and she nods. I should have known she'd still be cool as ice.

I step into the house and inhale a vanilla scent. I spot three lit candles on the mantel of the fireplace, an open paperback by a leather chair. I've clearly interrupted what appears to be a peaceful evening. Mia's dad, George, is standing next to a long white couch, his face neutral. He's lost a little hair and found a little weight around his middle. He shakes my hand but doesn't speak. I guess he hasn't changed.

Janice closes the door behind us. "When did you get in?" she asks.

"An hour ago. I came straight from the airport."

"No bags?" she asks, surveying me.

I shake my head. *I don't need any bags.*

"Your place, you've remodeled," I say, stalling. Not knowing how to begin the conversation I came to have as I take in the thick crown moldings, the sleek wood floors, the gas fireplace.

"Yes, it was quite a process, but we're happy with it now. Right, George?"

He nods again but still doesn't speak. He settles into a worn black leather recliner that looks out of place.

Janice sits on the sofa, and I take a seat across from her in the chair next to the book, which I can now see is Stephen King's latest. I place my hands chastely in my lap and look over at George, who is cracking his knuckles. I feel a bead of sweat form as I try to muster the courage to start the real dialogue. But it's so much harder now that I'm staring at the two people who would have been my in-laws.

Thankfully, Janice pushes me to start.

"So, Dominic, what brings you to see us?"

I clear my throat and tell them how I ran into Mia at the coffee shop and look for any signs they've already heard this story. No recognition passes through their expressions. I go on to tell them that we have a date planned. My voice catches as I confess I've never gotten over her. I also catch myself rambling about my regrets, my pain, my apologies for breaking things off, stopping myself when Janice's eyes begin to glaze over. But I want them to understand that I'm here because I care about Mia as a person. I'm not some creepy ex-boyfriend.

I'm not sure I pull it off.

Janice leans forward in her seat when I'm finished speaking, her eyes soft. "Dominic, you've got to let yourself off the hook here. It was a long time ago. I hope you haven't come all this way just to get our forgiveness."

"I know. I haven't," I say, my gaze falling on a picture of Mia and her sister as little girls. Mia's arm is wrapped around Hailey's shoulders. They have matching strawberry-blonde pigtails.

"But I do want to apologize to you both because I know I hurt Mia and that, in turn, hurt you," I say, meeting their eyes. George looks away quickly. I thought a lot on the flight about what I could say to Mia's parents to convey my remorse. To help them understand I'm truly sorry.

Janice glances at her husband, and they share a look. "We appreciate you saying that. But why now, after all this time?" she asks matter-of-factly. I don't blame her.

Obviously I can't tell them the real reason—that Mia burst back into my life like a gust of wind sent by the universe and now we're stuck in this cul-de-sac of time. And that I'm wondering if I need to reconcile my past in order to move forward. And that includes apologizing not only to Mia but to her parents as well. "I should have been in touch with you sooner. What I did to Mia, I broke her heart, and it wasn't okay."

"But what you did sent her back to us. We had this entire decade being close to her. We didn't think she'd return here—she's such a free spirit that we imagined her backpacking around Europe or something like that. But when she showed up on our doorstep after . . ." Janice pauses, not wanting to say it. "When she showed up, we were heartbroken for her but happy she was back. Does that make sense?" She pauses, as if thinking back on Mia's return. "We were able to get close to her in a way we hadn't been. It was good for our family and, I think, for Mia."

I find relief in Janice's words. I've harbored a lot of guilt for being the reason Mia moved back. She once told me part of the reason she'd chosen a college on the West Coast was to break free of them, of the small town she'd felt suffocated in. She'd grown up with all the same people and wanted a change. And her mom initially hadn't taken it well. Had told her she wouldn't pay for college unless she went somewhere in state. But eventually she'd come around. But now, hearing her return had been good for the family and for Mia eases my mind. Because I know Mia—she wouldn't have stayed if it hadn't been the right decision.

"I guess I'm wondering if there's a chance for Mia and me again?" It's out before I realize what I've asked. Before I face that it's part of the reason I'm here—to ask them this. To have them offer me hope. My earlier conversation with Lance has me questioning everything. I had been so sure that Mia had landed back in my life so we could try again. That by saving her life, I'd also be guaranteeing our future. But now, I'm rattled. Not knowing if one thing leads to the other. Maybe I'm supposed to save her so she can live happily ever after with Lance. Or it could be possible Lance is her intended savior. I'm no longer sure of anything, except that I love Mia.

Janice leans forward, her eyes kind. "Oh, Dominic. That's not for us to answer."

I'm not surprised by this. Yet still, I feel disappointed.

"I get that," I say, trying to read Janice's face for signs that Mia has confided things about me. I find none. "But can you tell me why she's back in Southern California after all this time?"

"Have you asked her?" Janice asks, her tone not as gentle now. I've struck a nerve.

"I have, and she avoids telling me," I admit and feel a small stab of desperation. Waiting to know.

"It's not for us to tell you either," George says, and both Janice and I swivel our heads toward him. Surprised by the sound of his voice. It's deeper than I remember.

"Okay," I say, trying to read his expression, but his face gives nothing away. He's a father protecting his daughter, and I can respect that.

"He's right," Janice says, mindlessly fluffing a pillow next to her. "Mia is a grown woman. She certainly doesn't want her parents sticking their noses in where they don't belong."

"Is that what I'm doing?" I ask her, suddenly hyperaware that I could be coming across not as apologetic but as greedy. Like I'm only after answers. I continue before she can answer. "Because I don't mean to pry . . ." I don't finish the sentence because we all know that is exactly what I'm doing—whether I mean to or not.

"I think you need to talk to Mia," Janice says simply. And I can tell by her clipped tone that it's time for me to go. I want to ask about Lance but hold off. She and George have made it clear they're not going to tell me anything, so I should leave well enough alone. *But if that's the big secret, guys, I already know!*

"Okay. Thank you for seeing me tonight. I appreciate it," I say and stand up. "It was good to see both of you after all this time."

George and Janice walk me to the door. I shake George's hand and Janice's and wonder if I'll ever see them again as I walk to the curb and wait for my Uber.

CHAPTER TWENTY

As the silver Ford Explorer heads down 94 south, I replay the conversation with Janice and George and wish I could go back and do it again. And then I think, *I could*. But what good would that do me? They are going to protect their daughter at all costs, and that's exactly what they should be doing. I sink into the seat and try not to look at the visit with them as a failure. It did feel good to come full circle and apologize to them. And maybe that needs to be enough.

As we get closer to where Mia's friend Tami works, I'm no closer to figuring out how to coerce her into revealing why Mia came back without coming off as a lunatic. I didn't miss the concerned look in Mia's parents' eyes when they realized I'd flown halfway across the country in a desperate attempt to get them to confide what's really going on. They clearly questioned my sanity. Probably thought I was more of a stalker than a forlorn ex-boyfriend, because they immediately called Mia after I left.

My phone starts blowing up. Mia texts that now she understands why I canceled our date. She wants to know what the hell I'm doing visiting her parents. Asking them questions about her. She tells me it really threw them off when they found out Mia didn't know I was coming. I slump farther down in the seat and shake my head at my stupidity. This is not going the way I thought it would. Now Mia is involved. And while I have every reason to believe tomorrow will erase all of this, it doesn't ease my anxiety that I've now upset Mia—*again*. I'm sorry is all I write. Because I am. I hate that I have to be here, sneaking around behind Mia's back—or trying to, anyway. And then, though I cringe as I do it, I mute her number so I won't see any notifications from her. I don't need any distractions to deter me from the rest of my trip. My argument with Lance forced me to see that there is a lot I don't understand about Mia. And until I do, there's no saving her. So hopefully her friends will be more forthcoming.

Tami works at a bar called the Sixth, conveniently located in Lincoln Square, a charming area slightly northeast of the city. Tami and Mia were roommates in an eighteenth-century walk-up somewhere in the area, and Mia commuted each day to Lake Forest, where she taught kindergarten. Rob, the dark-haired man with his arm draped around Mia in the photo, worked there as well as an art teacher but recently took a job at a graphic design firm in Chicago. Did he leave because she left? I know he lives in this area and pieced together his backstory pretty easily, as he clearly hasn't heard of privacy settings on his Facebook page either. I feel a stab of jealousy as I picture him and Mia carpooling to work, drinking hot coffee out of stainless steel mugs as they lament the weather. Rob knew Mia in a way that I no longer do.

The Sixth is hopping when I walk in, and I grab the last seat at the bar. The dimly lit room is juxtaposed with yellow booths and craft cocktails with brightly colored ice cubes. Heavy hardcover books line shelves against the wall. I spot Tami mixing a drink. She looks like she does on Facebook, except she's taller than I thought she'd be, and her bleached hair is more severe in person. She's pretty, but in a polar-opposite way to Mia. Mia's beauty is soft, so airy that you almost can't put your finger on it. Tami is angular, with sharp edges that feel like they could hurt if you rub them the wrong way.

As if she can feel me dissecting her, Tami looks over. I smile innocuously. She hands me a thick menu. "Need one of these?"

I point to a drink with the rainbow ice cubes. "I'll take whatever that is."

"The Silly Rabbit?"

"Yes. One Silly Rabbit, please!"

"You don't want to know what's in it?"

"I like to live dangerously," I say, thinking nothing could be further from the truth but liking how the words sound coming out of my mouth. Her gaze is intense. I don't look away. We stay like that for a moment before she turns to make my drink, flipping bottles in the air and catching them seamlessly. She glances over to make sure I'm watching her.

I am. It's impossible to look away. She's quite striking, her white-blonde hair a contrast to her dark-brown eyes. A couple of minutes later, she sets a small carafe of clear liquid next to a glass filled with perfectly square colored ice cubes, as well as a dropper.

"What is that?" I ask, pointing to the small glass bottle. "Are you trying to drug me?"

She laughs. "Maybe," she says and bites her bottom lip.

Good. I need her to like me.

"So what you do," she continues, "is pour this." She picks up the carafe and gently tilts the liquid into the glass. "And then you take this mint dropper—"

"Ah, so that's what it is."

"Yes. You take that and drop it in to taste."

I pick up the dropper. "This drink is more complicated than I am."

She raises her eyebrows.

I take a sip. "Delicious," I say and pause. "Hey, you look so familiar. Have we met?"

She leans into the bar. "Is that your pickup line? If so, it's pretty weak."

"No! I swear, I think we've met. Do you know Mia Bell?"

Her eyes light up. "You know Mia? How?"

"We worked together at her first teaching job," I lie. I remember Mia mentioning she hated her first teaching gig and left after one year. "The shitty one she hated."

"I hope not because of you?" Tami teases.

"Ha—no. But we kept in touch, and I'd see her occasionally. Sometimes with Rob?" I say and hope to hell I strike gold.

Tami nods. I'm in.

"I haven't seen Mia around lately. How's she doing?"

Tami pours vodka, ice, and olive juice into a stainless steel shaker. "She's back in California."

"She is?" I feign surprise. "Why?"

Tami shrugs. "That's a good question. She came home one day, not too long ago, and told me she was moving." She begins to shake the canister vigorously. "I was super bummed because she was the best roommate. Now I'm stuck with some flaky bitch who leaves her hair in the drain and is a salesperson at Anthropologie." She scrunches up her nose. It seems she's more disgusted about her workplace than her hygiene.

"That sucks she left." I shake my head. "And she didn't give you any indication why? That's a pretty big thing to do—quit your job and move halfway across the country." I pause before adding, "Didn't she have an ex back there?"

"The guy on TV?" she asks, and my heart starts to thump.

"She told you that guy was her ex?" My voice cracks as I push the words out.

Tami holds a finger up to me and walks away to deliver the martini. I try not to hyperventilate before she returns. Did Mia confide in her that she's involved with Lance? Or is Tami simply confusing him with me? We do both work in TV.

She takes another order before she returns. She grabs two snifters from under the bar. "Wait, is the guy in front of the camera the ex, or is it the other one? The one who works behind the camera?" She frowns. "I can't remember. But whoever it is fucked her up, big-time. She had trouble trusting guys for a long time." She pours scotch into the glasses and walks them over to two men at the end of the bar.

I let out the breath I was holding. I guess I am the aforementioned asshole who broke Mia's heart. Not that I'm surprised. But *if* there is something between her and Lance, what did he do to make her feel safe and ready to trust again? I'm lost in thought about Mia when Tami returns. I keep looking at the time, worried about her, that her life might be over soon. Or might already be over.

"I miss her," she says. "I guess I thought she'd always be here. I'm kind of hurt she didn't give more notice. I thought we were closer than that."

I search my mind for reasons she'd take off without warning. Maybe Hailey needed her? Maybe Lance needed her? The thought makes me queasy. I tell Tami that I'm struck by how quickly Mia up and left, hoping she'll reveal more. But she only shrugs in response.

"I get it," I say. And I do. People are easy to take for granted. Appreciating the time you have, understanding that time is a moving walkway that no one can stop, is the key. Circumstances change, no matter how hard we try to stand still.

We chat for a few more minutes, but it's clear after a while that she's more interested in what I'm up to when she gets off at midnight than why Mia left. I glance at my phone: nine o'clock.

I'm running out of time, and I want a chance to talk to Rob too. "Hey. Is Rob around tonight? I'd love to say hi."

A disappointed look crosses her face, but she recovers quickly. "Probably. He's usually out on Thursdays. Want me to text him?"

"Sure," I say, trying to contain my excitement.

Tami grabs her phone from her pocket. "Hey, I don't know your name."

"Lance," I say and reach my hand out to hers. Her handshake is confident and firm. Her phone pings almost immediately. "He's a few streets over. He said he was planning on swinging by." She points at my empty glass. "Another?"

"How about a beer?" I ask. "And thanks. I owe you one."

"You can pay up later," she says and winks before moving on to a guy wearing a black fedora.

~

It's another thirty minutes before Rob pushes through the door. He makes a beeline for Tami, a big smile on his face. She points to me, and I hear her mention Lance's name. Rob's eyes scan the bar before settling on me. I smile and raise my hand. "Hi."

Rob says nothing.

"What?" Tami asks him.

Rob takes a beat before speaking. "That's not Lance. That's Dominic, the guy who dumped Mia after proposing."

"Oh," Tami says, her lips curling down, and it's clear the offer to hang out after is now off the table.

It takes a few minutes to clear things up. Tami is not happy I lied. Rob is not happy I'm here. Basically, everyone at the Sixth thinks I'm a total dick.

Thankfully, the bar is so busy that Tami is forced to move on and take orders. I use the opportunity to grab a yellow booth and motion for Rob to join me. "I'll give you all the answers you want, if you sit with me a few minutes," I say. "Please," I plead when he doesn't move. "I'm here with good intentions. I'm here for Mia. I'll buy you a fancy drink with a dropper."

He rolls his eyes. "I drink beer."

Fine. I can work with this.

I order two beers as he reluctantly slides in across from me, his lips thin and narrow, looking nothing like the wide-smiling man who slung his arm around Mia's shoulders in the picture on Facebook.

"How did you know who I was?" I ask once he's settled.

"Mia showed me pics last year from your Facebook page."

I grin, happy she'd been thinking of me.

"You can knock that smile off your face. It wasn't a happy walk down memory lane," he snaps, then takes a long pull from his bottle. "I kept asking her who had fucked her up so badly," he continues. "And she finally showed me one night. You."

Okay. So I guess she didn't remember me in the best light. But still—Mia hasn't moved on in ten years either. Both Tami and Rob are insinuating that it has to do with me. Maybe there's a connection there—two people who have been stuck in quicksand for a decade are now stuck in the same day. It has to mean something.

"You might not care about this, but I've regretted hurting her every day since I broke things off," I say. "I wish I could go back and change what I did."

Rob shrugs. "She had moved on," he says, and the words pierce me.

"But you said—"

"We would joke about how jacked up we both were—I have trust issues, and she's a commitment-phobe. One night we were drinking, and I asked her to show me who you were. And she did. We laughed at your profile picture."

"What's wrong with it?" I ask defensively. It's a picture of my mom and me at her retirement party.

"Really, man?" He smirks.

"Whatever," I say. "I'm not here to dissect my social media presence."

"Then why are you here?"

"I want to know why she left. Why she quit her job. Went to California." I'm also curious what Rob is to her, but the other questions are more vital to figuring out how to save her.

Rob leans back in his seat. "Why do you care? After all this time?"

"Let's just say I have a vested interest."

I can see Tami out of the corner of my eye, glaring at me.

"Please," I try again. "If I told you why, you wouldn't believe me anyway."

"Try me."

I shake my head. This guy has never met me. His only view into my life is that I'm the asshole who dumped Mia and has what I now understand is a creepy profile picture.

When I interview people for stories, sometimes I have to try different tactics. Be a chameleon. It's obvious Rob cares about Mia. And so I try another way.

"I've thought about her most days in the last ten years. And now she's back, and she won't tell me why. And the more times I ask her, the more I can see in her eyes that there's something she's not telling me. And I get that she doesn't owe me shit after what I did. But I'm positive there's more to the story, and maybe if I understand that, I can save her."

"What do you mean, save her?"

I realize my slip and try to cover. "I mean be there for her. If I know why she's home, I can be there for her."

Yes, I'm trying to get Rob to trust me. But I mean every single word. My eyes glisten, and I wipe them with the back of my hand. I've been so focused on getting answers that I almost forgot how desperate I am to save the woman I love.

Rob is watching me carefully, but his eyes have softened. "Sorry, man, but I can't tell you why she went back to California. That's her private business, and if she wanted you to know, wouldn't she have told you?"

"Ouch," I say.

Rob laughs awkwardly. "I'm not trying to be a jerk. I promise you. You seem like a decent enough guy if we don't count the lying." He raises his eyebrows. "But you know Mia—she'll tell you when and if she wants to tell you," he says, then takes another drink, contemplating. "But I'm glad you care about her and want to be there for her. That makes me feel better about her being there."

"Why? Are you worried about her?" I ask, my skin prickling.

"I am," is all he says. He looks down at his beer and plays with the label.

"Rob, tell me why. I can't help her unless I know."

He says nothing.

"You love her, too, don't you?" I ask, a knot in my stomach forming. I hate thinking of her with anyone else, although I'm the reason she would be. "How long were you guys together?"

"We were never together. But you're right. I do love her. She said we were better as friends," he says wistfully. "Maybe she never got over you."

My pulse races. "Did she ever say that?"

Rob shakes his head. "No. But it makes sense."

"I tried to fix things with her after I screwed up. But when I couldn't, I didn't feel like I had the right to stay in contact," I say, my heart burning slightly at the memory of being told no and having to respect that.

"But she still knew what was going on with you."

"How?" I ask, my pulse quickening.

"Your friend. The one you pretended to be—"

"Lance?" I ask.

"Yes, Lance. They kept in touch."

My stomach does a flip and slams to the floor. So I was right—they have been in contact. And they both lied to me about it. "Oh. You didn't know?" He whistles softly. "That's interesting."

I nod. The confirmation of my worst fear making me speechless, the possible confirmation of their betrayal creating an emptier space inside my heart.

"Maybe he's not the friend you think he is?" Rob offers, then finishes his beer, signaling for another. "These are on you, right?"

I nod. It's the least I can do. I recognize the pain in Rob's eyes when he talks about his unrequited love for Mia. I feel for the guy.

"You might be right about Lance," I say.

"Sometimes you don't know people the way you think you do," he says, and I'm not sure if he's talking about Lance and me or Mia and him.

"I'm figuring that out more and more each day," I say and slide out of the booth, dejected, my insides crushing. "Thanks for your time," I add, then put money on the table to cover the tab—and then some. I walk out, and the warm night air slaps me in the face as I stumble onto the sidewalk, trying in vain to catch my breath and get a grip on the conflux of emotions raging inside of me. I walk toward the lights of Western Avenue and wonder if anything—or *anyone*—is authentic.

CHAPTER

TWENTY-ONE

JUNE 11, 10:00 P.M.
THURSDAY #6

I walk for what feels like forever, trying to make sense of what I've learned about Lance and Mia. I know I suspected it after seeing them at the Rustic Root, but there was still a part of me that hoped it might not be true. So now I can only assume I'm also right about their being involved. That idea makes me sick. After years of me pining for her, she ends up with my best friend. How does Lance think this is going to play out? That I'm going to accept it and we'll all be friends like the old days? I'll stand up in their wedding? I laugh out loud and hear a voice.

"What's so funny?" It's a homeless woman leaning up against the window of a dry cleaner. The light from the store's sign illuminates her aging face.

"Life," I say.

"You can say that again." She takes a swig from something wrapped in paper, and I shake my head. But I give her twenty dollars anyway, because who am I to judge? If I've learned anything today, it's that if you don't know your best friend, you can't begin to know anyone else.

I head down Western to Irving Park and finally turn on Clark. Before I know it, I'm standing in front of Wrigley Field. It's like I was on autopilot, my body leading me here while my mind wandered. I look at my watch. I've been walking for an hour and a half. I gaze up at the Wrigley marquee, remembering something Mia told me once when the subject of the Dodgers (my team) came up while we were at a hole-in-the-wall bar in Pacific Beach. She told me matter-of-factly that the Cubs (her team) deserved to win a World Series before the Dodgers did. We sparred for a bit until she stood up on her barstool and pronounced to the small crowd of patrons that the Cubs would win the World Series and the Curse of the Billy Goat would be gone. She didn't know when, but she knew it was going to happen. A couple of people clapped, but most didn't respond. It was Southern California, after all, where we have our own teams to root for.

But it's my reaction I remember most. I grimace at the memory. I was embarrassed for her, and for me, that she'd made such a spectacle of herself. My mind questioned, as it had more than one time before that night, if I was meant to be with someone who would do *that*. Make a spectacle. Draw attention. Embarrass. Because Mia, as much as she was so smart and fun and lovable, was also unpredictable. A word I had—and still have—a hard time with. I wondered if she'd outgrow it or if she'd always be that way. My skeptical side guessed it would be the latter. I never knew how to talk to her about this because it was one of the very things that had initially drawn me to her. Made me take notice. The day we first met, she was dancing in the quad to music she must have only been able to hear in her head. She was magical and magnetizing, and I couldn't look away. And before I knew what my legs had done, I was standing in front of her, introducing myself.

I thought of her the night the Cubs finally did win, clinching the series by one run in the eleventh inning in one of the most incredible baseball games I'd ever seen. It would have been nearly one a.m. in the Midwest where Mia was. I wanted to call her that night—congratulate her. But I didn't. Lance and I were at a bar, and he stepped away after the win. Was it to call Mia? My chest burns at the thought.

I head into the Cubby Bear and manage to catch the eye of a cute blonde bartender. I shout over the noise that I'll have a whiskey and to keep 'em coming. A seat opens up; I grab it and down the shot within moments of her setting it down.

"Bad night?" a woman next to me asks.

"About six of them," I mumble.

"What do you mean?"

I meet her eyes for the first time. They are dark blue, almost black, and almond shaped. Her complexion is olive. Her cheekbones are high. She looks nothing like Mia. This is a good thing right now.

"Nothing. And I have a feeling things are about to vastly improve," I say and offer a wan smile. She grins broadly in return, revealing two deep dimples.

"You look out of place here." She leans toward me. "Not like the typical slobbering-drunk frat boys that would frequent a place like this. Thankfully it's an away game tonight. Much calmer crowd."

"I'll take that as a compliment," I say.

"Trust me, it is!"

"You don't sound like a big fan of this establishment. So why are you—"

"Here?"

I nod.

"My friend ditched me for her boyfriend. This is just around the corner from my place. I took a risk."

"I'm glad you did," I say. Am I flirting?

"Would you like another?" She nods toward my empty shot glass.

"You buying?"

"What if I am?"

"I'd have to tell you no, but that I appreciated the offer."

She blushes slightly. "Sorry, I thought because you were here alone . . ."

"Oh no. I am!" I say a little too quickly. "I was going to offer to buy yours."

"Well, in that case, I'll have a Blue Label on the rocks."

"A whiskey girl!"

"Tried and true." She puts her hand over her heart, and I feel a jolt of satisfaction. She's flirting, and I'm going to flirt right back. I think of Mia and Lance and down the rest of my drink.

"What's your name?" I ask.

"Mia."

The hair on my arms shoots up, and a shiver runs through me. "No, it isn't."

Her smile fades. My tone was sharp.

"I'm sorry. I didn't . . ." I backtrack as I try to regain my bearings—as I try to ignore the throbbing in my chest at the coincidence. What it might mean.

"Bad experience with a Mia?" she asks, letting me off the hook, sipping her whiskey.

"You could say that."

"Well, I'm a good Mia."

So is she. I think.

I grab my drink and hold it up to hers. "To good Mias," I say.

"To good Mias," she repeats.

More drinks and a genuinely good conversation later, I'm nice and drunk.

"You know, there is a good thing about me having the same name as your ex." She licks her lips.

"What's that?" I ask, feeling her hand on my thigh.

She leans in, her breath hot on my ear. "You don't have to worry about saying the wrong name in bed."

Okay, so she's inviting me to have sex with her. But can I sleep with another Mia? Or with anyone in the midst of all this? In all the years I've pined for my Mia, I've never met another. But now, after she comes back, I meet Mia number two. Is this the universe testing me? Playing some kind of trick on me to see how invested I am in the real Mia? The good Mia. My Mia. Because I still think she's good. I get that all the signs point to her and Lance being together. But there is a part of me that refuses to believe that it's true. Or that if it's true, it makes her bad. After all, I left her. She owes me nothing. Lance, on the other hand—that's a different story.

Mia number two is giving me the eyes, waiting. Any guy in his right mind would say yes to her. Not to mention I have my Four Seasons penthouse suite where I could take her. And come tomorrow, it will be washed away.

But the universe will remember. And so will I.

I hear myself telling her no. I pretend not to see the hurt look in her eyes. Because we connected, dammit. If I weren't stuck in this time loop with the Mia I love, if I didn't know I were going to wake up tomorrow and this girl would never remember me, I'd tell her no but that I'd like to take her to dinner. Because she's worth more than a one-night stand. The revelation surprises me—I haven't been this instantly attracted to a woman since Mia. Is it because I'm worried my Mia might never be mine?

I ask for her number, but she shakes her head. "That's okay. You don't need to get my number to make me feel better."

"No, I do want it." Because I do. I do want it. There's something about her. Maybe in another life. Another loop. Another something. "I have an early morning. I have to be in California."

"For business or pleasure?" she asks, toying with me again. Making me rethink my no.

"Business," I say. Which is true, because right now I can't think of anything pleasurable about going back to the two people I care about most in this world, who are both lying to me. I hold my phone out to Mia, and she punches in a number. She hands it back to me. She's logged herself in as *The Good Mia*. I walk her out to her Uber, and as she pulls away, I wonder what I'm doing. Why I'm chasing a Mia who clearly hasn't come back for me. Who it seems has come back for my best friend. When this Mia—this good Mia—is clearly interested.

I hope I'm not making a mistake. That the universe wasn't sending me this Mia so I would move on from the other one.

CHAPTER
TWENTY-TWO

I wake before the alarm and turn the power off so I don't have to hear the damn song that only mocks what I can't do for Mia. I'm not remotely surprised I'm in my own bed and not the one at the Four Seasons—although that one was exponentially more comfortable, with a Heavenly mattress and a billowy down comforter. Lance called as I was slipping into that bed, thinking about how I could have been sharing it with Mia number two, wondering if I'd made a mistake letting her walk away. I let Lance's call go to voice mail, already anticipating what was coming. When I listened, Lance informed me Mia's sister had told him Mia had been in an accident at home. She'd slipped in the shower and died. I wasn't surprised, but it didn't hurt any less to hear Lance's tears. To know she was gone again. In fact, it hurt more than it ever had. Because I'd come all the way to Chicago to try to make sense of everything, and I'd only be leaving more confused. I cried myself to sleep. My last thought was, *Why am I stuck in this day with Mia when I can't do a damn thing to save her? Why doesn't the universe assign Lance the task? He's clearly the one she wants.*

I sneak out of the house before Lance sees me. I can't face him right now. I can't rehash the lunch with Mia. His contact with Mia over the *years*. I can't deal with any more lies.

I head down to the intersection to save Amanda. Despite the circumstances, I'm looking forward to seeing her.

On the way, I hand Chuck $200, the Mucinex, and a bottle of water. I urge him to take the medicine while I watch. He's confused, doesn't know why I suddenly give a damn. I tell him I've heard him coughing several times when I've walked by. That I want to help. He balks at the pills, so I promise him that there's more cash if he takes the medicine. He finally relents. I hand him another hundred and head to meet Amanda.

After, I don't rush off, and we talk for a while. For longer than we have on any of the other Thursdays. It's nice. I learn that she grew up in San Francisco, went to San Francisco State, and got a job as a PR assistant with a large hotel chain after she graduated. She moved down here six years ago when she got an opportunity she couldn't pass up as the public relations director for Hornblower. She tells me she had a long-term boyfriend up until a year ago and since then has been flailing, hence the snoring douchebag from last night. She also says she doesn't know why she's telling me all of this, and it's bizarre, but she feels like she's known me for a long time. I smile as we exchange business cards and tell her nothing about what she's saying is the least bit odd. And for reasons I don't understand, that's when I tell her. That I'm reliving the same day. Maybe because I know so much about her. All I know is it feels good to be honest with her. To tell it like it is to a perfect stranger. Although I guess I wouldn't put her in that category anymore. I'd now consider her a friend.

She cocks her head when I'm finished. Asks me if I'm joking, her voice nervous. A twinge of concern pricks my temple, and I glance at my business card in her hand. I wonder if I should grab it back and run. Tell her I'm only teasing. But there's a part of me that needs Amanda to believe. To be on my side. Lance has clearly disappointed me, but Amanda and I have a clean slate.

I double down and tell her it's all true. Confide all the details that will happen later to prove it. Tell her that she'll see. That I'm not crazy. And then I turn and go, feeling a flutter in my stomach when I think of the email from her I know I'll get later. I head back toward the condo, but I don't go inside. I've been thinking about the constants each Thursday—Amanda. Chuck. The plane. How they must play a pivotal role in changing my fate. I've clearly helped Amanda. Saved her life. But what have I done for Chuck, besides throw some cash and a package of cough medicine at him? Today, I'll try to actually get to know him.

"Medicine kick in?" I ask when I walk up.

Chuck is sitting on a blanket, leaning against a newspaper stand filled with copies of the *San Diego Union-Tribune*. "Yes, thanks," he says, pulling his flannel tighter across his body, despite the heat. "Don't take this the wrong way, but why do you care all of a sudden? You've walked by me a million times without so much as a glance. What's in it for you?"

I cringe, although it's a fair question. From his perspective, I've done a one-eighty overnight. "Will you trust me that I want to help you?" I say.

"I don't need your charity. I'm doing all right."

"Are you?" I survey his stuff.

"Better than most."

"Why do you have to be so prideful?" I ask. "I'm trying to help."

"Until you bore of it. I've seen your type before. You don't get it. It's not as simple as a couple hundred bucks and a bottle of medicine."

"I'm not saying I think I can solve your problems. In fact, I haven't thought very much of this through. I want to help. Can I take you somewhere?"

"Fine, what do you have in mind? Let me guess—hot meal?"

I shake my head.

"And the shelter is full today. Already checked."

"Wrong again."

"Then where?"

"You'll see."

He looks over his shoulder. "I can't leave my stuff."

"I'll replace it if something happens," I say. "Come on." I'm a few steps along when I realize he's not with me.

"I don't know. It's my stuff," he says, and I feel a pang as I watch him looking at his shopping cart filled with miscellaneous items that most people would write off as junk. But this is everything he owns.

"It will be okay, and if it's not, I'll buy you better things," I say.

"It's not about replacing the stuff. It's all I have that I can call mine."

I consider his words, finally getting it. "I have an idea."

I put his things in my storage unit in the garage and lock it. He seems satisfied with this. We walk several blocks to our destination, and Chuck has a hard time keeping up, breaking into several coughing fits along the way.

"No way, man," Chuck says when he sees the sign for the free clinic.

"Don't you *want* to feel better?" I ask.

Chuck sighs. "I get that you're trying to be a do-gooder here, but I don't need to be your special project. The cough medicine is enough."

"Let me help you this one time," I say, knowing I only need to get him inside the door.

He holds his hands up, his fingernails overgrown and yellowing. "Fine."

"How long have you been on the streets?" I ask as we walk inside.

"Too long."

The free clinic is run down and somewhat depressing. There are worn polyester chairs and large plastic barriers separating the patients from the medical assistants. Because it's still early, there's no one waiting, and we get right in to see the physician, a thin young man with dark circles under his eyes who looks like he finished his residency about five minutes ago. He checks Chuck out quickly and diagnoses him with a bad cold.

"That's it?" I ask. "A bad cold? It seems like something more."

"It's not," he says abruptly as he writes something in the file.

"Can he get a chest x-ray, at least?"

He looks back up at me. "Does it look like we have the budget for chest x-rays here?" He unlocks a cabinet and pulls out a bottle and hands it to Chuck. "This is an antibiotic. Take it and get some rest."

"He's homeless. Where is he supposed to rest?" I interject.

"Shelter is usually full," Chuck adds.

He looks at us blankly. "I don't know."

I grab the bottle from Chuck's hand. "Let's go." He follows me outside, and I tell him that he can stay with me. I can't leave him on the streets tonight, knowing he's sick.

"No way, I can't let you do that," Chuck says.

"It's already done," I say.

Chuck bows his head, and I'm not sure if it's from embarrassment or exhaustion or a little bit of both.

We Uber back to the condo, and I don't miss the looks our driver gives us in the rearview mirror. Being in a confined space with Chuck only reinforces my decision to let him stay with me—this man needs a bath. We pull up in front of our building, and I smile at the driver and mouth the words *thank you* as I shut the door. I put my hand on Chuck's back and lead him inside to the elevator. I show him to the spare bedroom and bathroom. When I hear the water turn on, I text Lance.

I need to talk to you.

Where are you?

Home.

I'm at work. That ass Devon went to the editorial meeting this morning and now Alexis is all over me, asking me why I can't be more like him.

Can you come home?

I told you, I'm in a shit storm over here

Tell Alexis you heard about a plane crash in Oceanside and you're going to investigate.

But there hasn't been one

Check the police scanner

He texts a few minutes later.

Holy shit. It just happened. How did you know?

Tell her and come home now please. It's urgent.

∿

Chuck is sleeping when the front door to the condo opens thirty minutes later. It's 11:35 a.m. I wonder if Lance still plans to try to make his lunch with Mia. I imagine her sitting at the table, looking longingly at the sidewalk, wondering when Lance will show.

Lance walks around the corner and tosses his keys on the counter. "Hey," he says. "What's going on?"

I let out a breath. "I know about Mia. I know you've been in touch with her. I know that you have lunch plans today. I know everything." It all comes out in a burst.

He looks away, and my chest tightens when he doesn't deny it. "She told you?"

"It doesn't matter how I know; I just do."

"Okay," he says. "For what it's worth, I'm relieved that you know. I've felt terrible keeping it from you."

"Oh, have you? What a burden! Lying and being disloyal to your best friend!" I snap. I think back to their lunch. The *one* time I've seen them together. They looked pretty cozy. Lance certainly didn't look like he felt terrible.

Lance looks up and meets my gaze. He doesn't respond to my rant. He's always been hard to read. It's probably what makes him such a great newscaster—no matter what's going on in the world, you can count on Lance to deliver the news objectively. Except when he reported on me and the fall from the Zipper. That was the only time I heard raw emotion in his reporting—was that because he and Mia had a relationship? I search his face now and see something shimmer in his eyes. Regret, possibly? For hurting me? Or because he got caught?

"How long have you kept in touch?" I ask, not sure I want the answer but desperately needing it.

He doesn't look at me for what feels like an eternity. "Since she left," he finally says, and then I see what he's feeling more clearly—it's regret with a little bit of fear thrown in. *Since she left.*

My head spins with disbelief, my gut clenching. "Since she left?" I yell.

"Everything okay out here?" It's Chuck, wrapped in my robe.

"What the hell?" Lance asks. "Is that—"

"Yes, it's Chuck, the man who lives outside of our building."

"I should probably . . ." Chuck turns around and heads back down the hallway.

Lance points after him. "What's he doing in our place?"

"Don't worry about it." I dismiss Lance.

"Don't worry about it? This is my home too."

"Yes, it is. But right now I don't give a shit what's yours or mine. Aren't we into sharing everything right now?"

"It's not like that."

"Right." I flash back to their hand-holding across the table. Their sharing a fork. I look at my phone. It's after twelve now. "Have you forgotten your girlfriend is at the restaurant waiting for you?"

Lance rubs the back of his neck. "Dom, it's not—"

I interrupt, not wanting to hear his empty excuses. "So every time I've mentioned Mia in the last ten years—" I pace the room, and Lance stands eerily still, his back like a rod as he watches me.

"Which was a lot," he finally says.

I feel rage build in my belly and clamp my jaws shut, trying to hold it together. I take a deep breath. "Yeah, I'm aware of how often I talked about the love of my life," I spit.

Lance runs his hand over his face. A nervous habit of his. "Dom—"

"No." I shake my head. "I'm doing the talking right now," I say, and Lance gives me a look like he's planning to shut the fuck up. "So every time I brought up Mia, every time I wondered how she was doing. If she was okay. Thinking of me. Hating me. Loving me. Every single fucking time, you had the answers to the questions. And instead of telling me, instead of coming to me, you looked at me blankly." I stare at his face. "Like you're doing right now."

Lance raises his voice. "It's not like that—"

"Did you sleep with her?"

"What?"

"Did you have sex with her?" I'm yelling now. "You could have any girl you want in a hundred-mile radius, but I'm asking if you slept with the only one *I* wanted."

"How could you think I would do that to you?" Lance walks toward me until we're only a foot apart. He lets out a long, low sigh. His face is flushed.

"How could I *not* think that?" I move closer to him, the space between us growing even smaller. I can see the vein pulsating in his neck. And I'm so angry that I'm afraid of what could happen next. I've never lost control. No matter how many beers I had, how much shit was talked, I can honestly say I've never felt a rage like I feel in this moment. I've often wondered how people snap. Because they do—I see it every day at work in the stories we report. Right now, I get it. Because I feel like I'm going to explode—all the stress, fear, and anxiety of the last seven days becoming a powder keg.

Lance, seemingly sensing this, puts both his hands up. "Dude. Yes, we've kept in touch. She was destroyed when she left, Dom. And I think talking to me made her feel connected to you." His voice is thick.

This is hard to hear.

He continues. "So at first she'd call and ask about me, but it was obvious she wanted to know about *you*. What *you* were doing. If *you* were dating. But somewhere along the way, she started to become genuinely invested in me. And she'd fill me in about her life. Her job. Her latest roommate. Who she wants to set me up with, by the way." He gives me a look when he says this.

I nod without thinking. "You'd love her," I say, picturing Tami behind the bar. She could give Lance a run for his money.

Lance cocks his head. "How would you know?"

Because I've met her.

"Because Mia does," I say quickly. "If everything with Mia was so innocent, then why not tell me?"

"She begged me not to in the beginning. I think she didn't want you to know how hard she was taking the breakup. And then . . . I don't know. She became this thing to you, man."

"What do you mean?"

"It was like she wasn't real. A celebrity you idolized. Dom, before Tuesday, you hadn't spoken to her in almost ten years, yet you've searched for her in every woman you met."

I think of the "other Mia" I met yesterday.

"But the thing is, and I'm not saying this to be an asshole, but the Mia you knew back then and the Mia you reconnected with two days ago are different. You don't know the first thing about the person she is now."

He isn't wrong. Flying to Chicago made me realize how out of touch with her life I am. It was almost as if I'd seen her as an unattainable object. She represented a crossroads in my past that haunted me. And I now know that I need to use our next date to ask her about not only how she is now but *who* she is now. *If* Lance is telling me the truth about there being nothing sexual between them.

"But I have a chance now, and I'm ready."

"I know you think you are," Lance says, then takes a deep breath. "All I can say is that you need to get to know who Mia is now."

"Like you do? Intimately?"

"You're wrong, Dom. You don't know what you're talking about."

These words echo the ones he spoke last time we fought. Different circumstances but the same words.

"Back then, when you told me not to marry Mia, was it because you wanted her?" I'm pissed again.

"No."

"Then why? Why, *really*?"

Lance stiffens. "Because I was twenty-three. You were twenty-three. What the fuck did either of us know? But Mia, she knew. She knew back then who she was."

"But you said she's different."

"She's older. She's had more experiences. She's grown. She's wiser."

"And so have I!" I am yelling again.

"She was hurt. So hurt," Lance says quietly. "So if you want to know the truth, I was protecting her."

"From me?" I point at myself. "I thought I was your best friend."

"You are. But I didn't want to see either of you hurt again."

"Bullshit."

"It's true."

"It wasn't your place to keep us apart. It wasn't up to you."

"I had planned to tell you. But then she stopped asking, man. After a while she didn't start every conversation with you. Sometimes she didn't bring you up at all. And then it became a friendship. Nothing more."

I stare at Lance. This guy I thought had my back. Who I believed I could trust. And now I realize I don't know a damn thing about him or our friendship. He gives me a strange look, like he's not sure if I'm going to punch him. I'm not, for the record. But I'm okay if he thinks I might. If he doesn't let his guard down. I'd like to keep him on his toes as I process his betrayal. It feels so out of place, like a red sock in a white load of laundry.

I thought I knew everything about Lance for fifteen years. I've known about his secret love for cartoons on a Saturday morning and how he's deathly afraid of the dentist. And things I didn't want to know, like his brief bout with crabs. The realization that he's kept something so important from me, even for what he thinks were the right reasons, is something I'm going to have to work through. And I don't know how many more Thursdays it's going to take. But the fact that it wasn't more than a friendship makes me feel a little calmer.

"You still lied to me," I say.

"By omission."

"Come on, dude. That's such a bullshit loophole. You lied when you acted like you didn't know anything." I walk over to the window and stare out at Petco Park. "Have you seen her since she's been back?" I ask without turning around. It's a test.

Lance takes a beat before answering. "You're right that we're supposed to have lunch. Okay if I text her to tell her I'm not coming?"

I pause, surprised he's telling me the truth.

"Did she ask you or the other way around?"

"She asked me." He takes his phone out of his pocket. "I got a text this morning." He says it so quietly I almost don't hear him. Like he feels bad telling me. "I can show you."

I think about this for a while. I could stop him. Tell him I forbid him to see her. And he might listen. In fact, after this conversation, I'm sure he would. But Mia. Mia wants to see him. She invited him. And I want her to have the things she wants. "No, you should go." I think back on the day I spied them together. Hugging. Laughing. Two friends who have kept in touch for a long time. Who share a common bond.

Me. I was their catalyst.

"You sure? Because you seem upset," Lance says.

I picture Mia, her red hair flowing around her face. How happy she looked when she saw him. He was there when I wasn't. In a twisted way I owe him for being the one who didn't abandon her. "Yes, I'm sure," I say. "And for what it's worth, I'm canceling on her tonight," I add, deciding right then. I won't be able to hide from her that I know. And she might confront me, because I'm sure Lance is going to tell her when he sees her. I will start again tomorrow. When the deck is clear. I feel nauseous thinking about her impending death and how it could happen. But today—on *this Thursday*—I know I can't help her.

"She'll be disappointed," he says.

"You don't have to say that." I stare down at my feet.

"It's true." His voice is steady.

"Well, forgive me if it's a little hard to believe right now. I need to digest all this. Okay?"

"So are we good, man?" Lance asks, rocking on his heels.

"I don't know," I answer him honestly. "I need to think."

"That's fair," he says, then points down the hallway. "What about him?"

"Only for tonight. I promise."

"Fine," he says, knowing he has no room to argue after his duplicity.

"I'll find a place for him tomorrow," I lie, knowing there is no tomorrow. Only today. Again.

⁓

"Do you believe him?" Chuck asks when I check on him after Lance leaves.

"What?"

"Sorry, couldn't help but overhear."

"I do. But that doesn't make it any easier. I still feel betrayed. Like this was all going on behind my back and I was stupid enough not to see it."

Chuck lies back on the pillow, and I lean over and pull the covers up over him. He's pale.

"I don't know the guy. But he seemed sincere," Chuck says.

I give him a half smile. "Can I ask you a personal question?"

"Sure," Chuck says.

"How did you end up on the streets?"

Chuck leans back against the pillows I set out for him. "That's a long story."

I sit on the edge of the bed. "Tell me. I have the time."

It seems like I have all the time in the world.

"It wasn't drinking or drugs or anything like that, if that's what you're thinking."

I feel my cheeks redden but say nothing. I assumed that one of those two factors was involved. I couldn't understand how someone could end up homeless otherwise.

"I spent eight years in the army. Did two tours in Iraq, back in the late nineties."

"And you came home with PTSD? I can't imagine what it was like there."

Chuck's expression is pensive. "No, I was an officer. Didn't see a ton of action. I mean, yes, it was a depressing and sad place, but I came home in one piece. Mentally and physically."

"Then what happened?"

"I left the army and went into the loan business. I started my own mortgage company, in fact."

I try to picture him in a suit and tie, pushing contracts in front of people to sign.

"In the early 2000s, it was off the charts. We had more business than I knew what to do with. I worked twelve hours a day, seven days a week. I had no wife, no kids, and the only friends I had were like me—workaholics trying to close as many deals as possible before the bubble burst."

"So you knew it wasn't going to last?"

Chuck begins to cough again, and I hand him the glass of water off the table. He takes a long sip. "Did I know people were going to lose their houses? No. But did I believe a lot of the loans didn't make sense? Yes. Was I surprised at how easily the bank would approve them? Absolutely. But I'd built my entire life around it. And when you do that, sometimes you choose not to see what's going on right in front of you."

Is that what I did with Lance? Choose not to see? Did I stop crying my Mia tears to him because I sensed there was more he wasn't saying, so I closed down the topic entirely?

He grabs a tissue and blows his nose. "And then 2008 came, and people started losing everything."

I think back to that time. I'd recently graduated from college, and the economy was a mess. Mia and I had been dating for about a year. But thankfully, the fallout didn't affect her new job or mine.

My parents know people who were caught up in the refinance trap—taking out money based on the inflated equity in their homes. My mom and dad had been locked into their thirty-year mortgage for twenty years at that point and didn't take the bait. But they know people—a lot of people—who fell into the refinance-and-no-interest-loan trap. Some of their friends lost everything. My mom was so mad.

"So what happened next? How did you go from making money hand over fist to being on the street?"

"It wasn't overnight. It was gradual. First came the crash. Then loans came to almost a standstill. By 2009, my business was gone. I fell into a deep depression. My work had been my life. And it all disappeared."

"What about your family?" I ask, thinking again of my parents. No matter how badly I screwed up, they'd never let me hit the skids.

"My parents had passed in a car accident in the nineties. It was one of the reasons I joined the military after finishing college. I had no siblings. I felt alone."

"And so the soldiers became your family."

"Yes. But I'd lost touch with them all since unenlisting. I was so caught up in my own life. First I lost my business. Then my house. Then the depression set in and I couldn't function. I told myself being on the streets would only be temporary. But ten years later, here I am."

I touch Chuck's arm. "But why not—"

"Stop," he says gently. "I can think of a million things you were about to say. And yes, I probably could have figured things out. Gotten help. Called my old army buddies. Dominic, have you ever felt alone? Not, like, lonely once in a while. Have you ever experienced true loneliness?"

I think about the past six Thursdays. I've felt more alone than ever. But in the back of my mind, I've known that I'm not. That I have a whole network of people willing to help, if I'd let them. "No," I say, feeling sheepish that I ever thought I was truly lonely. That I ever thought I had the right to judge Chuck's past or any homeless person's past and the choices that landed them on the streets. "I haven't. I've always known I have a safety net."

"Right. But it's different for me. I've always struggled with depression, and when my world came crashing down, I couldn't get back up. And when you feel alone in this world, it literally feels like it's sitting square on your shoulders, preventing you from rising up again."

"I'm sorry," I say.

"For what?"

"For not asking about you earlier. For not caring enough. For everything."

"Better late than never," he says, his eyes smiling.

I get up. "I'm going to make you some chicken noodle soup the way my mom always made it for me," I say.

"That sounds amazing. Thanks for giving a shit. Most people don't."

I'm surprised to feel a bubble of emotion rise in my throat. "Well, I do," I say and walk out, gently closing the door behind me.

CHAPTER TWENTY-THREE

I'm heading out to the store to buy some ingredients for the soup, and it takes me a second to process who is standing outside my front door. It's Erik Tavares from our rival station, Channel Nine.

"What are you—" I stop midstride and start to ask him why he's here, but he interrupts me with a series of questions.

"Dominic, is it true you believe you are living the same day every day?"

"How did you know Amanda Bradford would be in danger?"

"Do you think you have psychic abilities?"

He throws questions at me like grenades.

I turn away from him, trying to assess the situation—how he knows. My breaths are hitching, and my skin tingles. When I turn back, he has his cell phone out, recording me. I stare at his stout frame, thinning hair, and beady eyes. I have to think fast. At this point, on this seventh Thursday, the only person I've told about the time loop is Amanda. And she must have gone to the press. A part of me is bummed that she'd sell me out, but then again, she doesn't know me the way I know her. That has to be the most frustrating part of all this—that I'm developing relationships with people, and they are none the wiser the next day. And then I have to build them back again. Although I have to believe the conversations linger, and the feelings aren't forgotten. Especially with Mia.

And of course Channel Nine took the bait. Who knows if Amanda called them first or last. All I know is the other stations would have told her to pound sand. It would be a nonstarter. But Erik would see this as an opportunity to discredit me.

"Believe everything you hear, Erik?" I say, puffing out my chest, though inside I'm nervous about where this is going.

He laughs. "Care to comment?"

"Nope," I say and start to push by him.

"Why aren't you at work, Dom?"

"What do you want?" I swallow hard.

"A comment on this thing you told"—he pauses and finds something on his phone—"Amanda Bradford after she says you saved her from being hit by a car this morning. And that you confessed to her you are reliving the same day."

"No comment," I say, my scalp prickling as I hear him say the words.

"So it's true, then, that you said it?"

"I have to go," I say, a wave of heat circulating through my body.

"Have you ever been diagnosed with any mental health issues?" He puts his phone in my face. The question makes my entire body tense. I am *not* crazy. I turn back to him. "Fine. You want to know how I knew she was going to get hit if I didn't pull her back from the curb?" I say, my voice high. "Let me tell you." I stare at the screen of his iPhone and tell my story, and then I give the guy verbal permission to use the video.

Maybe I am nuts after all. He could track down Mia. Ask her for a comment. But if Thursday arrives tomorrow, it will all be erased. It's both depressing and encouraging that, at this point, nothing really matters.

I rush back up to the condo and find Chuck asleep. I leave him a note that I had to go in to the station and there's food in the fridge. That I'll make him the chicken noodle soup as soon as I get back.

I begin to regret the interview with Erik as I drive in to work. The smug look on his face as he hit the end button on his recording. After I get to the station and park, I text Mia to cancel again, telling her something has come up and I'll need to reschedule. The frustration of not being able to save her is wearing on me. There's a numbness that has set in, a hopelessness that is beginning to haunt each thought. And the frustration I feel over what I learned from Lance is wearing on me. I need to regroup. Unlike when I canceled yesterday, she does not let me off the hook today. She tells me we need to talk. She admits that she saw Lance. She wants to see me. *Why?* I wonder. My heart spikes with the thought that somewhere inside of her may be a scrap of memory of the days we've spent together.

Regardless, I tell her I can't. I feel bad for letting her down, but it's for her own good. *Our* own good. Because I don't want to see her under these terms. I want to see her when it's about us, not about who lied to whom. Knowing what I know now will only help me when we go out on our date tomorrow. Because according to Lance, I don't know her now, and it's become clear I'm supposed to use what I learn on these Thursdays to get closer to her. What other explanation could there be for reliving them? As I walk into the station, the Channel Seven sign above the door is a reminder that I need to focus. The thought of her dying again tonight without me there makes it feel like my body is crumbling into itself, but I push it away, and I wish I could fast-forward to tomorrow and begin again.

CHAPTER

TWENTY-FOUR

JUNE 11, 2:30 P.M.
THURSDAY #7

I get a series of texts from Alexis as I'm entering the building. There is one that says: You gave an interview to our competitor? Another that says: You're reliving the same day??? WTF? And one that's a series of red-faced angry emojis and the words: come to my office immediately! I keep my head down as I enter the newsroom, passing a group of interns, who stare at me and then bury their noses in their phones as I walk by. Clearly they've seen the video of my interaction with Erik. I hear Alexis's sharp voice before I see her. "Dominic! Get your ass in here!"

I look around for Lance, but I don't see him. "Close the door behind you," Alexis says when I enter. She pulls something up on her computer screen and flips it around for me to view. Not surprisingly, it's the video Erik took of me.

"That's not my good side," I quip.

Alexis doesn't laugh. "What's going on?"

I throw my hands up. "I saved some girl from being flattened by a car on Seventh this morning, and now she thinks I know the future."

"You seemed pretty passionate and assured when you talked about being in a real-life *Groundhog Day* here." She plays the entire video.

Oops. I might have said that.

"Dominic. What's going on?"

Before I can answer, Alexis's assistant, Trent, pops his head in. "Channel Nine's Facebook post of the video has already received five thousand hits," he says, then glares in my direction. "And there's a *Groundhog Day* GIF."

"How?" Alexis asks as she rubs her temples.

"Erik has twenty-five thousand followers on Insta," Trent says.

"Another thing he's beating us at. How many followers do you have, Dom?" Alexis scrunches up her face.

"I don't have Instagram," I say, biting my lower lip. I don't miss Trent's smug expression.

Alexis pounds her fist on her desk, and I jump a little, realizing the weight of what I've set in motion. Understanding I didn't think things through.

"Dammit, Dominic. We are supposed to report the news. Not become a part of it! Especially by Channel Nine. They're doing this to embarrass us. To ruin our credibility. And it's working!"

"I'm sorry," I say. "He pissed me off by coming to my house like that."

"Why were you home and not here?"

"I was taking care of some things," I say, hoping she doesn't press me for details.

"Are you trying to get fired?"

"No, of course not!" I retort, panic rising, though I understand that tomorrow she won't remember this.

"Well, it gets worse," Alexis says, then pushes play on the video.

Amanda appears on the screen. She's no longer in that bandage dress. She's wearing jeans and a pale T-shirt, her hair falling past her shoulders. I watch as she recounts exactly what happened. How I saved her life. The things I knew. How I told her I was reliving the same day. How she can't explain why, but she believes me.

I smile, thinking of how she was unsure when I told her—she must have come around.

"Wipe that shit-eating grin off your face!"

"*She* believes me."

"She's obviously a quack!"

"Amanda is not a quack."

"How the hell would you know that? She said you didn't meet before today."

"Because of the time loo—"

"Stop!" she says, waving her hands in the air. "Don't you get how this looks? A news producer who's predicting car crashes? Says it's because he's trapped in a time loop like some bad eighties *movie*?" She blows out a long sigh through her puckered lips. "It takes away from what we're trying to do here. We have enough problems being accused of reporting fake news without one of our producers claiming he can predict the future!" Her lips curl. "I have to suspend you," Alexis says.

I stand to protest, and my chair falls over. "What the hell?" Yes, I will be gainfully employed here again in the morning with a clean slate, but it still stings to know that when things get sticky, she doesn't have my back.

"Calm down," she says.

"You want *me* to calm down?" Alexis starts to talk, but I cut her off. "Where's the loyalty? I've been here for a decade. And you suspend me so easily?"

"I need this to die down. And I think you should use the time to see someone who can help you."

I bristle at her insinuation. "Alexis—"

"I need you to go home. Now," she says and walks around her desk. "Don't make a scene."

I slam out of her office, making a scene anyway. So much for the ten years of dedication I've given Alexis. This station. Lance matches pace with me as I storm through the newsroom and past the set. He pulls me aside behind one of the cameras. "Dude, is what you said in the interview true?"

"Yes. Every damn word of it," I lash. "It's how I knew you were having lunch with Mia. Why I didn't blow a gasket that you'd kept in touch with her. I already knew. I flew to Chicago yesterday."

Lance blinks hard before answering. "That's impossible. You were here yesterday." He waves his hand around the studio. "During the tape piece about the semitruck overturning on the 163. You told me my tie had hot sauce on it, and I licked it off. Remember?"

"Yes, but that was a week ago!" I scrub a hand over my face, not wanting to explain this *again* but knowing that I have no other choice.

"You couldn't have been in Chicago . . . we went to Barleymash," he says, his tone uncertain.

"I know we did. But I flew to Chicago on *my* yesterday, which was the sixth Thursday, June eleventh, that I've repeated."

Lance turns away for a moment, gathering his thoughts, then pulls me into a side room. "Are you fucking with me?" he whispers.

"I wish I were," I say. "Listen, I have to go—Alexis wants me out of here. But I promise you it will all make sense at some point," I say more to myself than to him.

My phone rings as I walk out to the parking lot. It's my mom. I take a deep breath before answering.

"Hi, Mom."

"Dom! Are you okay? Someone sent me this nutty video! What's going on?"

Her voice is comforting—thick and soft, like the soft blanket she made for me three Christmases ago. "Nothing. I'm okay; don't worry."

"Then why would you say you are in a time loop? That's insane!" my mom shrieks, and I pull the phone away from my ear.

I decide it's easier right now if I lie to my mom. In the moment with Erik, it seemed like the time, to be honest. But that didn't go very well—I'm now suspended from my job, and my roommate is looking at me like I have two heads. And while it's true that Amanda believes me, that's probably only because she's a vital part of each day. And therefore possibly more open to trusting me about something so seemingly far fetched. Because somewhere, deep down, she knows it's happening to her too.

"It's not true. I don't think that. It's a long story, and I promise to explain everything later."

"Is it some sort of prank?" she asks, her voice hopeful.

"Yes. That's what it is, a prank." I squeeze my eyes shut as I say it.

"Praise God! I didn't know what I was going to say if you told me you believed that!" She laughs, the relief obvious.

"I know, right? You'd have to send me to an institution." I laugh awkwardly, but the thought sends a chill through me as I recall how I narrowly escaped being committed.

"I sure would. Straitjacket and all!" My mom laughs. "Dinner tomorrow night? I want to make sure you're okay."

"Sure," I say, suddenly feeling sad. Because I know we're not having that dinner tomorrow. And maybe we never will. Maybe I'll never escape today.

Worse, maybe I'll never find a way to save Mia.

～

I leave my car in the station's employee parking lot and walk four miles back home, wanting to be alone. It takes me two hours, but I enjoy the anonymity during my journey. On the crowded streets of San Diego, I'm simply another khakis-and-polo-shirt-wearing guy with somewhere to be. But the truth is that I no longer know where I belong. Before I got stuck in the same twenty-four hours, I was going through the motions every day, but at least I *knew* I could count on the motions to be the same. Within my control. It's taken time literally standing still for me to realize that I didn't have a clue what I was doing. That I didn't know anything about Mia. About Lance. About me. And that's the scariest part of all.

Once home, I tiptoe in to check on Chuck and find him asleep. The quilt pulled up around his chin, his breathing soft, as if he's finally found some comfort. Is this what he experienced when he lost everything? Did he feel like no one understood him? Like no one saw the world the same way he did? He spoke about everything weighing heavily on his shoulders. I feel that now, too—the heaviness almost too much to bear, the only bright spot when I picture Amanda's face as she looked into the camera and said she believed me.

My phone pings with a text from Mia. She's seen the video of me and is concerned. Would I please see her? We need to talk—especially now.

I turn my phone off and walk into my room, close the shades, and crawl into my bed. I block the thoughts of how Mia will die tonight and pull the pillow over my head to shut out the rest of the world until I fall asleep, not quite sure anymore where my place in it is.

CHAPTER

TWENTY-FIVE

I wake up at 5:30 a.m. in a full-blown panic. My ears ringing and my heart feeling like it might explode. My *eighth* Thursday has begun. I grab my phone and calculate. Seven days = 168 hours = 10,080 minutes. All that time, and I'm no closer to saving Mia. I have another blank canvas, but what the hell will I do with it?

I know one thing for sure: I won't be giving any interviews.

I wince at the thought of my video from yesterday but find myself smiling when I think of Amanda's, knowing I did some good. After seeing it, Lance texted me that I should be skeptical about her because she went to the press, that she was trying to get her fifteen minutes of fame out of it, but I didn't believe that. I think Amanda was genuinely happy she'd been saved and wanted to spread the word about the miracle she now considered her life to be. What I couldn't explain to Lance was that

I felt the same way. After watching Mia leave this earth multiple times, I have a new perspective on how fleeting life is.

I make a pot of coffee, pour myself a mug, and glance at the bar cart. "Why not?" I say to myself. I grab the bottle of Jack and pour some into the coffee. I step out onto the balcony and watch as the sun rises. Rays of light grow brighter until they light the entire sky. I walk to the railing and feel a shiver at the memory of Mia sitting there but shake it off. Today is a new start. A new chance. A new life. I observe the city below me as it comes to life. Trash is being collected, the claw from the truck grabbing each can, one by one. The street sweeper brushes the debris into the gutters. Men and women in suits are walking briskly as they grasp their stainless steel coffee mugs for dear life. Everyone is living Thursday, June 11, oblivious that they've done it seven times before. Déjà vu the only inkling that they have. But I am acutely aware of every minute of every Thursday that I've lived.

I sip the coffee and decide adding some Jack Daniel's is definitely the way to go. I should have listened to Lance seven Thursdays ago! My nerves are settling, and I'm suddenly clear on how to approach this day. I'm not going to do *anything* the way I've done it before. I won't save Amanda in person. I won't go in to the office or advise Lance to go to the editorial meeting. I will avoid my job and all aspects of it. No heads will be shaved. No tattoos will be inked. Everything will be different, if only slightly. But the one thing that will be undergoing a *major* change is my attitude. I will embrace Mia's carefree and, dare I say, risky approach to life. Every principle my mom taught me about being double careful or extra cautious will be thrown out the window in exchange for freedom. How blissfully free I will feel to not worry about Mia. I will lean into the person she is instead of fighting it, and hopefully I'll see the answer to saving her. I've been coming at this from the defensive. But today I'm going on the offensive.

I stand up and raise my arms toward the sky. "Thursday number eight, you are my bitch!" A woman on a neighboring balcony looks over and shakes her head—at my language or behavior, I'll never be sure. All I know is today, I don't mind being the person someone shakes her head at.

A plan begins to form, and I know exactly where I'll take Mia. I text her to make sure she's free to leave at nine a.m. She has to cancel her lunch plans, but she's in. I can't take Chuck to the urgent care clinic today, so I head into the kitchen and make him some hot tea with lemon and my mom's chicken noodle soup. I pour the tea and the soup into two thermoses, grab the Mucinex and a large bottle of water, and head downstairs. When I walk out, I find him in his usual spot.

I set everything down in front of him, and before he can speak, I tell him it's not charity; it's a neighborly gesture. "We are neighbors, technically." I point toward my building and smile.

He nods and says thank you.

I skip giving him money today because now that I know him better, I understand that he doesn't want to feel like my vanity project. So I ease in to the cash part of things. I have an idea on how I'm going to help him and can't wait to start putting my plan into place. But first, my focus is on Mia.

When I get back upstairs, I email Amanda about the accident she needs to avoid at the intersection of Seventh Avenue and K Street. I add all the other details I know about her and sign my name and wish her luck. She writes back immediately, WHO THE HELL IS THIS? For some reason, it makes me laugh so hard that I cry.

Lance walks into the kitchen and is wearing that same oxford shirt that I'm so sick of I could burn it. He asks me about the source who never showed at the coffee shop. We're back to having the conversation about work and his future there, and it feels a lot better than talking about how he hid his friendship with Mia for the past decade. To my surprise, Lance tells me he dreamed he should go to the editorial meeting this morning and impress Alexis. I tell him I think that's a great idea.

"Will I see you there?" he asks.

"Where?"

"The meeting?"

"No. I'm taking the day off."

"Oh?" He raises an eyebrow. I've never taken the day off. Never so much as called in sick—no matter how bad I felt.

"Mia and I are going to Palm Springs."

Lance gives me a look. I keep going before he can speak. "Got any plans today other than work? *Lunch date?*" I ask.

Lance shrugs. "Nope. I'll probably send an intern to grab In-N-Out."

Mia didn't invite him to Rustic Root. It's probably because I got to her first. Nice and early. This news gives me an abundant amount of pleasure.

He starts to walk toward the door, then stops. Here it comes. The speech about Mia. The lecture. "You sure you know what you're doing, Dom? With the exception of Tuesday, you haven't seen her since your *Say Anything* moment." He pauses, and I expect him to smirk or make a joke, but he doesn't.

"I'm aware," I say, the memory of me on her front lawn burned into my brain in a much different way now than it was then.

"You're sure spending an entire day with her so soon is the right decision?" He draws his eyebrows together. "Because the fair was a much better idea, I thought."

Of course he has no clue that I know why he's so concerned about where I'm taking Mia. I search his face for the secrets that Mia has confided about me. It's a burden. This information I have now. It makes it hard to take the people I have trusted for so long at face value. I do realize it's entirely possible that his protection of Mia is innocent—that he's only looking out for a friend.

"I don't know if this is the right decision. But it feels right. I want to spend time with her. I want to get to know her again. And what better way than in a long car ride?"

"I get it, but be careful," he says, giving me a long look before closing the front door behind him, heading out to live Thursday, having no idea how many times he already has.

~

I Uber down to San Diego Prestige, a luxury car rental company, and pick up the cherry-red Ferrari 458 Spider convertible I reserved on a whim this morning. The price tag hurts, but it will be well worth the cost if both Mia and I make it to tomorrow. And if we don't, it won't have cost me anything. I gun it up the 5 freeway to get Mia, the 540-horsepower engine in full effect. A number of people honk at me and give me a thumbs-up. I laugh and push the pedal down a little more, loving the sound of the engine. When I pull up to the bungalow, Mia, who is waiting outside in the driveway, squeals.

"Fancy!" She smiles as she slides into the lush leather seat. "I love convertibles. The whole wind-in-my-hair thing, you know?" I breathe out. *So far, so good.*

I've made a deal with myself that I'm not going to think about Mia's lie about not being in contact with Lance and her subsequent admission that she has been. My confusion over what she feels for him and what their relationship is has grown stronger than ever, but it's not my focus today. Instead, I plan to get to know her—*again*. I fire a ton of questions at Mia as we drive. I ask her about her favorite and least favorite foods (orange chicken and asparagus), best and worst places she's traveled (Costa Rica and El Paso—she got the stomach flu), and best and worst relationship (me to both.) She lobs the same ones back to me. We both try to guess if our tastes have stayed the same or changed. Not surprisingly, hers have evolved a lot more than mine. Each question leads into a fun discussion, and we are laughing more than we have yet. I'm on to something here, I think. We are passing the windmills on the 10 freeway, their large white blades spinning, when I ask her about her goals for the future. She stares out at the desert, and then back at me, her head tilted. "I'm trying a new approach," she says.

"What's that?"

"Living more in the moment. Not being so worried about what's around the corner."

"I like that," I say.

"You do?" She looks over at me, grabbing her hair so it stays out of her face.

"That seems weird to you?" I ask, holding the steering wheel with one hand, my other on the gear shift.

"Well, the Dom I knew, the one I was engaged to marry"—she raises an eyebrow—"he would not have been into that idea."

"True, but this guy right here"—I pat my chest—"this guy behind the wheel of this Ferrari, going a cool eighty miles per hour, *he* likes it."

"Duly noted." Mia smiles.

We pass a big rig, and Mia does the pulling motion to get the driver to honk his horn. He does. We laugh.

We pull into the parking lot of the Ace Hotel and Swim Club thirty minutes later. Like many resorts in this area, it is a kitschy throwback to the seventies and known for its pool parties in the summer. In the past, there was nothing Mia loved more than sipping a drink and meeting new people. It was as if she drew her own energy off those around her. I would sit back and observe, in awe of her ability to float from person to person with such ease. I felt proud that she could talk to anyone but had chosen me. I've brought her today so I can soak her in, the Mia she is now.

"You brought your swimsuit, right?" I ask as we step out of the car, the sun reflecting off its shiny hood.

She holds up her bright-yellow beach bag. "Yes, sir." She takes in the simple two-story building and colorful sign. I haven't told her yet that I reserved a room so we can stay overnight. It's not so I can rip her clothes off and go at it with her (not that I would mind it) but because

I'm hoping sleeping here, together, is part of the key to making it to Friday.

"I've heard of this place. They throw one hell of a pool party. The ski shots are legendary!"

"They are!" I say, having done a fair amount of research this morning while choosing where to take her. I wanted a place that screamed fun and reckless abandon. A place people would go to hide from the real world and let loose. According to the Yelp reviews, this was the spot. I give my keys to the valet and grab my bag out of the trunk. Mia eyes it. "I didn't want to be presumptuous, but I booked a room since we'll be drinking. But don't—"

Mia smiles. "Trying to get me into bed already?"

"No!" I put my hands up. "I swear. And we don't have to stay. It's just in case we drink too much to drive."

She gasps. "Drinking too much and losing control? Not the Dom I know."

"Maybe you don't know me anymore," I say. I mean it as a joke, but the truth of my words sits in the air as we walk into the lobby. I hand the clerk my ID, and she tells me the room won't be ready until four p.m.

After checking in, we follow the heavy beat of the bass coming from the speakers to find the pool. "Nothing like an all-day pool party to get to know you again," Mia quips as a well-built man in a bright-pink polo shirt hands us wristbands and towels.

There are tons of people in and around the pool holding colorful drinks and floating in bright-pink and yellow inner tubes. A DJ spins tunes in the background. Mia opens her arms up, almost as if she's embracing every single person in the pool. "I love this place already." She turns to me. "Thank you. This is exactly what I needed."

"Me too," I say and point to the bar. "Drink?"

"It's five o'clock somewhere, right?" Mia throws her head back.

My phone buzzes. It's Amanda. The subject line of the email reads: Psychic? She tells me she avoided the intersection at the time I told her, and then when she walked down to it a few minutes later, she found the aftermath of the exact accident I described. She asks if I can meet later for coffee. She wants to thank me in person, give me a proper hug. She looked me up, and I don't seem like a serial killer. Plus if I were one, I wouldn't have warned her she could die this morning. And she's sorry she was rude when I emailed earlier. But she gets a lot of weirdos writing to her. Then she writes that she's thankful a dozen times and tells me she's reevaluating her life. I quickly respond and tell her I'm out of town so I can't have coffee, that I am sort of psychic but it's a long story, and I'm glad she listened.

"Who's that?" Mia asks.

"Huh?" I look up from the screen.

"Who are you emailing so intently that you didn't even hear my question?"

"Sorry," I say and shove my phone in my pocket. "It's no one as important as you."

The bartender saves me from having to say more by choosing this exact time to make his drink recommendations. He tells us about his favorite, the Desert Facial, a bright-yellow drink topped with a mint leaf. I start to protest, to say that I'll take a beer, but then I remember my plan. Out with the old Dom, in with the new. Ten minutes later we've changed into our suits, I've put my phone in my bag so as not to be distracted, and we're floating in the pool, my foot hooked on Mia's tube so that she can't float too far away. Mia's wearing large sunglasses, an even larger straw hat, and a striped one-piece with cutouts that make it incredibly sexy. *Focus*, I tell myself. *You aren't here to have sex with Mia. You're here to save her life.*

The sun is beating down, and I move us into a shaded part of the pool to escape the heat. "Mia, why are you here?" I ask, the Desert Facial combined with the hot sun giving me the courage to ask.

"Because you asked me, silly," she says and sips her drink. Deflecting. Again.

"You know that's not what I'm asking you," I say. Her parents wouldn't tell me. Her friend Rob either didn't know or wouldn't tell me. If Lance knows, he hasn't let on. And each time I've asked before now, she's changed the subject.

Not today—we are floating and drinking these goddamn Desert Facials until I get some answers.

She doesn't reply for a few minutes, and I don't press, wanting to give her the time to tell me what she's thinking. "I missed it here," she finally says and reaches up as the server leans over to hand us another round of cocktails.

I down mine in two gulps, and a man wearing flamingo board shorts raises his glass. "Cheers, man," I call out.

Mia lowers her sunglasses to look at me. "Who are you, and what did you do with Dominic Suarez?" She laughs and then knocks back her drink too. "Things. Just. Got. Interesting," she says and wraps her foot around mine, pulling me closer. "I missed it here, but I also missed you."

"I've missed you too." My heart flutters at her touch. "We're just getting started," I say and signal the server. It feels good to step into the shoes of the man Mia always seemed to want me to be. To not worry about whether we are drinking enough water. Wearing enough sunscreen. To not obsess over how she may perish. It's possible that this may be the answer—that I need to live in the moment in order to move forward. And so I push any worries away. "Two more of these, please," I say to the server, then pull Mia in for a deep kiss, surprising us both.

She pulls away a minute later, and we sit there, nose to nose. "Why are you back, Mia?" I whisper. "Tell me."

Mia opens her mouth to speak, but before she can, we are drenched by a rotund man who cannonballs into the pool.

"Way to ruin the moment, dude," I joke, which conjures a smile from Mia. The server drops off our drinks, and we sip them as we float through the sea of people, the earlier moment gone. But I'm still giddy from the kiss. For once in my life I've stopped getting in my own way. And things are moving forward—Mia and I are having a great time. And I'm more relaxed than I've been since this all started. Maybe that is the lesson—to be more like Mia.

"Rescue Me" by Marshmello starts to play, and I pull Mia toward me. "I love this song. Let's dance," I whisper and kiss her again. Her mouth tastes like the Desert Facial—sweet and supple.

"Where?" she asks, looking around.

"There!" I answer, pointing toward a patch of concrete in front of the DJ booth.

Mia touches my forehead with the back of her hand. "Has the heat gotten to you? You hate dancing, especially if you are the only person out there!"

I navigate our floaties to the steps and hop out of the pool, then reach back for her. "You coming or not?"

She holds her hand out to me. I take it.

I'm pretty sure I'm dancing horribly, but for once in my life, I don't care. And I must admit, there is an adrenaline rush that accompanies that freedom. The not caring. Is this how Mia feels all the time? When she dances on tables or skydives or sings karaoke? If so, then I've been missing out.

People begin to join us on the makeshift dance floor, and we high-five them as they arrive. Soon the small area is so crowded that we've shifted back toward the pool. I take Mia's hands and spin her around, watching her beautiful face whirl past me several times. She squeals in delight. It takes me a millisecond to process when my sweaty hand slips from hers. I reach out to grab her back a beat too late. She starts to fall backward, her eyes wide, almost as if she knows what's coming. Images of our very first night on the Zipper flash through my mind, and I think

I see them also register in Mia's eyes. Could it be possible she remembers the sensation of this happening to her before? The people around us are still dancing and don't seem to notice as she hits the back of her head on the side of the pool and falls in. I dive in after her. I pull her out and set her on the concrete as I scream for help, my voice cracking in the desert heat. Tears flow freely down my face as I give her CPR, the last of the lyrics of the Marshmello song not lost on me as I try to rescue her. I realize as I pinch her nose and blow into her mouth that Mia has died again. But one major thing about this death is different.

This time, I was the one pushing us to take chances. To drink. To dance. I am to blame.

CHAPTER TWENTY-SIX

JUNE 11, 7:01 A.M.
THURSDAY #9

I have a master plan for my date with Mia tonight on this ninth Thursday. The theme? Complete and utter vulnerability. I'm so raw at this point that it won't be a stretch. My theory is that for us to move forward, I must put it all on the line—release any scrap of fear I have left.

But first, I need to check off my Thursday to-do list: Chuck, Lance, Amanda, the plane crash. I put on a T-shirt and a pair of jeans and head downstairs. Chuck is starting to set up in his usual spot. I can hear his rasp from several feet away, and a chill slices through me. No one cares about Chuck. They've forgotten him. They've forgotten that he fought for our country—something I only found out when we talked on the other Thursday. And I'm positive no one knows it was a few bad choices that any of us could have made that landed him on the streets. I realize I was one of those people before I started looking *at* him instead of *past* him. Because time has literally stopped for me. Now I can see. Not only

Chuck but myself. My loop has been a mirror. It's forced me to take a hard look at my shortcomings.

I hand Chuck the chamomile tea I brewed him this morning and the Mucinex. Our usual back-and-forth about why I'm helping him goes faster than ever because I know exactly what to say to convince him to go to the doctor. We get to the urgent care as the doors are opening. Today I take him to the one I've been to a few times rather than the free clinic. The last time I was here was when I'd come down with the worst flu of my life but was on deadline and refused to miss work, and I was impressed with the staff.

The medical assistant looks from me to Chuck as I sign him in. "We'll need his insurance card," he says, an air of superiority about him. His nose wrinkles enough that I can tell he's not into charity cases. "If he has one." He maintains eye contact with me, won't look at Chuck.

"I'll be paying cash," I say through gritted teeth and glance at Chuck, who is staring at the floor. So much for the impressive staff I remembered. As I sit here, I'm already mentally prewriting my negative Yelp review.

He darts his eyes to Chuck again, who is now wheezing. "It's going to be expensive."

I throw my American Express card on the counter. "Charge it to this," I say as I take my business card out and slide it toward him so he can also see where I work. It's not my usual style, but he's pissing me off. Maybe because his attitude reminds me of the one I used to have. "Any other issues? Or are you going to give this man some badly needed—expensive—medical care?"

He reads the card and swallows hard. "We'll call him back right away."

"Thank you," I say, swallowing my annoyance. Chuck and I sit side by side in soft blue chairs that feel like Barcaloungers compared to the ones at the other clinic. The look I saw on the medical assistant's face when he read my business card sparks an idea that I mentally log for later.

"Should we go? They obviously don't want me here," he says, with a small laugh that quickly turns into a coughing fit. An elderly couple who came in behind us glances at him nervously. I stare at them until they look away.

A few minutes later we are ushered into a room, and the physician knocks before opening the door. She introduces herself as Dr. Sheila Keys. She's a petite blonde with kind eyes who explains she completed her residency and fellowship at the Balboa Naval Hospital and the San Diego VA. She looks Chuck square in the eye as they chat briefly about his time in Iraq, and she thanks him for his service. She takes her time examining him.

"We'll need a chest x-ray to know for sure, but this looks like a bad case of pneumonia." She picks up her pad and begins to scrawl. "Maybe the beginnings of COPD."

"Antibiotic?" I say and reach my hand out for the prescription.

She draws her eyebrows together. "Chuck needs to be admitted to the hospital. We'll do the chest x-ray there."

"No!" Chuck cries out and tries to sit up. "No hospitals."

Dr. Keys touches his arm. "Chuck. You are very sick. You need IV antibiotics. We can't mess around with pneumonia." She turns to me. "I'm assuming he doesn't have a permanent place to stay?"

"I'm working on something permanent, but in the meantime he can stay with me."

Dr. Keys looks back and forth between us, probably trying to figure out our connection. "Okay, Chuck, here's what we're going to do. I'm going to secure a bed at the VA hospital, and we're going to make sure you get what you need."

"No!" Chuck flaps his hands.

I start to step in, but Dr. Keys gently pushes me away and leans toward Chuck. "I worked at that hospital for five years. I promise they'll take great care of you."

Chuck looks at me. "But my stuff?" he asks, his voice small.

"I'll continue to store it all for you," I say, reminding him it's safe in my locked storage unit, where we put it before we came.

"Are you sure?"

"Yes. I promise. Let the doctor help you. Let me help you. I know you ended up on the streets because you didn't have family to be your safety net." I pause, thinking of the way his face twisted when he said the words. "Let me be your family now."

Chuck's eyes brim with tears. "How did you know?" he asks, because, of course, he doesn't remember that conversation.

"Trust me, okay?" I say, and he nods.

"For some reason, I do." He smiles, revealing the missing teeth, and I fight the urge to hug him.

I nod to Dr. Keys to get the ball rolling on his admission.

An hour later, Chuck is settled in his hospital bed at the VA with the promise that I'll be back in the morning.

≈

I have to sprint the last block to the intersection where I know Amanda will be standing. She's already taking her first step off the sidewalk, and I am running so fast that when I grab her, we both fall onto the safety of the concrete behind us as the Toyota Camry crashes into the bus.

"What the—"

"I didn't mean to knock you over." I stand, then help her up.

She stares at the steam rising from the Camry's engine. "The way you came running at me. You knew that car was going to hit me. But how?"

I take in her narrowed eyes, her small, pointed nose, and I hug her. She starts to resist, but then she leans into me. "Thank you," she breathes into my ear.

When I pull back, I look at her. "I had a bad feeling," I say, glancing at the airbag deployed in the front seat of the Camry, its driver sitting next to it on the street.

"Well, I'm thankful for your bad feeling!" Amanda smiles. "I was a little out of it this morning and wasn't paying attention." She pauses. "Late night, as you can see. Too much right swiping."

I've grown to love her smile. It never gets old. Then I can't help myself, and I caution her again about Tinder and snoring douchebags.

"How did you know?"

"Studies show most guys on Tinder snore loudly," I joke.

"Is that so?" She pokes me playfully, in a way people do when they're familiar with each other. And I wonder if subconsciously she knows me more than she realizes. Then she pulls out her business card and hands it to me. "If you need anything—or want to give me more advice on bad dating apps . . ." She trails off.

I look at her card, and an idea forms. I tell Amanda and ask her if she can help.

"Anything for you," she says. After we make plans and say goodbye, I go back over my checklist.

Help Chuck—check. (Although I still need to break the news to Lance that Chuck will be staying with us until I can find him something permanent, but that can wait until I make it to tomorrow.)

Save Amanda. Check.

Now I need to make sure that Cessna doesn't take off from Palomar Airport. The last nine Thursdays I haven't put much effort into this one—left a message and moved on when I could have done more. But no one has been hurt. No one has died. It hasn't seemed significant. But maybe it is? And I'm not taking any chances today. I have to get it right.

I duck into a liquor shop a few blocks down and grab a Smartwater and a burner phone. I dial the number for Palomar Airport. I wait as it rings, hoping I can get a live person on the phone. After pushing zero several times, I finally do! I clear my throat nervously. There's no easy way to tell someone you've hidden a bomb at their workplace. She doesn't say anything, so I repeat myself. I don't want to stay on the phone for too long, so I deepen my voice and tell her how serious I am and then hang up. I toss it on the blacktop and crush it into a million little pieces with my foot.

That should ensure no flights take off from that airport for most of the day. Hopefully that will be enough. I leave the alley and insert myself into a crowd of oblivious people heading to work. To school. To brunch. All of them having no idea how determined I am to get us to tomorrow.

CHAPTER
TWENTY-SEVEN

I head back to my place and get into my car. I turn the radio on as I pull out of the parking garage and listen for the news report I'm hoping to hear—that Palomar Airport is shut down.

I get to the station a little before the nine a.m. editorial meeting. Lance is already there. I open Lance's office door and shut it behind me. He doesn't look up from his computer. "Palomar Airport is shut down. Bomb threat."

"Really?" I say. "Is it legit?"

"They don't know yet, but they've grounded all flights."

I exhale. Item number three is handled.

"Should we do a story on it?" he asks.

"Yes, get over to the editorial meeting and pitch it."

"It's weird you say that—that's why I'm here so early. I had planned on going."

"Good. Because Devon will be there."

"How do you know that?"

"I have my sources," I say, and he laughs. "I also want to talk to you about a piece I want to do."

"I'm listening."

"I want to educate the public about homelessness." I tell him about Chuck and my experience with him at the urgent care. What I learned about his past.

Lance nods, but his expression is tight. "I feel like this has been done before."

"Maybe. But they haven't done it right. I'm talking about humanizing the homeless population. They aren't all drug addicts and alcoholics. Chuck owned his own mortgage company! And he served our country, but he isn't on the streets because of PTSD. Think of all the others we could find. People who had productive lives and simply fell from grace and couldn't get back up. Who didn't have families, safety nets. Not to mention the angle of how these people are treated because no one really looks at them. It will be a multipart series that starts with Chuck. You should have seen the way the medical assistant looked at him. Like he was trash that didn't deserve proper medical care. It was disgusting. They're human beings too. With past lives. Stories. Like you or me."

Lance purses his lips. "I like this angle. But you'll have to convince Alexis."

"You mean *we'll* have to convince Alexis."

"You don't need me to pitch. Get her on board, and then we'll talk."

"I want you in there with me," I say, and I can tell by his face that he's touched by this. "*We'll* tell Alexis the goal is for people to see the homeless as human beings. If we do this right, it could mean Emmys for both of us," I add, although that is not my motivation. But I need to get Lance on board. Regardless of what he kept from me about Mia, I don't want to do the series without him. We've both lost our way a bit over the past few years. Let the news cycle numb us to the real struggles of others. And because of that, we've also lost our edge. Lost the part of ourselves that wanted to use our platform to do good things. But if I've learned anything, it's that I want to make change. And Chuck is the perfect place to start.

Lance still hasn't agreed.

"Have you ever talked to Chuck?" I ask.

"No, but neither have you. Until today. What's bringing this on, anyway? Is this about Mia?"

"It is, but not in the way you think."

"What do you mean?"

I pause. "Sit down," I say and point at his chair. "This may take a while."

Lance's jaw hangs open when I finish the story. I left nothing out—I detailed each day, almost breaking down when I told him about Mia dying at the pool in Palm Springs. A happy ending had felt so close that day. As if I could reach out and touch it.

His eyes are watery too. "This is all so haunting—I can't believe she is dying over and over. It's so awful." He puts his head in his hands.

"Try being there," I say.

"I'm really supposed to believe this? Do you have any proof?"

"I do, but Lance, it's not about that. This is about needing you to be there for me. I've never lied to you—not once." I stop. "Wait, one time—when I told you that purple pin-striped suit worked." I stare at the ceiling, the weight of the past eight days crushing me. There are so many parlor tricks I could perform to convince Lance—predict today's entire news lineup or tell him I know he has lunch plans with Mia. That they've been in touch. That he is the one who told me. There's Brian the audio guy and his girlfriend—the story he's told only me. But I don't have the energy. What I'm realizing now is I need my best friend to simply trust me. So I tell him as much.

"I want to, Dom. But think of it from my point of view. What you're describing is impossible." He stops, thinking for a moment. "It's so strange. I'm having déjà vu right now."

"It's not déjà vu. We've had this conversation before."

He rubs his face. "Really?"

"Yes," I say, then look him in the eyes. "I need you if I'm going to make it to tomorrow. If you don't do this for me, do it for Mia. She needs you too."

He doesn't respond right away, but his face tells me he understands. Then he says, "No, Dom, I'll do it for you."

"You will?" My heart leaps. Because we need to tell Chuck's story. Today.

"Yes. But I'd better get a damn Emmy out of it!" he quips. "I'm kidding," he adds when he sees my face fall. "You're right. You've never asked me for a damn thing."

"So you believe me?" I ask.

"Is it all right if I say I don't need to? I have faith in you, and that's enough."

I nod. It is. "You don't think I'm demented?"

"I do. But you're my best friend. So I'm going to be demented with you." He slaps my shoulder. "So let's get our asses to Friday. Because we all know it's always been a much better day than Thursday!"

"TGIF!" I say, and we high-five. "Thank you."

"Let's get to work," he says and opens his laptop.

I look at the time. It's almost nine. "First, go to the editorial meeting and impress Alexis. There's a shark-attack story she'll be into after you pitch the bomb scare," I say and don't miss his eyebrow rising. "I'll start with vetting Chuck's story." Before I left the hospital, I asked Chuck for his full name—Charles Samuel Dunguard—his Social Security number, his last known address, and any information about his military service he could provide.

Thirty minutes later I'm on a roll with my research, and a very happy Lance is back from the meeting. Alexis was pleased, not only that he came but with his pitches. Lance also couldn't help but notice and take a certain amount of pleasure that Devon sulked in the corner.

And two hours later, we've been able to verify Chuck's story—records of his military service and of his mortgage company and its ensuing bankruptcy. My chest feels heavy as we confirm his spiral from the top of the world to the streets. I had hoped to find some living relatives, but my searches came up short.

"I can't believe it," Lance murmurs. "He had it all."

I think about this for a moment. "But did he? Yes, he had money, but no family. I can't find a single person. No real friends—he said he lost them all when he went bankrupt." I shake my head. "From my vantage point, he didn't have much of anything. Because if you don't have people you can trust, who you can count on at rock bottom, you have nothing."

Lance looks over at me, his face tight. "There's something I need to tell you. About Mia."

I try to keep my face neutral but fail.

"You already know, don't you?" he asks.

"Do I know you've kept in touch with her all these years and that you have lunch plans with her today at Rustic Root? Yes. I do."

Lance's face goes slack. "*Had* lunch plans," he says, glancing at his phone. "I told her I was working on a really important story." Lance twists his chair so he's facing me. "Dom, I want you to know that nothing is going on—nothing has ever gone on. It isn't like that. I promise you."

"We had a fight about it several Thursdays ago, and I wasn't sure if I believed you, but I've had some time to think about it, and I trust you. I still feel weird that you were in contact with her and I didn't know it, but that's my penance to pay. You guys were friends too. But I do appreciate you telling me on your own today—or wanting to."

Lance looks down. "When we fought, did we talk about why she's back?"

A shiver rolls down my spine. "No."

"You should ask her."

"I have. She's evasive."

"Ask her again," he says as his phone pings. "We have clearance to film at the VA in Chuck's room. And there are several replies to the Facebook post asking if anyone knows someone in a similar situation that we can use as follow-ups." He stands. "Let's pitch Alexis and grab a camera crew."

I nod, but my mind is reeling. It's become clear that in order to move on, there are things about Mia I need to uncover, specifically the reason she's back. As we march into Alexis's office, I hope I can find a way to get Mia to trust me enough to tell me.

"This is quite a departure for the two of you." Alexis pulls her glasses off and sets them on her desk, which has papers strewed across it. "What's bringing this on?"

"Does it matter?" I answer. "It's a good story. And one that needs to be told. Have you walked downtown lately?" I press, knowing Alexis jumps onto the freeway each day and heads to her cushy Mission Hills neighborhood. "The homeless problem in this city is growing. And until our community leaders and the public truly understand the why of it, there won't be any real solutions."

"So what's the solution, then?" Alexis fires back.

"Jesus, Alexis, I don't know! This isn't a simple problem, and it's not going to be fixed overnight," I assert, and her eyes grow wide. Lance nudges me and moves his hand up and down to signal I need to calm down. But I don't want to calm down. I'm tired of not caring. I'm sick of playing it safe. Of not doing the right thing because it's not what's best for me. "Listen," I continue, lowering my voice. "These people have been forgotten. So yes, it's going to be a great story with legs, and that's why you should approve it. But you should also say yes because we have a chance to make real change. And at the end of the day, isn't that why we're here?"

Alexis stares at me, saying nothing for several seconds. I sit perfectly still. "Dom, I have no idea what's gotten into you—"

"Alexis—"

She raises her pointer finger. "Stop. What I was going to say is that I have no idea what's gotten into you, but I like it. This is the passion I've been looking for. This is what we need to get back on top."

"And it's also the right thing to do," Lance adds with a smile.

Alexis waves her hand. "Yes, that too." She pushes some papers around her desk. "Take Brian and the backpack to the hospital. I want to air something on the six p.m., so you'll need to get moving." She sets her glasses back on the edge of her nose. When we don't move, she shoos us. "Go!"

~

An hour later we've gotten what we need with Chuck and the VA. "That was solid," Lance admits as we walk out the glass doors into the blinding sun. Chuck was great on camera, telling his story with equal parts humor and heart. I think I saw Lance tear up at one point.

Brian, who shot the footage, nods. "I feel like an asshole. I've always assumed they're all drug addicts."

I put a hand on his shoulder. "Some of them are. But I think the lesson here is that we can't give up on them. That we can all do better." I glance at the time on my phone. "Lance—" I begin.

"Go," he says. "I'll get it produced."

"But Alexis—"

"I'll handle her. Don't worry, dude. I still remember how to work the Avid. And this is something I care about. I'll make sure it's perfect for six o'clock." He pulls me in for a hug. "Thank you."

"For what?" I ask when he pulls back.

"For helping me give a shit again. Now go get your girl," he says. "And I'll see you Friday morning."

CHAPTER

TWENTY-EIGHT

June 11, 3:30 p.m.
Thursday #9

The ocean that meets the San Diego harbor shimmers like glass in the sunlight. The comforting presence of the sun has been one of the few constants on every Thursday—the glowing bulb rising in the east and setting in the west. No matter what happens to me or to Mia, I know I can count on a cloudless bright sky.

A fish jumps from the sea and does a flip before diving back in. I stare at the disrupted water, wondering if it's a sign. Or maybe it's exactly what it appears to be—a fish jumping out of the water. I'm so turned around at this point that it's hard not to read into every little thing. To not see the most unremarkable happening as a signpost.

"Dominic?" I turn and see Amanda standing on the dock to my right. She's wearing a conservative cardigan and striped sundress that tickles her knees as she walks toward me. The only thing that gives her late night away is the messy bun atop her head. I give her a tight hug when I reach her, and she shoots me a quizzical stare. She has no idea the history we have. No clue that she's played a large part in shaping these nine Thursdays. That she's helped me in a way she'll never understand. Amanda and I begin to walk, the dock ahead of us. I've known for several Thursdays that she does all the public relations for Hornblower, a large company that charters a fleet of impressive yachts, but this morning when she asked how she could repay me, I had a vision of Mia and me out on the ocean. Alone. And so I asked Amanda if she could arrange it.

"You really are a hugger, aren't you?" she says as we walk.

I shrug. I wouldn't have described myself that way before, but now I understand that life is short. That you can't take for granted that you'll see someone again.

"It's okay. So am I!" She checks something on her phone. "So, I had to call in several favors to make this happen," Amanda says now. "You don't seem like a grand gesture sort of guy."

"What?" I ask, surprised by her comment. Because she's right. I'm not.

"I didn't take you for the romantic type."

"But we've only recently met," I lie.

Amanda chews on a cuticle. "Right. But for some reason I feel like I know you. Is that weird?"

"Not at all," I say lightly. "But for what it's worth, you're right. I'm not into this kind of stuff."

"So then why the pomp and circumstance?" She points at the sleek blue-and-white yacht to our right.

"Long story," I say.

She presses her lips together, and I wait for a quip, but it doesn't come. She directs her attention to the boat. "Well, regardless, there she blows," she says and motions toward the yacht. "It's the *Newport*. Captain Emert and eighty-five feet of pure luxury, at your service."

"She's perfect," I say.

She taps her watch. "I could only get you an hour. I hope that's okay. There's a private cruise booked at six o'clock, and it needs to be back to be stocked and serviced prior."

"That's all I need."

"Hey, before you go, I want to say thank you again for this morning. I'm not sure this boat favor is a fair exchange for saving my life."

"You're welcome. And you don't have to do anything to repay me. This is more than enough."

"How did you know that car was coming? And the other details about where I'd been, the douchebag, the snoring?" Amanda cocks her head. "It's been eating at me all day. And please don't tell me you had a bad feeling. Or that it's a long story."

I take a deep breath. Mia will be here any minute. I want to confide in Amanda. Tell her everything. So I do. All of it, including how I haven't been able to save Mia. And this time I make her promise to keep it between us.

"Wow," she says, chewing her nail again. She catches me watching her. "Sorry, bad habit. When I'm nervous."

"Do you think I'm losing my mind?"

"I can't explain it, but no. I don't. And now I understand why I feel like I know you. Because apparently I do."

"You do," I insist.

She's quiet for a moment. "What if you haven't been able to save her because you've been saving me? That maybe you only get one chance to save a life, and you've used it up on mine?"

The notion hits me in the gut. That the universe would make me choose between two lives. I shake my head. "I can't believe that—that I can't save you both."

"Because you truly think you can, or because you don't want to decide who lives and who dies?"

"Both," I conclude, doubt swirling in my stomach. I push it away and cling to the faith that I can do it all—save both Amanda and Mia and move forward to Friday.

Amanda reaches out and grabs my hand. "I hope you can save her tonight." She pauses. "But if you don't, I'll understand if you don't save me tomorrow."

I start to protest, but she presses her pointer finger to her lips, and I close my mouth. We stand in silence, holding hands. A seagull calls out, and we both turn to look out to the ocean; the only sounds we hear are the harbor waves as they slap against the yacht. I almost feel like I can hear Amanda's heartbeat in the wind.

"Hello?" Mia's voice breaks the spell between us. I pull my hand away and swivel to see Mia, who is frowning at us. "What's going on?"

I shake my head. "Nothing. I was thanking Amanda for setting up your surprise."

"Yes. You certainly looked grateful," she inserts sharply.

Mia is jealous. Despite myself, my heart does a small leap. It means she's invested. That she cares—maybe more than I realized.

Amanda steps between us. "He saved my life this morning. I was almost hit by a car. Dominic pulled me out of the way."

"More like tackled you," I quip, and we laugh.

"Wait. What?" Mia asks.

Amanda explains in detail what happened at the intersection and that she was holding my hand because she got caught up in thanking me again for saving her.

Mia touches my arm. "Sounds like you're a hero!" Her tone has shifted. It's now light and airy. She likes when I do the unexpected, and, I realize, so do I.

My arm warms to her touch. "Not really," I say. "I was in the right place at the right time."

"No, she's right. It's heroic." Amanda smiles that smile. It's contagious.

"I'm happy you're okay."

"Me too," she says, and we share a look.

I gesture toward the majestic boat. "You ready?" I ask Mia.

"Always," she says, leaning close to me. I'm not sure if it's because of Amanda, my earlier bravery, or her excitement to cruise the harbor. Whatever the reason, her ease with me makes me grab her hand and lead her to the dock. I glance over my shoulder and smile at Amanda, who is still watching us.

～

"Is this really necessary?" Mia tugs on the bulky red life vest as the *Newport* slowly pulls out of the harbor, the captain at the helm. I insisted we both wear them.

Amanda rolled her eyes when I asked her earlier to have them available. "You're cute but also very odd," she observed. But to her credit, they were sitting on the bar waiting for us when we boarded.

"What are you talking about? These are all the rage right now. Life vest fashion!"

Mia laughs. "It clashes with my romper, but whatever."

Amanda has set up a single table with two chairs on the sundeck. A bottle of Veuve Clicquot sits unopened in a sterling silver wine bucket. I point to it. "May I?"

"I thought you'd never ask!" She smiles and watches me as I pop the cork, both of us jumping slightly at the sound.

I pour two glasses and hand her one. "To new beginnings," I announce, and we both sip. I'm sure she thinks I'm referring to us. But my toast is a nod to the universe. I'm asking for Friday. Begging. I'm ready to be free.

Mia walks over to the railing and leans against it. Her hair flies in the breeze as the boat picks up speed. The afternoon light hits her face perfectly. Her freckled shoulders reflect the sun.

I've realized that I may never love anyone the way I love Mia. I love her in that desperate way you do when you lose something and fight like hell to win it back. I love her in a way that transcends time and place. "What?" she asks when she catches me staring at her.

"I want you to know how much I've changed."

She looks me up and down, and I know what's coming next. I didn't change my wardrobe for her today. I dressed the way *I* wanted to dress. "I beg to differ on that. Still wearing your shirt tucked into pants and buttoned up to here." She tugs at my collar. "Same haircut. If you tell me you still have a flip phone, I'm going to scream!"

I pull out my iPhone. "No need to get hysterical. I may not have changed much on the outside—which I would like to argue is a good thing—but I have advanced technologically."

"I'll be the judge of that." She grabs my phone and scrutinizes it. "Password, please."

"So soon?"

She laughs.

"Eight seven one six nine four," I say.

"What are those numbers?"

"Totally random," I say.

"Really?"

"Yep. You can never be too careful."

"Aha!" she says, and I instantly realize my mistake.

"No! Wait." I laugh. "Cybersecurity doesn't count."

"Anyway," she says, then asks me again for the numbers she's already forgotten and types them into my phone. It springs to life, and she starts scrolling through. "No Instagram. No dating apps. Not even Pinterest."

"I think if I had Pinterest, it would be concerning," I deadpan.

"Hey, never underestimate the ability to get an appetizer recipe or a costume-party idea at a moment's notice!" She laughs, but it gets a little lost in the sound of the motor. "My point is, back in the day you were resistant to new things. And it seems like you still are," she says.

"I have Facebook!" I argue.

"When was the last time you updated your status?"

"Oh, I've never done that. I use it to be a voyeur into other people's lives."

"Like mine?"

"Like yours."

"Learn anything interesting?"

I shake my head. "Only left with more questions."

"Me too—about you."

"Me? Really?"

"How do you think I know you don't update your statuses?"

I'm not sure why it's so hard to believe that she would have wondered about me. Lance told me she'd asked early on, and then he said she'd stopped.

"What do you want to know?"

"You said you've changed on the inside. I want to hear." She leans forward. "I'm having a serious case of déjà vu right now. Like we've had this conversation before."

"Really?"

"Are you having it too?"

I nod. *If you only knew.* But I also feel a spark of hope. Lance, Amanda, and now Mia have all experienced it. It must mean I'm close to breaking free.

"Anyway, sorry, that was just really weird. So tell me what's on your mind. How are you different, Dom?"

"It's not so much how I'm different, because to be honest with you, I'll probably always be the guy who looks both ways before crossing the street." I think back to Mia's getting hit by the car in her sister's neighborhood. Of all the ways she's died. No matter how many precautions I've taken, I haven't been able to prevent tragedy. It's forced me to realize that you have to live, regardless of fear. But to Mia, I say, "But what I have now that I didn't have when you knew me is perspective."

I tell her everything heartfelt I've told her on the other Thursdays. But I also add one important detail that I haven't said before. I'm taking a huge risk, but I can't hold back now. If this is going to be the night that will make the difference, then I have to tell her *everything* that's in my heart. "I still love you, Mi."

"Wow," she says and turns toward me, her eyes soft and glistening. "I don't know what to say."

Say you love me too.

"You don't have to say anything. I know it's out of the blue. But I figured, Why hold back? It's how I feel, right? The worst that can happen is you can tell me to turn this boat around."

"I'm not going to do that." We watch a seagull swoop down in front of us as we sip our champagne. "But Dom, how could you still feel that way? We were so long ago." She thinks for a moment. "You said it's always been me, but haven't you . . . hasn't there . . . been anyone else?"

I shake my head, trying not to be dissuaded that she doesn't reciprocate. *Stay vulnerable,* I remind myself. "I haven't been celibate—"

She holds up her hand. "TMI."

"Sorry! But what I mean is, I've dated. But it's never come close to what we had," I say.

She nods as if she understands. So I ask, "What about you? Have you been serious with anyone?"

"I have," she says, then adds, "I was engaged."

I stifle a gasp, my skin tingling. Is that why she's back? Is that what Lance wanted me to find out?

"Engaged?" I repeat the word, trying to mask the painful tightness in my throat as I say it.

"Yeah," she says, her voice flat. I wonder if it makes her sad to think about it.

"But?" I ask, my mouth dry.

"But it didn't work out."

My heart soars, but I keep my face expressionless. "Why not?" I ask, then add, "If you don't mind me asking."

"He wasn't you."

I'm stunned that she's admitted this. I raise an eyebrow.

"Don't get that look!" She points at me.

"Well, I am a hard act to follow."

"I can't believe I'm telling you all this." She puts her hand over her face.

"I'm glad you are." I pull her close, our life vests bumping awkwardly. "I'm happy to be here. With you."

"Dom," she whispers.

"Shhh," I say. I'm tired of trying to navigate the complications of who we were. Of who we've become. She has no idea how many times I've apologized for what I did. For who I was. I mean, maybe subconsciously she does. I think back to the many conversations we've shared on our Thursdays and attempt to articulate the words that will convey what she needs to hear. That will help us move forward.

"I'm sorry. And I've changed. And I'm sure you've changed, too, in so many ways. I know it will take more than one night and a romantic boat ride to fix what happened, but I think us running into each other is a sign, and now that I understand that, I can't rest until I do everything I can to save us." I'm out of breath as I say the last words. I inhale and continue. "Do you want to? Save us?"

She stares at me. "That's quite a speech," she whispers, almost to herself. "Especially when we've only had half a glass of champagne." She laughs softly.

"You haven't answered the question," I push.

"I think it's more complicated than that."

"Say yes, and we'll figure out how to uncomplicate us."

She looks out to the water and then back to me. "Yes," she breathes, her skin flushing, her lips parting.

Hearing this makes all of my senses burst like in a kaleidoscope. My breath quickens. My nerve endings tingle. I kiss her. Softly at first, like it's a question I'm asking. She takes her hand and cups my chin and pulls me in close, and our embrace intensifies. I can taste spicy bubbles of champagne on her tongue. We stay like this for a few minutes, making out as the boat rocks side to side as it heads out to the open ocean, where we will all be free.

"Dom," she says again when we pull away. The sun is lowering. A wind has kicked up. Her arms are covered with goose bumps. I rub them possessively. "What if—"

I put my fingers to her lips. "Shhh. We only have an hour out here. Let's enjoy it. Reality can come later," I plead. Because I know better than anyone that it's going to take more than a romantic speech and a kiss on a yacht to make this work. We have ten years of separate experiences. A decade of regrets and resentments. I know this. But there is still love here. It's like a fire that appears to be extinguished but roars back to life when blown on. We are that fire.

Mia runs her hand through my hair, surprised. Because the Dom she knew cared a lot about reality. He didn't make romantic speeches. He anguished over every detail, not wanting to make a mistake. But he made mistakes anyway. Because that's life. No matter how much preparation you do, you'll never be truly prepared. I know that now. And I need Mia to understand I'm not the same person who walked away from her ten years ago.

"You know what? You're absolutely right. Who needs reality?" Mia says, and she grabs me by the neck and pulls me back into her.

CHAPTER

TWENTY-NINE

JUNE 11, 4:00 P.M.
THURSDAY #9

"By the way, you got a little jealous back there," I say as the boat blazes back toward the harbor. Mia and I are leaning against the railing, our faces pointing into the wind. I'm still flying high from the kiss—it's as if an electric current is buzzing through my veins.

"Of Amanda?" Mia asks, holding her hair away from her face. Her cheeks are coloring, but I'm not sure if it's from embarrassment or the cold.

"Was there another woman I don't recall?" I poke her in the side, and she turns.

She lets out a nervous laugh. "Maybe. I guess after I ran into you and you asked me out, I took it as a sign that we might still have something between us. And then I saw you holding hands with this beautiful woman, and my heart froze. All that bravado vanished. It made me feel like maybe I was being naive to think . . ." She trails off.

"Think what?" I press.

"That this is meant to be, after all."

I grab her and pull her into me, feeling her hot breath on my neck. "It is," I say into her hair. I say it over and over until she pulls her head up to mine and kisses me softly in response.

She pulls back a few moments later and plays nervously with the ends of her hair. "And this is going to sound strange, but that déjà vu I mentioned earlier is still with me. This all seems familiar. Like we haven't been apart."

"That's not strange at all," I say with a sly smile.

She lets go of her hair and moves back so she can look me straight in the eye. Goose bumps rise on my arms.

Mia chews her bottom lip. "Do you ever worry we've wasted so much time already? Ten years, lost."

"I don't see it that way." I think back to the tidal waves of infinite sadness and joy as I lost Mia only to find her again over and over this past week and a half. If anything, it has taught me that nothing is guaranteed. "I think that no matter what's happened in the past, we're here now. And we should make the most of each moment moving forward," I say and pull her close, inhaling her sunflower scent.

"But you don't know me, Dom," she whispers back. "Not anymore. And this is nice"—she waves her hand around—"but we can't jump right in after a decade."

"I know that. But for tonight let's pretend we can," I plead. I've done every single thing I can to save Mia. To save this day. And in this moment I want to enjoy every second with her.

"Okay," she agrees. "For tonight."

~

After we dock, Mia heads to the restroom, and I pull out my phone. I've purposely avoided my mom for several loops—six of them, to be exact. After the way she laughed with relief when I lied and told her I didn't mean what I'd said to Erik at Channel Nine about the time loop, I moved on from the thought that had been in the back of my mind—to tell her everything. I've always told my mom everything, so it felt strange to avoid her during the most critical time in my life. But she also has a way of seeing right through me like I'm merely a pane of glass. But now, I'm so buoyed (pun intended!) by my conversation with Mia that I can't wait to tell her.

"Dom!" she exclaims. "I've missed you."

"Mom, it's only been two days."

"It feels like longer," she says, and goose bumps sprout up on my arms. Does everyone have the sense they've been stuck in this Thursday? Maybe to them it's more a feeling. Something they can feel but can't quite touch.

"Dom?"

"I'm here. Sorry. I know; I've missed you too. I have something I need you to know," I say, glancing toward the restrooms. Wanting to get this out before Mia comes back.

"You can tell me anything."

"I hope that's true," I say, thinking of how adamant she's been that I get over Mia, not get back together with her. I could wait to tell my mom until I safely make it to Friday, but something tells me that she's part of this. That her knowing—and accepting—is a piece of the puzzle I need to solve.

"What does that mean?" she asks.

"It's about Mia."

My mom sighs.

"Mom, please, listen."

"Okay."

"I still love her, and I told her so. And hopefully we're going to give it another try. I made a mistake ten years ago, and I'm not going to make it again. She's the love of my life. Always has been. She's perfect for me. And I need that to be enough for you."

"Are you sure this is what you want? What *she* wants?"

I flash to our conversation on the boat. How she saw our reunion as a sign. "Yes," I say.

"Dom. If this is what you want, I'm happy for you. But I want you to be careful. Not painting her to be perfect. Don't get me wrong—she's a nice girl. But no one is perfect."

Perfect. The word jolts me slightly. But then I spy Mia walking toward me, and I wave. When she smiles, my heart swells. What's wrong with thinking the person you love is perfect? We will have the rest of our lives to discover each other's blemishes. I think back to the seashell on the beach the day I proposed. Am I making the same mistakes? Putting Mia on a pedestal, and it's only a matter of time until she falls? Until we fail?

No, I decide. She was brought back here for a reason. And I'm meant to save her. And that means saving us as well. "Can I bring her over in the next couple of weeks?" I ask.

"Of course," my mom says brightly, but I can hear the hesitation in her voice. I don't blame her. She needs time. And then she will understand I'm ready.

"I have to go—talk soon, okay? I love you."

"I love you too."

I hang up as Mia is approaching.

"Who was that?"

"My mom."

"How is she?"

"She's good."

"What were you guys talking about?"

"You," I say and grab her hand. "I told her you are madly in love with me," I joke and feign outrage when Mia swats me. "I told her we're happy we've found each other again."

"And?"

"She's supportive but apprehensive. Scared a little, I think."

"That makes two of us," Mia says.

"Don't be. I promise you, I'm ready this time. I will show you every day how ready I am. But we can take it as slow or fast as you want," I say, and I let the warmth of her palm in mine comfort me.

～

An hour later, a man in a fluorescent vest flails his arms, directing me to a parking space between a cherry-red Tesla sedan and a shiny black Escalade.

"Are you ready for the fair?" I say and try to swallow the fear that hits me, being back here, where I first lost Mia. Where this journey began. Some people would argue that the circle of life is a loop. If you think about it, most people die as helpless as they were when they were born. That's why I came back to where my loop started. Because maybe the way to close it is to open it right back up.

Mia unbuckles her seat belt and turns to take me in. What does she see, I wonder? Does she see me as determined? Or desperate? The truth is I'm a little bit of both. I am a man who has everything and nothing to lose. But I'm also a groundswell of hope. Hope that I can escape this. Hope that if Mia is alive in the morning, then we'll live the rest of our days together. I pray that this is the man she sees as she stares at me with those blue eyes.

"I am," she says and arches her neck, planting the softest kiss on my lips. It takes everything not to lose it right there. It feels as if I'm holding the world's fate in my hand. And I sure as hell hope I know what I'm doing.

"Then let's go. There's a corn dog with our names on it," I say. We hop out of the car, and I hold her hand tightly as we walk united toward the entrance.

CHAPTER THIRTY

As we did last time we were here, Mia and I stop at the giant yellow stand with the pictures of polish sausage dogs, all-beef hot dogs, and corn dogs.

We order two corn dogs, baskets of fries, and lemonades. We sit on the same bird-poop-stained bench and watch people walk by, their shoes kicking up dust behind them.

She has a tiny bit of ketchup on the right corner of her mouth. This time I don't hesitate. I take my index finger and wipe it off. She blushes.

Goddamn. I love her. "I like this Dom," she says and leans sideways to kiss me. I taste ketchup and salt with a mix of lemonade. It's delicious. She's delicious.

I run my finger along the frame of her face. "I think I do too."

"You think he's going to stick around?"

"That depends. Are you?" I ask, kissing her deeply this time, only pulling away when a group of teenagers walks by yelling, "Get a room!"

"Too much?" I ask, our faces still inches apart.

"Just the right amount," she says as she stands and reaches for me. "Come on. Let's hit some rides!" On the way, I ceremoniously dunk the basket to win Mia the grand prize of her choice, and I try my best to act surprised when she points to the large brown bear with the pink bow.

"I'm going to call him Beary." She beams as she hugs the stuffed animal to her chest.

"I think that's perfect," I answer and try not to think of him sitting alone in that folding chair as my world ripped apart for the very first time.

We make our way down the winding path of rides. I refuse to be afraid. To let the screams we hear as we pass sound like anything other than delight. We walk past the Zipper, and I force myself to look at it. Mia squeals when she sees it and dares me to ride with her, and I can tell she's disappointed when I shake my head no. I know we are recreating our first night, but I've also decided it's important for us to learn from our mistakes. And for that reason there's no way in hell we're riding that hunk of junk. I blame the corn dog swirling in my stomach and convince her to move on by promising a ride on a less speedy choice, the Ferris wheel. We walk away, and I keep my arm encircled around Mia the entire time. She holds Beary, and I grip Mia's small waist, holding her so close that we eventually sync our steps. I try my best to feel confident that I've made enough changes to alter her fate, but only time will tell.

The six o'clock hour arrives, and it's time for the piece about Chuck to air. I wasn't sure that we were going to be able to pull it together so quickly, but Lance texted me earlier that Alexis had brought all hands on deck to make it happen. I pull Mia away from the crowd, and we watch the story on my phone. She wipes tears from her eyes as Chuck describes his fall from grace and the life he's led since. It's edited beautifully, and Lance's commentary is pitch perfect—asking how and why the city has left these people behind. It's an impeccable blend of emotion and hard facts with a promise of more to come. A home run.

"I love it, but I have to say I'm surprised," Mia says when it's finished. "Two days ago you were chastising me for giving that guy at the coffee shop cash, and now this? What changed?"

I shove my phone in my pocket and ponder her question. The time loop has turned my life upside down. It has taken my heart and smashed it into tiny pieces again and again until I felt as if I had nothing left. It has made me face my past over and over. But it has also taught me that living cautiously is not living at all. That you can't fix your past blunders if you don't learn from them. "Everything has changed," I answer. "Every single thing," I add and reach my hand out to grab hers.

Dusk arrives, and the lights of the rides become brighter. We find ourselves in front of the Ferris wheel, which looks taller from its base. I find comfort in how slowly it moves. That it stays upright. That there is little movement in each of its cars because they appear to be securely attached to the frame. And I don't hear one scream from any of its riders.

"God, you look terrified," Mia laughs. "Dom! It's nothing more than a big wheel that goes around at a snail's pace."

I swallow hard. "I know. It's—"

"Tickets, please," a throaty voice interrupts me. I turn and see Theo. The operator from the Zipper. He's wearing the same Avenged Sevenfold T-shirt from eight Thursdays ago. The one that's a bit too snug, exposing the bottom of his belly. I look away when I see the hair above his navel. I can't decide if I'm terrified or relieved that he's here. Is he a signpost for me to follow?

"Can I bring Beary?" Mia squeaks as she holds her stuffed animal up for Theo.

Theo glances between Mia and the bear. "Sure, why not," he says as he walks over to the cab and swings it open. He motions toward us. "Come on now."

Mia starts to walk, but I hesitate. I'm frozen. With fear. With anticipation. With trepidation. All of it at once. Because we're close to either the beginning or the end. I can feel it in every fiber of my soul. But instead of letting the fear paralyze me, I lean in and let it propel me forward.

Mia turns back. "You ready?" she asks and holds out her hand.

"I am," I say with confidence as we lift ourselves into the cab of the Ferris wheel and watch the world become smaller as we graze the night sky.

"I love it up here," Mia says. The cab is rocking slightly. We are one car from the top. A flash lights up the sky to the east. "Was that lightning?" Mia asks, her voice sliding up a notch.

"I think so," I say and am drowned out by thunder so loud that our car shakes slightly. Another flash, this time closer. Mia jumps and grabs my hand when the thunder claps a few seconds later. From down below, there is some commotion. Theo comes over the microphone to announce that there is a minor mechanical problem and to tell everyone not to panic. To sit tight. That we *should* be moving again shortly. My stomach clenches as we feel the first raindrop. There is no escape from this cab. I look over at Mia—her mouth is set in a straight line. As another flash of light spikes through the sky, panic boils to the surface. I ponder the significance of the drastic weather change from any other Thursday—have I broken the pattern? But I'm also concerned that we are sitting ducks out here, and our time may be short.

I decide to tell Mia the truth. It may be our only hope.

"Mia," I begin, clearing my throat nervously as I brush a raindrop off her face. "Have you ever heard of a time loop?"

She shakes her head slightly and glances nervously toward the ominous sky. "No."

I jump in, anxious to explain it. "It's when time keeps starting over. I don't know how to say this." I pause, taking in her tiny nose, her soft lips, the freckles speckling her cheeks. I have to trust her and trust myself. "I've lived this day nine times."

"Like in *Groundhog Day*?"

"Exactly!" I say, picturing Bill Murray's face. "Or that show *Russian Doll*."

"The one on Netflix? I've been wanting to watch that! It sounds so good!"

Fear takes hold. She thinks I'm joking. It's raining harder now. People below us call out, asking when the ride will move again. There is no answer.

I grab Mia's hand. "I'm being serious," I say, and I hold her gaze before continuing. "Every morning I wake up to this same Thursday. And to the song 'How to Save a Life.' Which I now kind of hate, by the way."

"Hating on our song now? What did the Fray ever do to you?"

You have no idea.

She scrunches her nose. Her hair is soaking wet now, plastered against her face. I tuck it behind her ear. "Are you messing with me?" She glances around the passenger car we're sitting in. "Is there a hidden camera in here somewhere? Am I being *Punk'd*? Is that ticket guy in on it? He seems like he'd be in on something like this."

I touch her arm. "I swear, Mia. This is real. Please, give me a few minutes, and I'll explain everything. Can you do that?"

She searches my face. "I can." Then she laughs nervously and looks to the damp, dark sky. "It's not like I can leave anyway."

I quickly launch into the same story I've given Lance. When I finish, we sit in silence for several seconds. Mia leans back against her seat before speaking, letting out a shriek when another bolt flashes. We brace for the thunder, which comes five seconds later. It's getting closer.

"Dom, I *want* to believe you. But it's so—"

"Crazy?"

"Yes, crazy."

"I can prove it," I say.

"Okay," she says, but her lips are pressed into a fine line.

"When I flew to Chicago, I met your old roommate, Tami—she's feisty! And Rob—he admitted to being in love with you but said you told him you were better off as friends."

"You could have gotten in touch with them through Facebook. It doesn't prove anything." She flaps her hand, and I lose a little steam.

I struggle to think of a better example. "I saw the *inside* of your parents' house. They redid it." I describe the crown molding, the floors, the fireplace, the vanilla candles, the Stephen King book.

"Sorry, again, something a phone call could accomplish." She juts her chin. We are both soaking wet now. But I barely notice. I must make Mia believe me.

"I've been to Hailey's house as well. I've seen that too." I tell her the address and describe it down to the royal-blue-and-white tile with a flower backsplash in the kitchen, the type of coffeepot, the brand of almond milk in the fridge.

"Now you sound like a stalker. What, are you following me? Going through my trash?" She half laughs, but the look in her eyes tells me I'm losing her.

Another flash. Two seconds to thunder. Closer.

I rush the next words out. "Mi, I promise you, what I'm saying is real."

The look on her face is clear—she does not believe me. I take several deep breaths and try to focus on how to convince Mia. Then it hits me. A secret she confided that she's never told anyone else. "I know something. You told me on one of our dates—the one where I saw the inside of Hailey's house. That night I came to the Midwest and tried to win you back, you tried to find me the next morning before I left. You had second thoughts."

Mia gasps. The sky opens up, and the rain falls sideways in sheets. Mascara runs down Mia's face. I can hear the cries of a child in the car below us.

"No one knows that. How do you—?" She stumbles over the words.

"Because *you* told me."

Mia doesn't say anything for a moment, squeezing her eyes shut as if she's trying to make sense of everything. "How can this be real?"

"I know it's hard to comprehend."

"So I'm going to die tonight?" she asks, her voice shaking. There is a flash behind us, followed instantly by a tremendous boom. People are screaming. Mia is trembling.

Hearing the fear in her tone makes me want to take back what I've said. I try to cover her with my body, to shield her from the rain or whatever else may be coming. "No. I'm not going to let that happen."

"Is that what you said to me the other eight times?" she asks, not unkindly, but her eyes are wild. "If what you say is really true—how can you make any promises? What makes today, this Thursday, any different?" She's shaking harder now. I explain to her all the different choices I've made. How everyone's subconscious, including hers, seems to be having a breakthrough.

"But these are only guesses on your part—you don't know."

Her words punch me in the gut. She's right. I don't. And I probably have no business telling her I can save her. If the past dictates the future, then we're screwed. And right now we are trapped at the top of a Ferris wheel in a fierce storm. But I have faith. It's something I can't prove or touch or explain. All I know is that it has everything to do with convincing her that this is real at the same location where it all started. Mia is going to live to see midnight—even if it means I have to swap my life for hers. "I need you to trust me. Can you do that?"

Theo gets on the microphone, asking everyone to stay calm. No one is calm.

Mia puts her hand on my heart. "It's beating so fast. What are you so afraid of? The storm?"

"No—I'm afraid that you won't believe me."

She lets her hand fall to my arm. "I do. It's almost too nuts *not* to believe. But I'm scared, Dom. I don't want to die." She says this last part so softly I barely hear it. She starts crying. I can't imagine what she's feeling—to be told your life has been ending over and over and have no control over it. I start to panic. Maybe I shouldn't have told her that part.

I take her in my arms, and over her shoulder I can see the ground below, most people having scattered to take cover from the storm. "I will protect you. I *will* save you." I kiss her, letting my lips linger on hers. She presses her mouth against mine, both of us hungry for more. But she pulls away, leaving me breathless. The rain subsides slightly, and I let out an audible sigh. Maybe I've broken whatever spell we were under.

"I wish it were that simple," she says, her tears mixing in with the rain.

"It will be. Because I love you. It's you. It's always been you."

"I love you too, Dom," she says.

"You do?" I'm shocked. I figured those words would come later for her, much later.

"I do, dammit." She pauses. "And believe me, I didn't want to. For a long time I fought it. You know, I used to call Lance to find out about you? I wasn't very sly—but he never called me on it." She laughs to herself. "I have always loved you. I should have said it back to you earlier, but I couldn't. Or I didn't think I could."

"Why not?" I ask, my stomach churning. She can't second-guess us now. Not when we are so close.

"Because I haven't told you something."

My heart freezes. "What?"

She sucks back fresh tears. "I'm sick."

I feel light headed. "What do you mean?"

Mia takes a breath. "I've been diagnosed with stage four ovarian cancer."

I stare at her. "What?"

"They tell me it's pretty much terminal. So that means I'm dying." She looks at me. "Ironic, huh?"

"What?" My breath is becoming ragged. Yes, I knew there was something she wasn't telling me. But I never in my wildest dreams thought she was dying.

She touches my hand, which is clammy with shock. "It's why I came here. I got diagnosed three weeks ago."

"What do you mean by 'pretty much' terminal?"

Mia's expression is grave. "It's spread to my liver and spleen. There's not much they can do at this point. My parents were so upset that I refused to even consider treatment that I had to get out of there. So I basically packed up my stuff and left. I freaked out."

"Mia, you need to at least try," I plead.

"Stop. This is my choice. Not yours. Not my parents'. Not Hailey's," she says, her eyes flinty.

I suck in a long breath, my heart burning. I bite back my tears. Finally, I find my voice. "Why come back here?" I ask.

"Some of my happiest times were out here," she says, looking down. "I wanted to feel happy again. I wanted to feel the sun on my face and smell the salt air every day. I thought that would be enough. And then I ran into you."

"And?"

"And that made things more complicated. Because when you're trying to come to terms with the fact that your time is short, it's hard to reconnect with someone who makes you want to live."

The lump in my throat bursts open. "Then try. Live. Please." I wipe the tears from my eyes. It's possible this is why I've been reliving each day. To save Mia from herself.

"Dom. If I do all those things, the prognosis is still terminal. And I'll be miserable. I don't want to be miserable. I want to enjoy the time I still have where I still feel decent."

"Why didn't you tell me sooner? Call me when you found out?"

She rubs her hand over her mouth. "I thought about it. But we hadn't been in touch. I thought it would be a strange phone call to make to you out of the blue." She pauses, looks down, then back up at me. "Lance knows. I called him after I ran into you. He didn't take it well—he was sad for me and also for you, and I invited him to lunch to talk more and discuss how to tell you. He was adamant I explain right away, but I wanted to find the right time on my own."

"What?" I exclaim, my voice sharp. The rain has ceased. The child below us has stopped wailing.

"Don't be mad at him. I made him swear not to tell you. I felt I owed it to you to hear it from me," she says, then adds, "He was trying to protect you."

I sniff loudly. "It's so fucking unfair. No matter what I do, I can't save you. If we can make it to Friday, I'll lose you anyway," I say, my voice cracking. Anger rises in my chest.

Mia grabs my face with her hands. "Dom. Promise me one thing. No matter what happens—whether we wake up tomorrow morning and it's Friday or we start over on Thursday again—I want you to swear you'll let go of what we could have been. That you'll forgive yourself for breaking up with me. I refuse to be the reason you can't move forward."

"You're not," I protest.

"Yes, I am!" she yells, and it stuns me. Her loud voice in our small car. "You're literally in a time loop because of me!" She takes a breath, and her next words are much quieter. "I need you to promise me, no matter what happens, you won't spend another ten years regretting us." She sniffles softly.

"What are you saying, Mia? That you don't think we're meant to be together? Because the universe has stopped time so that we can be."

Mia holds my gaze. "Have you ever considered that I'm not the one who needs saving?"

I think of Amanda. Chuck. The airplane. "No." I shake my head stubbornly. "Sure, there are other chess pieces, but you're always the catalyst."

"What if the point to all this is to free yourself from the guilt you've held for the past ten years? That maybe you've let your fear hold you back from truly living?"

I look down and shake my head. But as I do, there is a spark igniting in my head—the truth of her words lighting a fire. That maybe this was never about Mia. That it was about me and my refusal to look ahead. I force my eyes up to meet hers.

"You know I'm right," she says. "It's okay, Dom. It's okay to save yourself," she whispers and kisses me. "I want you to be happy. With or without me. Promise me you will."

The realization of the truth in her words hits me hard in the chest. A sob escapes my throat. I nod to let her know I understand. Because she's right. She's so fucking right that I can't speak, can't move. The acceptance paralyzes me. For most of my adult life, I've thought one thing. And I couldn't have been more wrong. So we sit in silence, holding on to each other for dear life, the realization that she's dying and I can't save her swirling inside of me. "I promise," I finally utter.

A flash breaks through the sky, and a collective scream tears through the crowd. The rain comes quickly once more, the drops angrily pelting our car. We pull away from our embrace as the thunder shakes the ground. "Do you think this is a sign?" Mia asks as she burrows back into my shoulder. "That if we can survive being at the top of a Ferris wheel during a thunderstorm, we can survive anything?"

I don't know what comes first—the blinding light, the deafening crack, or the realization that we're now the target. I hold on to Mia as tightly as I can, my last thought before blacking out that no matter what happens, no matter where I wake up, I won't forget Mia's words.

CHAPTER THIRTY-ONE

I hear the chorus of the song. Our song. "How to Save a Life." Fuck. It didn't work. I'm back here again in my Thursday prison! I'm crying suddenly. So hard I can't stop. I can't catch my breath. I try to open my eyes, but they are cemented shut. The lyrics of that damn song are on a loop pounding through my skull, feeling like a headache I can't get rid of, the pain more and more acute, the song louder and louder. Then everything fades away.

The song has stopped playing.

There is a steady beeping sound.

And my thoughts, louder than ever.

Mia. Where is Mia?

And pain. So much pain. My head is pounding. A pain in my leg is throbbing.

My eyes fly open, and I try to sit up, but when I jerk my arm, it's connected to something, and it burns. I look over to the source. It's an IV connected to a bag hanging above. I turn toward the beeping. It's a machine monitoring my vitals. I'm in a hospital room, which means I survived the lightning storm. But did Mia? My chest constricts, and I try to breathe, but I can't. The beeping on the machine becomes more urgent, and an alarm signals. I wince from the sound. A woman in pastel scrubs runs in. She switches the alarm off.

"Mia!" I scream. "Mia!" I try to get out of bed, and that's when I realize my leg is in a cast. I grimace.

"It's okay, Dominic. You are okay. I'm Janet, your nurse. You're in the hospital," the woman says, attaching oxygen to my nose. "Breathe."

"What day is it?" I ask, but she doesn't hear me.

"Dom!" My mom runs into the room, coffee spilling over the top of her cup. "I left for a minute to get this. Your dad is in the cafeteria." She jerks it, and more liquid flies out, and she tosses it in a trash can, cursing in Spanish. "What's going on?" She sees the mask over my mouth.

"He's okay. This happens sometimes when a patient wakes up from being unconscious and is disoriented," Janet says.

"Mom, what day is it? And where is Mia?" I ask, my eyes wide, physical pain radiating through my body, yet my emotional pain is numb. As if fear is freezing my ability to feel. My body somehow trying to protect me from what my gut tells me is coming. My mom doesn't answer. She keeps her eyes trained on the nurse. I turn to see the nurse switching something on my IV bag. My heart starts pounding as I take in her short dark hair streaked with gray and realize she's the same nurse who took care of me the first Thursday I was here, after we flew off the Zipper. So maybe that means it's still Thursday!

"You need to be resting right now. You also lost a lot of blood. We gave you a transfusion last night. And you have a broken leg and—"

"Broken ribs, I know."

"You are pretty in touch with your body," Janet says.

I've also lived through this before. Different ride. Same injuries.

My mom dabs at her eyes and puts her hand on mine. "When you were first brought in, it was touch and go—"

"I'm here, Mom. It's okay," I say, squeezing her hand.

My mom sits on the edge of my bed as my dad walks in. "Son, we are so thankful." My dad kisses my forehead. His eyes full of tears.

"Mia?" I ask again.

My mom and dad exchange a look. "They tried, but they couldn't . . ." My dad's strong voice trails off.

"No!" I cry. My mom tries to comfort me, but I push her away.

"But isn't today Thursday, June eleventh?" I press. Because if it is, that means Mia isn't . . .

"It's Friday, son," my dad says.

Tears fly down my face, and I pull off the confining oxygen mask. Emptiness radiates through me at the realization that there is nothing I can do to change Mia's fate. That I'll have to move forward without her. It feels like nothing will ever be right ever again. All hope is lost.

My parents move toward me, and this time I lean into them. My dad holds one of my hands, and my mom holds the other as my dad gently explains that the Ferris wheel car Mia and I were in was hit by lightning, which detached it from its frame. We plummeted eighty feet to the ground, and Mia was thrown from it. "She didn't suffer," he says, and I don't ask for more. I don't need more.

"It's a miracle you survived," my mom says, her eyes filling with tears. "When we got the call . . ." My dad pulls her in to comfort her.

I squeeze my eyes shut. One of the last things Mia said to me rings in my ears. That the point of all this was never to save her but to save myself. And maybe she was right. Because here I am, on Friday morning, June 12, without her. She made me promise I would go on without her. It had never occurred to me that I'd have to. When she told me she was dying, I was already thinking about how I'd convince her to seek treatment, to try everything. I thought about using every resource I had, every connection, to help her. She was going to fight it, and I was going to help her. But at the very least we would live out her final days together.

I start to cry harder. For Mia. For what we could have been. And for the fearful part of myself that I've shed the last nine days. I will never be that person again. Mia's death will not be in vain.

Eventually I fall back into a drug-induced dreamless sleep.

~

I wake up several hours later to the instant reality that Mia is dead. Still. I close my eyes, want to go back to sleep. To when I didn't have to feel this gut-wrenching pain. Lance is slouched in a chair next to my bed. He pops up when he sees me stir. "I'm so sorry about Mia," he says, his eyes red and filling with tears. "God, I'm sorry. She was finally back, and now she's gone. The irony of all this. It's not fair."

"I know," I say, and we both sit in silence for several minutes.

"She told me why she was back," I finally say. "Right before . . ." I can't finish the thought. I point to the pitcher of water on the table, and he pours me a cup and helps me drink it.

"I'm so sorry I didn't tell you."

"It was her story to tell, not yours," I say, thinking back to the night sky as we sat on top of the Ferris wheel. As she told me about her inevitable fate, she was more concerned with mine. With helping me understand that it had always been my own soul that needed saving. I tell Lance the story, pausing a few times to catch my breath.

"She's an amazing person," he says, wiping his eyes.

"I know."

"I should have told you she was asking for you; maybe you two could have had more time."

"What's done is done," I say.

"Is it? Maybe we can figure out how to go further back and repeat a day where I could tell you, somehow change all this?"

"Lance."

"I know. Wishful thinking."

A sob rises in my throat at the realization that it's over and that I'll never see Mia again. Never hear her laugh. Breathe her in. Never have another chance to start over. Never know who we could have been together, if given a second chance.

I have several missed calls and frantic texts from friends and colleagues, asking if I'm okay. If I need anything. But there is only one person I need to connect with right now. I pull up her name and pray she still has the same cell phone number as she did ten years ago.

Hailey answers on the third ring. She sounds like I feel—defeated, inconsolable, miserable.

I announce myself to her and am met with silence. "Hailey?" I say, wondering if she hung up on me.

"I'm here," she says.

"I'm so sorry," I say and begin to cry again. Lance looks away from me, but not before I see him wipe his eyes.

"I want to blame you," she says. It's an angry statement, but there's no anger in her voice.

"You can, if that will help," I answer, wanting to add that I blame myself too. It was my fault we were reliving the same day. My fault we were at the fair. My fault that Mia had to sacrifice herself so that I could be free.

"It won't help. It won't bring her back. Hating you accomplishes nothing." I hear her gulp down a sob. "She was dying, you know."

"I know."

"But I thought I had more time. I thought, if I waited her out, that she'd come around and get treatment. I had hope," she cries, her voice rising. "And now I have nothing."

I don't know what to say to this. Because I know how she feels. Empty.

"I'm sorry. I can't do this," she says a moment later, and the line goes dead.

I stare at the phone until Lance takes it and sets it back on the table. "Maybe let's wait on phone calls," is all he says. He grabs the remote control and turns on the television to ESPN, where there is a replay of an old Bears/Packers game from last season. We sit and watch in silence, both of us quietly crying, grieving Mia and what could have been, until I fall back asleep.

CHAPTER THIRTY-TWO

Saturday, June 13

Another day has come and gone. It's odd. I'd almost become used to the repetitiveness of my days, the knowing. It's made me realize how much of my life I've spent needing to know. Letting that need drive my choices. And now I look forward to the uncertainty of each new day. I tell myself Mia would like that.

I miss her. The thought of her sends shots of pain through my chest. None of the medicines they offer me here can take away the pain of losing someone like her. Yes, I will heal. My ribs will fuse back together. The bruises will fade. But losing Mia has created a fissure within my heart that will take much longer to heal.

Today I woke with a small sense of purpose. I made myself recall her last words to me. Her insistence that I not stand still if she leaves again. My promise. I play them over and over in my head as I lie in this hospital bed. I remind myself that I told her I would try. And I will. Try.

The reaction to Chuck's story has surpassed my expectations. I knew it would strike a nerve, but I couldn't have anticipated the number of emails that have poured in, not only from viewers who admitted they'd been judgmental and wanted to know how they could help him but also others in similar situations. Alexis also called me to say she'd heard buzz from many in the industry that this could be another Emmy winner. And while that felt good to hear, that's not what sharing Chuck's story was about for me. And maybe that's exactly what will make the difference—that I didn't do it with the intention of winning an award. The door to my room swings forward. I brace myself to be poked and prodded again by the stern-faced nurse who was on the morning shift. To my surprise, Amanda pushes through the doorway, smiling tentatively. "Dominic?" she says, my name a question. Asking if it's okay she's here.

"Amanda!" I exclaim and use my good arm to wave her in. I'm happy to see her.

"Hold on, I have something for you," she says and leans back into the hallway. My heart leaps to my throat when I see what's in her arms—a giant brown bear with a pink ribbon around its throat.

"Where did you—" I stare at the stuffed bear, the memory of winning him for Mia coming crashing back. Beary? My heart hammers as I try to figure out how Amanda found him.

Amanda blushes. "Sorry—is this too cheesy? I saw it in the gift shop, and I bought it on a whim." She walks in and sets Beary's identical twin on the bed. "I thought he might cheer you up." When I don't respond, she adds, "I can take it away . . ."

"No," I say, adding, "Sorry," when I see I've startled her. I bury my face in Beary, somehow comforted by the fact he's not the same bear, but still rattled that she found one that looks exactly like the stuffed animal Mia held in her arms just days ago. "He's perfect. Thank you," I finally say and point to the chair next to my bed. "Sit?" I ask, trying to sound calm, but my mind is reeling.

Is the bear a sign from Mia? Letting me know she is okay? Reminding me I promised to move on with my life? Or a gift from the universe, a confirmation that I didn't imagine the whole damn thing?

Or maybe it's all of the above. I breathe out hard and wince, my broken ribs protesting. I've spent the last twenty-four hours flip-flopping between peace and angst. Between believing I experienced something uniquely profound and wondering if I should check myself into the psych ward. And then in walks Amanda with this bear.

An affirmation of what happened.

"I hope it's okay that I came," Amanda begins. "I saw what happened on the news, and I couldn't stop thinking about you. About Mia," she says, her eyes downcast. "I know what she meant to you. That you thought you could save her. I can't imagine how you must be feeling."

"Thank you," I say. "It's hard."

"I thought you might get your happily ever after. Especially after what you did for me. You were due for some good karma."

"I thought I was going to get my happy ending too," I say seriously, and then we both laugh nervously at my unintended innuendo. It feels odd to laugh, as if I'm betraying Mia's memory. After a few moments, I add, "Now I feel lost."

This confession lifts some weight off my chest. I know the lessons I'm supposed to have learned. The ways that I'm now meant to live without fear. But I have absolutely no idea where to begin.

I look at Amanda, her green eyes sympathetic but not pitying, and I feel comfort wrap around me. I've been so focused on Mia that I never considered that the universe placed her into my life for a reason—more than to make sure she didn't get hit by that car.

She leans in, her hair falling forward over her shoulders. "Of course you feel lost. You spent a long time harboring feelings for her. And then she came back, and you dedicated nine days to keeping her alive. And now you have to figure out who you are without her."

Her words pierce. She is right. Without Mia in this world, I'm not sure who I am.

"Let me help," she says. "You've been a great friend to so many people—let me be your friend now."

A lump rises in my throat. I nod, unable to speak, my emotions swirling. Her kindness overwhelming. Amanda helped me when she didn't have to, believed me on pure faith. And moving forward from this experience won't be easy. It will be a battle to let Mia go. I can still feel her spirit lingering in my soul like a shadow as I try to understand why I couldn't save her. And absorb the harsh reality that maybe I wasn't supposed to. I realize now, as I look into Amanda's gentle eyes, that I will need every single friend I can get to help me accept that.

"You saved my life. Now maybe it's my turn to save yours." Amanda extends her hand to me, a life preserver to a drowning man.

I take it.

THE END

ACKNOWLEDGMENTS

It's hard to believe we've written *seven* novels together. Because each time we sit down to write one, we look at each other and ask, "How the hell are we going to do this again?" And then one of us inevitably adds, "Without killing each other?"

We'd like to believe that with each book, we've improved—in both our writing and our friendship. That we've evolved. Our ideas have grown. Our efficiency has heightened. But still, each book is its own animal. Some novels are like Labradors, easy and joyous, and others are monstrous and all-consuming, like killer whales. But whether the words flow easily like they did for *How to Save a Life* (thank you, writing gods!) or have to be pried out of us like stubborn teeth, we wouldn't trade the opportunity to live out our passion together for anything.

First, we must thank our book-blogging and bookstagrammer friends. It's been so fun getting to know each and every one of you! (That night out in NYC was epic!) Your support of our books does not go unnoticed. Whether it's a review on Amazon or Goodreads, a post on Facebook or Instagram, or an in-person recommendation over coffee, spreading the word about books is not something you have to do. It's something you want to do simply because you love reading. From the bottom of our hearts, thank you for that.

The two of us are only a fraction of why each book we write becomes a full-fledged novel. We wouldn't be able to bring each labor of love from inception to publication without our incomparable team.

Danielle Marshall, we will be forever thankful you took us under your wing and brought us into the Amazon Publishing family. Alicia Clancy, your keen observations and positive attitude help bring our books to a higher level. And Dennelle Catlett, thank you for never batting an eyelash when we come to you with our "out there" publicity ideas. You are a master at executing them! And Gabe, you are always there when we need you—thanks so much!

Tiffany Yates Martin, your *let us in* and *what's he thinking?* notes nearly kill us every time, but they elevate our books to a place they simply wouldn't be without your editorial expertise.

Elisabeth Weed, thank you for *getting us*. For always having our back. And for being you. We are grateful to have you as our agent and friend. Hallie—thanks for always being spot on!

Kathleen Carter, we are lucky to work with one of the best publicists in the business. You work hard, and you always deliver.

Ellen Goldsmith-Vein with the Gotham Group, thank you for believing in us and our books!

Thank you, Jake Minger at KUSI, for patiently answering all of our television-news-related questions. It was incredibly helpful!

Tony Jordan, thank you for your paramedic expertise!

Jackie Bouchard, your attention to detail makes you an invaluable early reader—we are so appreciative!

And to our families: we wouldn't be where we are without your love and support.

Xoxo,
Liz and Lisa

ABOUT THE AUTHORS

Photo © 2019 Ireland Photography

Liz Fenton and Lisa Steinke have been best friends for over thirty years and survived high school and college together. They've coauthored seven novels, including *The Two Lila Bennetts*, *Girls' Night Out*, and the Amazon Charts bestseller *The Good Widow*. In their former lives, Liz worked in the pharmaceutical industry, and Lisa was a talk show producer. They both reside with their families and several rescue dogs in San Diego, California. Find them at www.lizandlisa.com and on Instagram at @lisaandliz.